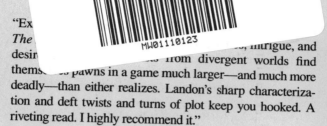

"Ex...
The ... , intrigue, and
desir... ...s from divergent worlds find
thems... ...s pawns in a game much larger—and much more
deadly—than either realizes. Landon's sharp characteriza-
tion and deft twists and turns of plot keep you hooked. A
riveting read. I highly recommend it."

—Linnea Sinclair, author of
Games of Command
and *The Down Home Zombie Blues*

"[A] promising debut novel." —*Sci Fi Weekly*

"With an interesting concept and deftly drawn characters,
this is a fantastic science fiction yarn. Landon's created a
world with plenty of intrigue and action and high-tech
devices while still leaving it accessible for readers new to
the genre. There are layers of complexity here, both moral
and political, that are sure to give readers plenty to think
about." —*Romantic Times Book Reviews*

"Kristin Landon has written a spectacular sci-fi thriller."
—*The Best Reviews*

"Kristin Landon's novel *The Hidden Worlds* is a space
sci-fi with a splash of romance and a dash of politics
mixed together to make a very interesting read . . . The
story is a great emotional ride."

—*Yet Another Book Review Site*

Ace Books by Kristin Landon

THE HIDDEN WORLDS
THE COLD MINDS

THE COLD MINDS

KRISTIN LANDON

ACE BOOKS, NEW YORK

THE BERKLEY PUBLISHING GROUP
Published by the Penguin Group
Penguin Group (USA) Inc.
375 Hudson Street, New York, New York 10014, USA
Penguin Group (Canada), 90 Eglinton Avenue East, Suite 700, Toronto, Ontario M4P 2Y3, Canada
(a division of Pearson Penguin Canada Inc.)
Penguin Books Ltd., 80 Strand, London WC2R 0RL, England
Penguin Group Ireland, 25 St. Stephen's Green, Dublin 2, Ireland (a division of Penguin Books Ltd.)
Penguin Group (Australia), 250 Camberwell Road, Camberwell, Victoria 3124, Australia
(a division of Pearson Australia Group Pty. Ltd.)
Penguin Books India Pvt. Ltd., 11 Community Centre, Panchsheel Park, New Delhi—110 017, India
Penguin Group (NZ), 67 Apollo Drive, Rosedale, North Shore 0632, New Zealand
(a division of Pearson New Zealand Ltd.)
Penguin Books (South Africa) (Pty.) Ltd., 24 Sturdee Avenue, Rosebank, Johannesburg 2196,
South Africa

Penguin Books Ltd., Registered Offices: 80 Strand, London WC2R 0RL, England

THE COLD MINDS

An Ace Book / published by arrangement with the author

PRINTING HISTORY
Ace mass-market edition / July 2008

Copyright © 2008 by Kristin Landon.
Cover art by Craig White.
Cover design by Annette Fiore DeFex.
Interior text design by Laura K. Corless.

ISBN: 978-0-441-01609-9

ACE
Ace Books are published by The Berkley Publishing Group,
a division of Penguin Group (USA) Inc.,
375 Hudson Street, New York, New York 10014.
ACE and the "A" design are trademarks belonging to Penguin Group (USA) Inc.

PRINTED IN THE UNITED STATES OF AMERICA

10   9   8   7   6   5   4   3   2   1

For the Harpies, without whom . . .

I thank Anne Sowards, for her gentle but thorough editing; my writing group (the Harpies: Patty Hyatt, Karen Keady, Candy Davis, and Skye Blaine), for getting me over the rocky bits; my agent, Donald Maass; and finally my family and friends, for their unfailing support.

ONE

TERRANOVA NEARSPACE

We're flying blind. Fear flickered in Linnea Kiaho's mind. She stretched out her perceptions into otherspace, searching for the feeling of *rightness* that marked their jumpship's point of transition to the safety of normal space. Her trainee, Joro, could not sense it, she was sure; she could feel him wavering on the edge of total panic. And the ship was in his control, not hers.

"Joro," she said, putting as much calm into her non-voice as she could. "Release control."

The eerie grandeur she not-quite saw, not-quite heard, did not distract her from the sense of rushing forward. Running out of time. Training jumps were short; if they did not drop back into realspace soon, they would overshoot, would not have the fuel to return safely to Terranova orbit. Through their mutual connection to the ship, she felt the shivering edge of the young trainee's fear. Pushed it away. It must not spread to her.

Joro's "voice" in her mind was faint, strained. "I can't breathe."

Locked down in the instructor's life-support shell, Linnea reached out tensely through her link to the old jumpship, to the main controls usually routed to the piloting shell. Her fingers and toes tingled, a ghost of sensation, as the connections awoke. "Joro. You are breathing. You just can't feel it in otherspace. Let go of that. Let go of your body. Float." Seconds spun past. "Joro! *Answer.* Can you feel the ship?" Here in otherspace her physical senses did not function; she could not see the ship around her, or the shell that enclosed Joro. But both the ship and her own internal sense told her that the time to drop back to normal space was only minutes or seconds away.

No time for calming drugs to take effect in Joro—he would botch the reinsertion. If they overshot, Linnea would have to bring them back to it, and she was still a new pilot herself—in an old ship, a half wreck they had managed to steal and repair well enough for training runs—had the pilot interface failed? "Joro!"

"It's too dark!"

"Reach in," she said tensely. "Get back to the center. The way I taught you. Feel for the ship, in your hands, in your feet—"

"Nothing's there!" His terror washed toward her along their connection, and again Linnea fought it back. It *must* not infect her.

"Joro. I'm taking over. You must not move. Don't move, in your mind, anywhere. You're still linked to the ship even if you can't feel it. Don't move!" As she spoke, she was collecting the threads of control that hung in her mind. Time whirled past. If she had five more seconds—

The ship gives direction. The pilot, volition. Her lover Iain sen Paolo's words rang in her mind, calming her. She had it, she had it now, clear in her mind, under her hands. Her mind *flexed.*

Realspace slammed into existence around her, the ship's air cold around her body, her eyes its eyes, the stars and glowing gas clouds forming familiar patterns. They must have—

A sharp *thunk*, a lurch, and the stars began to wheel around her. Joro had moved. Fired one of the attitude jets, that was all, but if he did anything more— "Freeze, Joro!" Her voice cracked as she fought the spin, fought it. She could do this.

She could do this—*Calm*. A mental twitch of two fingers produced a light tap on the necessary jets. *Steady*. Another. Another. Overcompensated—a twitch in the other hand—and the little ship steadied down, settled into normal flight.

"Keep still, Joro. I'll have you out of there in a minute." *Ranging*, she said to the ship, and a silent readout seemed to float before her eyes: They were within range of their beacon. Safe. She took a shuddering breath and set them on course for Terranova orbit. The great blue-and-green globe, whorled with white, half-lit, half-dark, began to grow slowly.

No more maneuvers would be needed for a while. Linnea brought her vision inboard. She had to blink hard to clear her eyes, closed and useless for so long while she was seeing through the ship. Here was the familiar piloting compartment of the jumpship, low and narrow, lit by two flickering old light panels and the glow of a few readouts. The piloting shell hulked in the center, gray, sealed, blank. The cold air still smelled of the oil that had coated all the bulkheads for so many years, preserving the old ship in case it should ever be needed for parts.

She heard Joro's muffled sobbing inside the shell. No. He would never make a pilot—not this one. He was not her first failure, either.

Anger flared again inside her. She had had hopes for Joro, and he'd let her down. And Iain, her partner in this work, would merely think: Here was further proof that pilots not from the Line might never amount to much. . . . But then he had been brought up on Nexus, a Pilot Master, and whatever he said, she knew that Iain's instincts, his prejudices, were still what they had been formed to be.

And maybe he had a point. Half a standard year of work, and they'd not found many likely candidates. Fewer than a thousand names on the list of those who had agreed to be tested—a dozen or so in each city they'd visited. And they had just this one decrepit ship for training— Iain's was a personal jumpship, made for him when he first became a jump pilot. He had stolen it when he escaped from Nexus to rescue her from Freija. A beautiful little ship, a commnet linker and quick as a fish—but it could not easily be adapted to other pilots. And with only one ship, the testing and training was a slow process. Maybe a hopeless one.

Linnea touched a control, then held carefully still as the microfine wires withdrew from her brain, back into the coiling silver leads that touched her temples and encased and protected the wires. Always it felt like the coming of a kind of blindness, the loss of that inner sight, that connection to the ship. Always a faint sense of absence, of being incomplete, lingered until the next time.

The leads curled back onto their spools. She unstrapped herself from the instructor's couch with a sigh. Three flights, she had invested in Joro; and now she would have to send him back groundside to his old work at the shuttle field in Port Marie. And move on to the next unlikely prospect. . . .

She floated free from the couch and toed herself over to the pilot's shell, cracked it open. Winced at the acid smell of vomit. Of course the ship's systems had cleared it from the air, but some still clung to Joro's naked body. He hunched in his straps, fists clenched against his chest, eyes shut tight.

She gripped his shoulder. "Joro, feel that. We're back. We're in realspace. On our way home."

"Never doing this again," he muttered.

"That's right enough," she said dryly. "Hold still. I'll get you out of there."

She had to tug him around like a child's balloon, but in the end she got him strapped onto the instructor's couch, without connecting him to the ship. Then she took his place in the sour-smelling piloting shell. In Joro's state he could not have managed the precise insertion into orbit, down the preapproved flight path that Station Six had assigned them, a path from which they dared not deviate or the Line patrols would spot them. Force them down at the very least, or simply shoot; it was their choice.

Stationmaster Segura had been willing to honor the dying request of an old friend, to help Iain and Linnea so far as he could; and without that help they would never have been able to carry out these testing and training flights. Terranova was a rich world the Pilot Masters valued, so the orbital patrols were numerous and vigilant—watching for any ships off-plan, off-beacon. Any ship that might mean a landing attempt by the Cold Minds. A single small ship, loaded with nanobots, setting down near one of Terranova's crowded cities. . . . Linnea shuddered, pushing away memories of the infested world named Freija, where she had been marooned, hiding for months with a handful of still-human survivors. The blank faces of their nanobot-infested captors, the sickly blue glow in their eyes, still haunted her dreams.

Freija was gone. But the threat remained. After six hundred years the Cold Minds had tracked humanity to its last refuge, the Hidden Worlds. Linnea knew with a cold inner pricking of fear that they were here still. Watching, somewhere in the dark between the Worlds.

Steadily, in frozen calm, Linnea guided the ship along

the docking pods of Station Six, past the upper levels, where the gleaming jumpships of the Pilot Masters lay in their cradles, down to the haphazard network of docks and fueling stations and cargo-transfer facilities that served the local-orbit ships and ground shuttles.

In public the Pilot Masters denied the threat of the Cold Minds—denied the news that she and the exiled pilot Iain sen Paolo had spread through the commnet from world to world. Worked to undermine them, sought to arrest them. It was better to preserve their monopoly than to allow ordinary people to learn the secrets of piloting, the secrets the Pilot Masters had long held under the pretense that only their sons, the sons of the Line, had the gift.

And yet here she was, piloting. Piloting a jumpship. She felt, again, a brief surge of triumph at that.

She had been the first new pilot who'd been born outside the Line. But the human race needed thousands more pilots to give them a fighting chance against the Cold Minds—to save not just the wealthy worlds, but the poor, small colonies like Santandru.

Not now. She pushed the thought of home away, home and worry. Nothing to be done, not from here. Messages took months to reach Santandru, and she had sent enough for now; her sister Marra had never once replied.

Once they were docked, anonymous among the smaller ships, she sent Joro off to clean up and get himself a spot on a shuttle down to the surface. Where he would, she hoped, stay forever. Then she worked doggedly for more than two hours to clean the filters in the air system and to clear and lock down the jumpship.

By the time she sealed the hatch with her palmprint, it was past midnight station time, and she was tired and sweaty inside her stained work coverall. She stood for a moment, alone in the long, curved sweep of dimly lit docking bay, and leaned her forehead against the cold metal bulkhead—just for a moment, just to rest. Here, at least, they were safe from Line Security, not like the crowds groundside, where any stranger might be looking for them. . . . And it was at that moment, of course, that Iain spoke behind her. "Linnea? Are you all right?"

She smothered a yawn, turned, and smiled at him. He was dressed in his best clothes, a night-black work coverall, clean and pressed. His long black hair was tied back in a simple tail. No longer a Pilot Master, exiled from the Line, he still carried "Pilot Master" in every line of his body, the lift of his chin, his dark, direct gaze. The pride, the breeding. For most of his life he'd believed he was one of them; and it told on him, of course.

"You're fancy," she said, caressing his arm.

"I had a meeting with the stationmaster. This is the best I can do." He caught her hand in his and kissed it.

She remembered him, in a time that seemed long ago, in his home on Nexus, in the sober, elegant, precisely cut black tunic and trousers of a jump pilot, his hair in a long, shining braid woven with the crimson lineage-cord. His face had been younger—his eyes had not seen what they had seen since. . . .

She found herself wanting to pull him close, and—she yanked herself back under control. "Do you want my report?"

He lifted an eyebrow. "Do I need it? You sent him off before the ship was secured. In my experience, that's not a sign that you're happy."

"It was a rough run," Linnea said. "He's not trainable. At least, I can't train him." And Iain, of course, had no time; always the next recruiting trip to organize, always an eye on Line Security.

"You could have commed me. I would have come down to help you lock things down."

She grinned. "You'd ruin your best clothes."

He smiled back at her, then picked up her flight bag,

and they started for the lift. "And so another one drops out," he said. "After three flights." He shook his head. "I wonder if they're really trying."

Linnea felt a flicker of annoyance. She took a breath to steady herself, and said, "You know they need more than just the gift." She kept her eyes on the worn plastic decking. "Being able to see otherspace doesn't do any good if they can't hold the flight clear in their minds. Or if they panic." She sighed in frustration. "These people aren't like you, they weren't born to the Line. They haven't been soaking in piloting culture since they were babies." They reached the lift, and she pressed her palm against the call switch. "They need better teaching. More time. Not to be pushed like this."

"We don't have time," Iain said reasonably. "You know that, Linnea. The Cold Minds could be anywhere. Massing for an attack here, for all we know. Or already established on one of the fringe worlds, just as they were on Freija."

As always, the careful patience in his voice only increased her annoyance. "Freija was not a fringe world—"

"A farming world," Iain said. "Producing only enough to supply its own needs."

"And so no use to the Pilot Masters," Linnea said, the old bitterness finally spilling over. "And so they let it fall, and in the end destroyed it. To save themselves, and the rich worlds." She and Iain had barely escaped the artificial bombardment of asteroids that had sterilized the surface of Freija.

The lift doors hissed open, spilling harsh bluish light into the docking bay. Linnea stalked into the lift, and when the doors had closed on them, she said, "I wish you would stop talking about fringe worlds. They are people's homes." Her voice shook. "If you dismiss them like that, you're no better than the Pilot Masters yourself." She took a breath. "And maybe that's true for me, too. Here we are, giving all our attention and help to Terranova—"

Iain spread his hands. "We are two people. Terranova has tens of millions of people we can search among, mostly concentrated in cities. Look how many have already come forward and volunteered. This is where we must be."

And, of course, in every sensible way, Iain was right. Linnea's shoulders slumped, and she let herself sag against the wall of the lift for a moment.

Iain looked down at her, his dark gaze full of thought. Then he set his hands on her shoulders, gently caressing. "Segura just gave us two more flights, tomorrow and the next day. I'll send down to have the next candidate come up. Then—let me take him out."

"I'm expendable," she said bleakly, as the lift halted and the doors opened on the bunkroom level. "You're not."

"Neither of us is expendable," Iain said, letting go of her. "I'm taking the flights."

Another good moment broken. She did not try to speak to him again as they threaded the narrow metal corridors, dim-lit for night, to their small room. A tepid, spattering shower, a packaged meal, and she climbed silently into her narrow bunk opposite his. "Are you coming to bed?" He still sat at the room's tiny table, a commscreen open in front of him.

"I need to do a bit more reading," he said. "There are some news feeds from the outer worlds I haven't followed for a few days." She knew what he was looking for: odd events, ship disappearances, breaks in communications—anything that might be a sign of activity by the Cold Minds.

"You know the Line is looking just as carefully as you are," she said, settling into the hard mattress. "And they have more resources."

"But they will not tell *me* what they learn," Iain said. "Go to sleep, Linnea."

She closed her eyes resentfully. Things had been better, lately, between them; she had been easing up, the long drought in her soul maybe coming to an end. But sometimes all the matters that still lay between them weighed on her like lead, everything they could not speak of: Their differing hopes for this effort. Her deep fears for her sister, so far away on Santandru. Her memories of Freija, the world whose death they had witnessed. And the Pilot Master Rafael, Iain's cousin. . . .

She shivered and turned on her side, her back to the hard metal wall. Rafael was dead. He was dead, his ashes stirring in the sterile dust of Freija. . . . So why could she not have peace?

Iain heard Linnea's breath quiet into sleep. He leaned back carefully in the creaking metal desk chair and looked at her. In the faint amber glow from the comm-screen, her face seemed young, peaceful. As she rarely looked when awake, even when they were alone together.

Especially when they were alone together.

He let his head roll back against the wall and considered, again, whether it would be easier for her if they lived separately for a while. They had been lovers again for a few weeks now, but it was always a fragile warmth, and fleeting. She had made clear after Freija that she needed peace, time to heal, and he had given her that; but he could see that the wounds were still there. Perhaps it was too soon.

Yet he could not let her go. To see her only when they worked together would not be enough. He needed her close, even when he dared not touch her. For it was not her body he needed; it was her honest mind, her generous spirit, her courage. She had hidden them away, even from him. Perhaps even from herself. He had to help her find them again, free them again.

He had seen her soul, for a while. For a while, in their first days on Nexus—before his father's suicide, his own arrest, her captivity with Rafael—for that brief time she had been truly open to him. If they could ever have a few days, a few weeks, of peace and safety together, he felt sure he could break through to her again. Yet that would not happen for years now, if ever. Unless his brothers forgave him, joined with him, took the burden of training from her.

But that could never be. Not—he took a breath, and finished the thought. *Not while Rafael is alive.*

He looked again at Linnea's peaceful, sleeping face. If she knew Rafael had survived the destruction of Freija, was even now on Nexus, was no doubt plotting to capture them again—if she thought Rafael might ever touch her again, Iain did not know what she might do. Certainly it would shatter the fragile structure of security that she had built for herself since their escape from Freija. And it would end their peace together.

No. He would protect her from the knowledge at all costs, for as long as he could. It was the only gift he could give her, the only way he could keep her at his side.

At his side, where she must be. For her sake, and for his.

In their small room, darkness pressed against Linnea's eyes. In the narrow bunk across from hers, Iain slept at last.

She would not sleep, not for a long time. She knew the signs: another long, gray night. She'd learned to hide them from him, this past half year.

The hard memories came in these dark hours, when

she lay alone, when Iain had gone from her into sleep. She no longer tried to fight them; it did no good. Instead she let them flicker past her inner eyes, trying—again—not to feel old grief, terror, pain.

Here, her last sight of her sister Marra, back home on Santandru, through a rainswept window at night: Marra smiling at one of the children, safe, warm, happy—because she did not know that Linnea stood outside, Linnea who was already dead to her.

A flash of those brief days on Nexus when she and Iain had been almost happy together, before his uncle Fridric murdered Iain's father and destroyed Iain's life. She sighed and turned onto her back, looked over at Iain's sleeping face. Back then she had been sure she loved him. For a long time, then, she'd felt only empty—of purpose, of hope, of feeling. Even for him.

And yet, and yet—she knew him in a way she had never imagined possible; he had changed the whole shape of her life, forever. Was that love? She didn't know. But the thought of breaking it hurt.

She had left him so easily, back in those other days, to make her attempted escape. She remembered being betrayed, and the Line Security tanglenet settling around her, gripping tight.

She huddled into herself and closed her eyes, remembering. *Oh, God. . . .*

Rafael. Iain's cousin. Ghost-pale, bone-thin, his red hair loose around his shoulders as he smiled at her. Here and now saliva flooded her mouth, and she fought back nausea, again.

And then Rafael had sent her to Freija, marooned her there. The doomed world, invaded by the Cold Minds. The infested, the few who survived, moving stiffly under control, their dead eyes flickering. Old Kwela, jumping to her death to escape that end. The men who accepted infestation so that she and Iain could escape.

So she and Iain could come here to Terranova and try to save the Hidden Worlds—with the equivalent of two sticks and a piece of string.

She squeezed her eyes shut tighter. Iain thought all was well, and he had important work to do. . . .

And he loved her. He must, or he would not endure this with such patience. Every day, she saw him at her side, as if she were seeing him through thick, watery glass. There he was, warm and present and willing.

There he was, patient, waiting, always kind. But at times like this she felt herself fading away from him, slipping down into the dark. She couldn't help it. She couldn't help herself.

She blinked back tears, fighting to keep the steady breathing of pretended sleep.

She'd tried to give him hope. That kindness was all she could offer him, when she was honest. The world was ending anyway—if they could not defeat the Cold Minds. . . .

TWO

NEXUS: THE CITY

Hakon sen Efrem entered the house of the Honormaster. His curiosity at this secret, late-night summons under firm control, he politely returned the welcoming gesture of the tall old man who had opened the great door to him.

The old man half bowed, a glint of humor in his eyes. "Pilot sen Efrem."

Hakon masked dismay. *The greeting of equals.* So this was no servant, but a man of the Line—a resident of the household. With a swift gesture of apology, Hakon made the proper bow of a young man to an elder and stepped across the threshold.

This house, deep in the City not far from the Council Tower, had been built in the fashion of fifty years ago: dark, vertical, severe. Hakon had never been invited inside a house of this age before. Young men did not take such houses, preferring the fashionable suburbs scattered up the mountainsides above the City.

When the door had sealed them in together, the old man said, "The Honormaster will see you in a moment. I am Isak sen Semyon, who shares his life. And therefore I must ask whether you have done as the Honormaster asked, and have told no one you were coming here."

"I have told no one," Hakon said.

Sen Semyon studied him a moment longer. The silence of the late-night hour seemed to hiss in Hakon's ears. The high, narrow entrance passage stretched up into shadow above them, smelling of stone and waxed wood. A tapestry, abstract in shades of red and black, warmed one wall; a tall painted vase stood in a corner. In the center of the space, gleaming in light from above, stood a life-sized bronze, a young man, naked, looking back over his shoulder with an infectious grin, gesturing as if to invite him farther into the house.

Sen Semyon turned and preceded Hakon along the stone-floored corridor, around an open stairwell, and to a finely carved wooden door at the back of the house. He opened the door and said, "Niko. Here is Pilot sen Efrem."

Honormaster Nikulas sen Martin looked up from his worktable and rubbed the bridge of his nose with obvious weariness. "Go on up, Isak. This won't take long."

As the other man left, and the door slid shut behind him, Hakon made a deep, formal bow, hoping the old man could not sense his eager curiosity, his hope. Yet perhaps this was it: his opportunity to distinguish himself from the rest at last.

The Honormaster, a small man with an air of wiry strength, nodded in courteous response. Facing him now, Hakon wondered that this was the same man who had taught him, years ago during his training; he seemed smaller in this informal setting, dressed in a plain house robe of crimson wool, with his thin white hair caught in a simple tail. The cudgel-staff of the Honormaster's office loomed in a wooden stand in a corner. Power. There was still power here. Hakon must not forget.

"Pilot sen Efrem. Please sit." As Hakon obeyed, sen Martin's sharp black eyes seemed to assess him. "I recall you from training—ten years ago now. And I have followed your career with interest. You have a superb record as a pilot."

Hakon only inclined his head in thanks, hoping none of his pride showed in the gesture.

"Your father must have been proud of you," the Honor-master said. "I was sorry to hear of his death. A good man—upright and reliable."

"I try to honor his memory," Hakon said over the stab of grief. After three years he should not still feel it, but his father's death had been sudden, leaving Hakon master of his own life and fortune—but also without ties among the old men, without influence to help him forward in the political career of which he had once dreamed.

Perhaps that was about to change.

"You are too polite to ask why I requested you to come to my house, and not to my offices," sen Martin said.

Hakon half bowed. "Any service I can render the Honormaster is an honor to me."

Sen Martin snorted. "You're too well taught, boy. . . . I require an errand of you. A private one. Nothing against your honor," he said quickly, and Hakon schooled his expression, which must have betrayed his surprise. "Merely—a message I dare not entrust to the commnet. To be delivered with discretion. I wonder if you are the man to deliver it for me."

And why can it not be trusted to the commnet? Hakon knew he must not ask. Yet this was an extraordinary sign of trust. "I will carry it, of course, Honormaster," he said, and waited.

"The message is for Iain sen Paolo," sen Martin said.

Hakon could not hide his surprise. "Sen Paolo? The traitor? Somewhere on Terranova, I hear he is. Line Security has not managed to arrest him in half a year—how can I hope to find him?"

Sen Martin smiled coldly. "Line Security could have swept him up at any time these last three months. They are holding back under orders. If he is taken into custody, Rafael sen Fridric, the son of the Honored Voice, will find a way to have him killed. And the Inner Council does not wish him to be killed."

Hakon looked away, frowning, then met sen Martin's eyes again. "And the message?"

"Verbal," sen Martin said. "You will offer him full reinstatement to the Line."

Impossible. Hakon let out a long breath. "Reinstatement! He betrayed our secrets to the Hidden Worlds. He spread lies about the Honored Voice—dishonoring his own uncle."

"Pilot sen Efrem." Sen Martin's voice was as cold as his eyes. "They are not lies."

Hakon could only look at him.

"We need sen Paolo," sen Martin said. "We need the work he can do for us. The new pilots he has begun to recruit."

Hakon took a breath to speak, and sen Martin shook his head firmly. "No, not to be admitted to the Line, to our oaths and ceremonies—never that. We need these men as cargo pilots, orbital patrollers, ground support." He leaned forward. "Under our control. That is vital. If this woman of sen Paolo's and their coconspirators on Terranova manage to create their own command-and-training structure, outside our purview and traditions, then when this crisis is ended our monopoly will also be at an end. The *Line* will end."

Hakon stared at him. *Impossible.*

Yet clearly this man, who was no fool, believed it.

Hakon searched for words. "I apologize, Master sen Martin. This is—difficult to absorb."

"For all of us, Pilot sen Efrem." The Honormaster's gaze sharpened. "Yet it is true. Sen Paolo's words are true."

"Not all, surely," Hakon managed to say.

"Yes, all." Sen Martin's dry voice betrayed irritation. "The Honored Voice himself is proof of the truth of all of this. Fridric sen David is not, in fact, the son of his famous father. Do you understand this? You must. The Honored Voice is servant stock. It cannot be proven, they say. But it is widely known."

Hakon looked away from the Honormaster's stern gaze, looked around the beautiful study, the orderly arrays of data crystals that covered one wall, a carved brass bowl dimly glinting on a shadowed shelf. Outside, he sensed the night crowding close, silence pressing down. Sen Paolo's lies—were true? "How can this be?" he said at last.

"A question a realist should never ask," the Honormaster said. "Instead ask, *How must I live now?*"

Hakon had to look away for a moment, reach down into his long training for the control he needed to speak steadily. Sen Martin wished him to be calm; he would be calm. A question, to show he was beginning to think clearly—"Why do we *need* these outside pilots, Honormaster?"

In answer, sen Martin touched the worktable between them, and a translucent page of text appeared, hanging in the air. "Dockmaster sen Joen has delivered an updated report on the damaged Cold Minds ships we recovered above Freija." Both ships had been intercepted as they attempted to escape the destruction, a disaster that had been widely reported as a natural asteroid impact but was actually, Hakon knew, a triple blow engineered by the Line itself. . . . Iain sen Paolo, damn him, had spread that news around the Hidden Worlds in his treasonous comm-net bulletins. At least Iain's dead father had known that some truths should not be spoken.

As, apparently, Honormaster sen Martin did not.

Sen Martin kept his assessing gaze on Hakon. "The Honored Voice does not agree that we need more pilots; he has drawn defensive plans that adequately protect Nexus and the major worlds without reinforcement."

"And the minor worlds?"

Hakon couldn't judge the Honormaster's expression—it *could* not be anger. "In the emergency," the Honormaster said, "sacrifices must be made." He let the words hang in the quiet of the room for a moment, then continued, "But tonight the Council was presented with further information. The autopsy of the human corpse found in the piloting chamber of the more complete ship is finished. And the human pilot was not infested with nanobots."

Hakon stiffened. "Not infested, Honormaster? Then he was a renegade—a traitor." He let his revulsion show in his face, his voice.

"They found none of the metallic network in his brain tissue," sen Martin said. "And his blood was free of any sign of the bots."

Hakon shook his head slowly. "Why would they choose not to control their pilots directly?"

"The investigators now believe," sen Martin said, "that an infested brain cannot guide a ship through otherspace, any more than a machine can. And thus that the jumpships of the Cold Minds are piloted by intact humans. Neurologically intact, at any rate."

Hakon saw an echo of his own horror in the Honormaster's face. After a moment, Hakon said, "So—if the Cold Minds did not control this man, this pilot, why did he serve them?"

"I said that he was not *infested*," sen Martin said, "not

that he was normal." Sen Martin touched the worktable, slid a finger along the surface, tapped. An image formed in the air between him and Hakon, and Hakon recoiled. A naked corpse, a dead man, with all the marks of violent decompression, lay half-enclosed by a sort of pilot's couch, partly concealed by machinery and connections. The worst was his face—his mouth was stretched wide, crammed with tubes. He had no eyes; silvery inputs snaked in from the walls of the piloting chamber and slipped into the smooth skin covering his sockets.

Hakon made himself look away, but the thing was too near. He got up abruptly, strode away from the worktable, stood for a moment studying an old painting, an exquisite little thing: a woman, her arched brows severe, her expression calm, holding on her knee a miniature human, perhaps a child, with a ring of gold around his head. From Old Earth, perhaps.

When Hakon had mastered his nausea, he said, without turning, "Why did they—do that to him?"

"Direct, permanent connection to the relevant portions of the brain," sen Martin said. "Very efficient." Hakon turned and looked at him. Behind the glowing image of the monstrosity, the Honormaster sat with his fingers tented on the worktable, looking down—so he, too, could not bear the sight of the thing. *Interesting.*

"Are they certain he was uninfested, Master?"

Master sen Martin took a breath. "Yes. Our investigators took the corpse apart. Every area of the brain that is necessary for piloting was normal, or somewhat hyperdeveloped. But this man had no more than vestigial motor function. Look at his hands, his feet—curled tightly, classic paralysis. From this and the condition of the soles of his feet it is clear that he had not walked in many years. If he ever walked at all." Sen Martin cleared his throat. "I suspect he had been in that piloting compartment since he was a young boy. The maldevelopment of his brain centers suggests that sort of—deprivation and confinement."

Hakon took his chair again, forcing himself to look at the image of the corpse. "So we are merely components, to them."

"Tools to be used," the Honormaster said. "And after the long jump from Earth, even with the time gain in otherspace, the pilots used by the Cold Minds must be aging, failing. To carry out their invasion, the Cold Minds need replacements." He met Hakon's eyes. "They need us."

Hakon was silent for a long time. Then he spoke in a carefully steady voice. "They cannot be allowed to do— that—to our brothers."

"That thing *was* our brother," sen Martin said quietly. "Twisted, hurt, used—but he must have descended from the first pilots, just as we did." He leaned forward. "That is why all pilots, Line or otherwise, must be under our control. We cannot allow pilots outside the Line to operate freely, out in the Worlds, without our traditions, without our discipline. The Cold Minds need human pilots. They will take them where they can. We must bring Iain sen Paolo's training program under our own control." He met Hakon's eyes. "We must call Iain sen Paolo home. You must do this, Hakon."

Hakon looked down at his hands. He had to say it. "Against the will of the Honored Voice?"

"It is the will of the Honored Voice that is keeping sen Paolo alive," the Honormaster said. "But"—he took a breath—"this must not leave this room. Fridric sen David is fading. His health . . . there are signs of weakness, hidden from most, but clear enough to those of us who are close to him. And as you have no doubt heard, his son Rafael's star is ascending. If Fridric dies, there is no question that Iain sen Paolo's death will follow soon after."

"Wouldn't that also solve the problem?" Hakon shook his head. "Master, as the plan the Honored Voice has published makes clear, we have enough pilots to protect all the *essential* worlds."

The Honormaster sat silent for a moment. "Not all of us," he said quietly, "are ready to accept the end of the Hidden Worlds—to abandon the smaller colonies to infestation and death. It would give the Cold Minds a foothold all around us. It is strategically unacceptable. And—it is not our way." Hakon heard sorrow in the Honormaster's voice. "I have always taught the traditions. How the Line's first fathers rescued humanity from lost Earth when it fell to the Cold Minds. Are we now to abandon them, to save ourselves?"

"A hard choice," Hakon said.

"And perhaps, in the end, the only choice," sen Martin said heavily. "But I am resolved that we must first try to do our duty." He touched the worktable, and the corpse-image flicked out of existence.

Hakon thought rapidly. A division in the Council made for dangerous times. Yet if the Honored Voice was dying, it would be better to have the Honormaster choosing the way than Rafael sen Fridric, about whom so many rumors swirled . . . odd behavior, secret vices. Spider-weave. . . .

The choice was clear. The tightness in Hakon's shoulders eased. "Of course we must do our duty," he murmured. A relief, to be committed.

The Honormaster looked at him, assessing again. "Did you know Iain sen Paolo? He would have been a new trainee, perhaps, just as you were completing your own training. Or perhaps you knew him socially."

"We met," Hakon said, "from time to time. I remember very little of him. He was always—reticent." *Never anything to be gained from him.*

"Now that you understand what is at stake," the Honormaster said, "are you willing to accept this task?"

Hakon knew in his heart what the cost of all this might be if the Honored Voice found out, if his son Rafael found out. Hakon might pay with his freedom, or even his life. All the advantages he might gain from this necessary service—advancement, a good position in the City, perhaps even Selection to father sons—counted for nothing compared to that.

But he had made his choice, and he must not turn aside out of fear. With the Council so sharply divided, a man could die as surely from failing to choose as from making the wrong choice. He looked up and met the Master's straight gaze. "I will carry the message to Iain sen Paolo."

The Master nodded slowly. "You will leave at once," he said. "The Dockmaster himself will clear your flight." He touched the worktable, and a data crystal rose from a hidden slot. He pushed it toward Hakon, who took it carefully. "This is the essence of what we are offering him," the Honormaster said. "Learn it, tonight, and destroy the crystal." He rose, and Hakon rose, too, as he must. "Travel well, Hakon."

"I thank you, Master," Hakon said. "I will find sen Paolo."

And when he found him, he would have some questions of his own.

THREE

TERRANOVA
TWO MONTHS LATER

Linnea Kiaho stamped her feet and shivered in the red twilight of the city, fighting back worry. Too tired to fight it back, after another day of searching for anyone with a spark of difference, who would be willing to be tested as a jump pilot, train as a jump pilot. Another day when she might at any time catch the attention of the agents of the Line. She wished again that she and Iain could stay on Station Six, where at least they would have seen danger coming. . . .

Linnea looked again at the chrono at the far end of the train platform. Iain should have met her here an hour since. By now they should already have gone to ground.

So—he must have found work today, that was all it was. They needed the money, after all. . . .

Terranova's sun, a fat red oval, hung just above the western ocean. On the high, open platform of Cape Hematite's elevated train, chill fingers of the rising breeze slipped through every seam of Linnea's old coat.

The others on the platform looked as cold as she felt, and almost as shabby in their worn winter gear. A woman in long braids, her thin face slack with tiredness, carried a sleeping child. An old man stood a little apart, staring down at the platform, half his face shiny with an old burn scar, his eyes flicking left and right. His oiled-wool coat with its rough toggles could have been made back home on Santandru. Again the stab of homesickness. Maybe that man had even come from there, from home. But she didn't know him. She didn't know anyone. She never saw any familiar face but Iain's. Strange faces, strange ways, strange voices. Behind her some men sharing a clay jug of beer talked loudly in an accent so thick she couldn't follow it.

Her eyes kept flicking from face to face, trying to spot anyone who might be covert Line Security. Which was ridiculous. They were too good. If they were here, she wouldn't know it until they laid hands on her.

She moved away from the noisy group of drinkers to the windy side of the platform, next to the high wire-mesh fence that looked west over low slate roofs toward the waterfront. No crowds here. She paced along the length of the platform to keep warm, keep alert. The evening sky blazed orange-red above the brown haze from the chemicals the smelters and refineries spewed into the air. Linnea tasted brass in the back of her throat. A rich world, Terranova, but rich because of the metals mined and smelted here, because of the goods and luxuries made here for the rest of the Hidden Worlds—because of the work that industry provided, and the people who crowded here to get it done.

Plenty of people. All day today, once again, she had haunted the workers' lunchrooms, and the shabby windowless alleyway shops where a man could buy beer and illegal liquor. Even here on the platform she watched for any man or woman with some spark of ambition, some sign of hope for a life beyond grimy daily work, cheap food and beer, sleep. People who might understand and accept the dangerous gift she and Iain offered: power and freedom—but also a place in the line of battle against the Cold Minds.

She paused for a moment, twined her fingers in the mesh of the platform fence, and blinked against the glare of the sunset.

People knew Iain, at least by reputation, everywhere they went: the Pilot Master who had been stripped from the Line by his powerful uncle's plotting, then had escaped prison to open the Line's long-guarded secrets to all of humanity. And she was known, too, in her way: a woman from one of the poorest colonies, who had been, for a time, Iain's servant. Who now was a pilot herself. Linnea leaned her forehead against the icy mesh of the fence. Half-educated, awkward, not beautiful—she knew how Line men saw her. Even if Iain said differently.

But he needed her. She could talk to the Terranovans more easily than he could. Even though they mostly didn't look or speak like her people, the plain, poor fishermen and villagers of Santandru, they had the same stubborn strength. They could stand hard work, they could grasp hard truths. They would be good help in the endless, dangerous fight to come.

Linnea squinted against the lowering sun. Other than the people, there was no beauty here. Off to the right she saw the lights of heavy machinery pushing gray mounds of garbage and industrial ash farther out into the cold salt bay. They made more land for Cape Hematite, which had long ago filled its narrow plain backed up against steep granite mountains. More low, damp land, good enough for cheap factories, or cheap lodgings for the swarms of workers.

The track beside the platform began to shudder and hum. Another train was coming, another train she would have to let go by, waiting for Iain. Only Iain knew where they would sleep tonight—in a packed bunkroom, or maybe, if they were lucky, in some dark cubby alone. They almost never had a chance to be alone, groundside.

The last spark of sun sank into the chill gray sea, and Linnea turned her back to the wind, dug her hands into her pockets. Then a hand settled on her shoulder.

Her heart slamming, she twisted away, turning to face the one who had touched her. "Oh!" It was Iain. Whole, safe, free. Relief flooded over her, and she smiled without meaning to. Still, always, he looked strange to her wearing shabby workman's clothes, with his long black hair knotted at the back of his neck. He should cut it; it marked him as different here. But she knew he would never do that—cut off the last visible sign of the honor he had once borne as Pilot Master Iain sen Paolo.

He did not answer her smile. He pulled her into an embrace, but it was a sham; his hands were tight on her back as he muttered into her ear. "A Pilot Master came into town today. Fresh from Nexus, they say."

Linnea took a sharp breath and hid her face in the cold, rough cloth of Iain's shoulder. A Pilot Master, in Cape Hematite—no doubt to be in at the arrest. There was no other reason for his presence in this grimy place, no other pleasure or profit it could offer.

"I stole two new transit cards," Iain said. "They won't have been missed yet." She felt the cold hard edge of the plastic as he pressed a card into her fingers. "This train. Off at the first stop. Then switch direction."

The familiar drill. *Keep moving.* Always keep moving. Line Security—Iain they might choose to arrest and return to prison on Nexus; Linnea they would simply kill.

Linnea gripped Iain's arm as they pushed through the crowd to the edge of the platform. The train thundered into the station with a strangled screech of brakes, and they boarded in the crush, waving their fare cards past the readers.

As always at shift change, workers heading home already jammed the car, filled every seat. She stood close to Iain and gripped a post as the train started up again. Iain smelled like tired sweat. Too hot, this car. Terranovans liked everything hot in winter. They had power to burn.

Linnea stood facing Iain as the car swayed, watching his back as she knew he was watching hers. On a moving train they were trapped; and stations were always bottlenecks, always watched, at least by security cams.

Yet they would find shelter—they always did. These were her people, and would hide them from Line Security. Iain did not seem to understand how deeply ordinary people hated the Line—even though that hatred was the best weapon they had, the most persuasive point she could use, when Iain was not there to hear. The Line had long kept humanity obedient, claiming their gratitude for rescuing their ancestors from the death of Earth. As part of that gratitude, all worlds accepted the Line's monopoly on travel, shipping, communication, paying a yearly tribute to Nexus that had made the pilots rich beyond these ordinary workers' dreams. She had seen it, as a servant on Nexus: the lavish wealth, the incredible luxury the Line took for granted, took as their due, even when people on other worlds went hungry.

People hated the Line for that. She wondered if Iain had realized it yet—if he knew that, often, the only reason people listened to him was the fact that she was there, too. Did he suspect that she was vouching for him? Knowing his self-contained confidence, she doubted it.

Her head swam with exhaustion. With Iain's arm snug around her, she felt herself drift toward a doze. Not many moments like this, where she could relish his nearness, relax into peace— Then she gasped and caught herself as

the car suddenly slowed, lurched, lurched again with a
screech of metal on metal. Stopped.

In the sudden silence, a mutter of surprise and protest
rose all around them. The windows, steamed over against
the bitter blue twilight outside, showed no platform, no
lights. Linnea drew a sharp breath. This was not a station.

Then the doors between the cars ground shut, and
with a heavy *clank* they locked. The indignant mutter
rose to a clamor. "They can't stop the train here," a tall
young woman said angrily. "It isn't safe. There's no way
to evacuate us."

But, peering through the fogged plastic of the nearest
window, Linnea saw lights ahead, up the curve of the
track, moving this way. She caught her breath. The lights
bobbed like handlights carried by hurrying men. Three
or four of them. There must be a catwalk along the elevated track.

They were coming.

Iain's arm tightened around her. He leaned down and
spoke softly into her ear. "Follow my lead."

She nodded mutely—all her breath had leaked away
somehow. This had to be an arrest. So there had been a
Line Security agent on the platform after all, who'd
seen them getting onto the train. Or—she pulled out her
new transit card and looked at it sharply. Nothing appeared to be different about it. But if the stolen cards
had been marked somehow, to alert someone when they
boarded—

The lights stopped outside their car. With a *click* and a
shudder, the door slid open.

Two helmeted transit police armed with stunrods entered first and took up places at each side of the door. Then
two more men in unfamiliar dark blue uniforms—officers,
they must be—stepped into the car. "Everyone will remain calm," one rumbled in an artificially amplified voice.

"This is a city security matter. The train will proceed momentarily." Linnea could not get a clear view of his face through the packed bodies in the car. "Everyone will produce their transit passes for rescan."

As people around her fumbled resentfully for their cards, Linnea struggled to think. She saw no way out except past those four men, past everyone in the car. The windows, of course, could not be opened or broken. All other doors stood shut, sealed. She straightened and took a step away from Iain.

And at that moment he seized her wrist and twisted her arm behind her back, held it almost painfully between her shoulder blades. She gasped, and Iain said in a bored voice, "Officer!"

The other riders near them melted back, clearing a space. From three meters away the officer, the taller of the two uniformed men, turned to peer at them. She could not see Iain's face, but she could tell that he had straightened to his full height. "What is this?" the officer asked.

"The arrest," Iain said, sounding unconcerned. "Come, man, they must have briefed you." Linnea heard a note in his voice now that she had not heard for many months—the cultured precision of Nexus. The unmistakable voice of a Pilot Master.

"And you are?" the officer said, clearly taken off balance.

"The man you were to meet here," Iain said. "If you speak my name in this public place, I shall see that you are dismissed from your position. You may call me Pilot Master." Iain's voice rang with supremely confident authority. His accent marked him as a man of untouchable power.

The officer's glance took in Iain's proud stance, his firm, high-bridged nose and clear dark brows, then flicked to the untidy knot of long black hair—neatly combed and braided, it would have been a pilot's mark. "You can't be one of *them*."

Iain dug into the pocket of Linnea's coat, pulled out her old transit card. "Scan that."

At the officer's nod, the other uniformed man stepped forward and waved a read-wand at the card. He looked at the officer. "This is one of the two."

"The man is already dead," Iain said. "A private Line matter. I boarded with his pass to make this arrest."

The officer's broad face darkened. "I was given none of this information."

"Are you so deluded as to think," Iain said icily, "that Line Security would share operational details with a minor local official? Your only part was to stop the train." His grip on her arm tightened. "I have matters to attend to," he said, a cold edge in his voice. "Stand aside."

Linnea saw the moment of decision in the officer's eyes, and just at that moment Iain wrenched her hand higher against her back. The nerves in her arm twanged painfully, and she gasped as Iain started forward. All around them people looked away, blind to power—deliberately blind, to protect themselves from its notice.

"You will remain on the train with your subordinates," Iain said in passing to the officer. "Do not leave or communicate with your superiors for twenty minutes. If anyone interferes with our progress, my displeasure will be shared at the highest echelons of the Line."

"You can't leave the train here," the officer protested.

Iain looked back at him, and Linnea could almost feel his freezing stare. "Private transport arrangements have been made. Why else do you think the train stopped precisely *here*?" In the doorway, Iain turned and faced the officer once more. "Move this train along. Now."

They stepped out onto the icy metal catwalk. Iain kept

his grip on Linnea's arm, forcing her forward. "If the train does not begin to move," he muttered, "run."

But it moved. Linnea huddled against the slender handrail as the cars flashed past. When the last of them receded up the track, Iain let go of her arm. "I'm sorry," he said, and kissed her forehead. "I had to do it."

"I know." Linnea rubbed her strained elbow. Darkness had already fallen. Dim bluish light filtered up from the street below. It had begun to snow, tiny dry flakes of bitter cold stinging the skin of her face. She thought longingly of warmth, safety, some enclosed place where no one could see them, where no one would ever find them. "We'd better move on. When that officer figures out what you just did, he'll call in reinforcements."

Iain nodded. They had both seen the dark ground cars parked beneath a service tower beside the track, not two hundred meters away. With a sharp motion, Iain flung their transit cards into the dark wind, which carried them fluttering away. "Hurry," he said. "The ladder is just up ahead there."

By the time they reached the ground, slowed by Linnea's twisted arm, her bare hands ached with cold from clinging to the metal rungs. Iain held them between his own for a moment. "Let's find some shelter."

She nodded, too frozen to speak. The warrens of worker apartments and barracks where they usually found refuge were out of reach—kilometers from this commercial district, closed down and deserted until morning. They'd pass a hungry night, and probably a cold one.

Linnea and Iain started away from the foot of the ladder, toward the street. But as they reached the edge of the pavement, a man's voice spoke, firm and cool, from behind them. "Stop there."

Linnea stood rigid as a man stepped out from the shadows of the trees. Her heart stuttered. This was a Pilot

Master—no doubt the one Iain had spoken of. He looked somewhat older than Iain—perhaps thirty subjective years. He was taller, more strongly built, with dark brown hair correctly and perfectly braided. He wore the black tunic and trousers of a working pilot, padded against the searching cold. In his right hand he held a neural fuser, the black mouth of its muzzle steady on Iain. "I mean you no harm."

She saw Iain glance at the fuser. Dryly, he said, "You have an unusual way of showing it."

"Perhaps," the man said. "But you see, I don't trust you, Iain." He did not grant Iain the patronym that would have marked them as equals.

"But I must trust you, Pilot Master sen Efrem?" Iain's voice was cool and polite, but she felt his tension in the hard line of his body close beside her. "You ordered the train stopped. Why not come aboard yourself?"

"Because I have been commanded to speak to you privately," sen Efrem said. "And, you see, I knew you would talk your way out of that car."

Iain's expression did not change. "Did you? So you are serving—is it my uncle Fridric? I thought you were an independent pilot. No family alignment."

"Times have changed," sen Efrem said. "More than you know. How long has it been since you were last free on Nexus? Two years? The generations move on."

Linnea heard Iain take a sharp breath. *Fear—of what?*

But Iain spoke steadily. "Say what you have to say."

"Certainly." Sen Efrem held the neural fuser steady. "I come with an offer for you. Amnesty. Return. Perhaps even reinstatement. You will not be imprisoned."

Through her own dismay, Linnea sensed Iain's struggle for calm. He wanted this so much. *Too much.* His voice shook a little as he said, "And the price?"

"Your silence," sen Efrem said, "on all those matters

about which you have been so vocal. A public admission, distributed on commnet, that you lied to discredit your uncle. And"—the muzzle of the neural fuser swung toward Linnea, and she tensed—"the woman's silence. Which we will have, however it can be obtained. Perhaps she should continue as your servant on Nexus."

Iain would not accept. He could not. Linnea could not find words or breath.

"And one other matter," sen Efrem said. "The names of any pilots you have discovered or begun to train are to be turned over to us. Not for arrest," he said, before Iain could speak. "We wish merely to see them properly taught, so they will be of use to us."

"You mean, under your control," Linnea said bitterly. "So nothing changes."

"So we are all safe," sen Efrem said, with only a flick of a glance at her.

"This offer," Iain said. "It comes from my uncle?"

"From the Council," sen Efrem said.

"From part of the Council, perhaps?" Iain straightened. "Does the Honored Voice know of it?"

Sen Efrem ignored that. "This offer will not be made again. Time is short. Your uncle swore to your father that he would never permit or command your death. But the protection that promise gives you will end with your uncle's last breath. Which may be soon."

Linnea saw that Iain's face had gone sallow. What could so terrify him? Again, Iain's voice shook, as he said, "You need not say more."

"And after his death," sen Efrem said imperturbably, "your cousin Rafael will take a very different view of the matter."

Suddenly Iain was gripping Linnea's arm. She swayed on her feet. *No, no.* Terror flooded her mind. *He is dead, he is dead. . . .* She closed her eyes and saw Rafael again—as clearly as if it had been yesterday, last night, that Rafael gripped her in pale hands, that his long orange-red hair slid like icy silk across her face. . . . She choked, sick to the pit of her stomach. *Rafael is alive.*

I will never be free.

With a clatter and rumble, another train passed on the track above, the light from its windows misty through the thickening snow. "Rafael is rising toward power," sen Efrem said. "Accept this offer. There will never be another."

At that moment, with harsh clarity, Linnea understood: Iain had known this. He had *known* that Rafael was alive, and he had kept it from her.

Iain would not look at her; he kept his eyes on sen Efrem. He spoke, his voice low and trembling. "And all I must do, in accepting this offer, is go back to the lie I grew up with. That piloting is a Line gift. That my father and my uncle were the sons of David sen Elkander, not of an offworld servant. That David sen Elkander deserved his glory."

The wind was rising. Dry snow skittered along the bare pavement of the street. "You wish to destroy what you can't understand," sen Efrem said. "Like some child."

"I loved the Line," Iain said. "Until my uncle forced my father to kill himself, to claim dishonor that was not his or mine. Until my uncle arrested and imprisoned me for treason."

She wanted to free herself from Iain's hold, run to darkness, safety—a place where Rafael would not find her. . . . But even in her panic she knew she could not lash out at Iain. Not with a neural fuser aimed at them both.

Sen Efrem looked hard at Iain. "This is your chance to put it behind you. Renew your oath. Return to your brothers."

"Your world," Iain said, "is simpler than mine, Hakon sen Efrem."

The neural fuser did not waver. "Do you accept? Will you and the woman return with me to Nexus?"

"Not at the point of a weapon," Iain said.

The fuser wavered, then in one clean motion sen Efrem put it out of sight.

Iain's face was impassive, but she felt his tension ease. "So you have no orders to kill me?"

"I had orders," sen Efrem said, "to deliver a message. I have done so. That's the end of it."

"Take back this answer, then," Iain said. "The Hidden Worlds will fight the Cold Minds. The Line may join *us*. Or not. As they choose." His voice was steady. "We are going to walk away. I trust you, brother, to let us both go free."

Hakon shrugged, and she saw how angry he was. This was one who did not like to fail. . . .

Iain released her arm, and they turned and walked away. Linnea waited for the spit of the fuser, for Iain to fall; but when she finally gathered the courage to look back, Hakon was hidden by swirling snow.

Darkness, light, darkness. Left into shadows. Out of the wind. A doorway, dark, chilly. She doubled over, her hands on her knees, struggling to control her breathing.

Then stood straight and faced Iain. "You knew. You knew Rafael was still—" Her voice broke. "How long have you kept this from me?"

He did not answer at once. Linnea stood rigid, staring down into the dry snow swirling along the pavement outside the shelter of the doorway. *Breathe.* She took a deep, shaking breath, and all at once a scent, the memory of a scent—cold, green, floral—filled her mind. Rafael's scent. Those few days in his power had burned it into her memory. Sickness choked her. She realized that Iain had taken hold of her again, stood facing her, gripping her shoulders. "It's all right," he said quietly. "We'll be all right."

No, we won't. She could not speak. Rafael was alive in the world again, and he might someday touch her again, and all the strength she had begun to regain slumped into rot and tatters.

Iain's arms enfolded her now, strong and gentle, and she did not let him see how sick the touch made her—how deep was the urge to fight herself free, slash out at him, run. Vanish.

"I know how difficult this is for you," Iain said.

She shook her head against his chest, her teeth clenched hard to keep them from chattering. Rafael had harmed Iain, too, long ago; but Iain was stronger than she was. She pressed her clenched fist between her breasts, over the scar Rafael had made.

"Let's go on," Iain said softly. "We'll find a safe place to rest, with friends. Torin and Zhen, at that winter camp where they're working—they will take us in for a while, keep us well out of sight that far back in the mountains."

For a moment a wave of longing for her home washed over her, so strong she almost cried out. But she could not go home. Not yet. Maybe not ever. Work to do. But Rafael lived— "I'm no use," she said. "This will break me." She began to weep.

"No," Iain said, "it won't." He stroked her hair. "You aren't alone, Linnea. I'll keep you safe."

A lie, and they both knew it.

She had no refuge, even in his arms.

No refuge anywhere.

I ain woke from a doze to deepening cold. His hands, his feet ached with it. For a moment he did not know where he was. Night. He sat in a hard seat, leaning against the wall of a dimly lit train car that shuddered as the distant engine labored to pull it up the mountain pass. Linnea slept, slumped bonelessly against him with her head on his shoulder. Careful not to wake her, he rubbed at the icy window with his hand. When he had cleared a patch, outside he saw the dark loom of mountains, spiked with tall plantation timber blanketed in snow. No lights anywhere but above—the stars. Stars and dust. The Cowled Man, ghost-pale against darkness, was just rising, on ahead eastward. The train crawled forward, higher, closer to the sky.

At least Linnea slept now. He did not have to face the accusation in her eyes.

He should not have lied to her. Once again he had tried too hard to protect her. And perhaps this time her trust had broken at last.

When they had reached the station that served the remote string of eastern logging camps where their friends Torin and Zhen had found winter work, he'd let Linnea assume the task she usually carried out for them. She had the gift of talking to groundsiders, putting them at ease; she had been born one of them, as he had not. It had seemed to pull her back into focus. It was Linnea who had talked them into a place on a supply train that did not normally take passengers, and Linnea who had persuaded the stationmaster's wife to sell them a bit of dinner, thick oatmeal gruel with oil and salt and a scoop of mashed red beans.

She had said almost nothing to him. Silence, and the closed door. The still face, the watchful eyes. Would she ever turn to him, open to him, again?

He sighed and watched the sky. They were traveling east again. Losing time, doubling back over ground they had already covered. But if the pattern of their travels was known to Line Security, they could not afford to continue a logical, and therefore predictable, progress south along the coast toward Terranova's capital.

Iain rested his head against the icy window and looked out and up, toward freedom. Someday he would taste that freedom again, in his beloved jumpship. And Linnea would as well. But the old free days would never return, the days when he had gone wherever it suited him, wherever the honorable service of the Line required.

When he had been master, a man among brothers. Seeing Hakon sen Efrem had hurt: a reminder of that effortless fellowship, which now excluded Iain. Which had moved on without him.

Which he had rejected, again.

The train snaked higher along the wall of a stony canyon. More and more of the star-frosted sky stretched out ahead, behind, across the canyon against the forested peaks. The ache in his chest became an ache in his throat, and he looked away, into the car, at anything but the stars. At Linnea. Her hand lay near his, on his lap, and he thought about taking it. Last night he would have. But now, with Rafael stirring like a snake in the depths of her mind, with Rafael between them—

He could not.

He slid his cold hands into the pockets of his work coat. There was no question of returning to Nexus, of bringing Linnea within Rafael's easy grasp. But how he wished it had been possible. Freedom again, honor again—to be, again, what he had once believed he was.

Whatever Linnea thought, this was a necessary alliance, one he must bring about somehow. If he could not work on Nexus, he must find a way to bring it about from here. A man like Hakon might have been the key he needed—a professional, another true pilot; and an ambitious man, a man with friends and, no doubt, followers. If Iain could ever win men like Hakon to his side, others would follow. Iain did not see, could not imagine, any way they could hope to fight the Cold Minds without the help of the Line. Or how the Line could fight, without the additional pilots he and Linnea could find and train for them. They must join forces.

But he did not see how it could happen. Not now.

Yes, Linnea and people like her made up an important part of the puzzle. Yes, some of them had the gift, the oddity of neural wiring that made it possible to pilot a ship through otherspace without blindness, without going mad. He had it himself, and he was no true son of the Line.

But it took more than that simple ability to be a pilot. It took discipline, courage, and the willingness to face danger for the sake of others. And where but among his brothers would he find all these things?

But he had refused them now, unequivocally. That door was shut.

His eyes closed. Dreaming, he drifted, dreaming of flight. Rising, rising, into the night, into the sky—to find his lost home.

FOUR

Linnea woke instantly when Iain touched her shoulder. She found herself lying along a hard bench seat with her own coat and Iain's over her. Iain reached out as if to help her, but did not touch her again as she sat up stiffly.

The train had stopped, the distant rumble of the engines stilled to eerie silence. Sunlight flooded the car, and outside a loading yard blazed white, pristine snow stretching away to a distant line of snow-covered trees. She rubbed her eyes. Near the track a sign, dusted with snow, read MALLY'S RIVER. "We're there already?"

"You slept hard," Iain said. "We should get to the lodge. The train won't stop long."

She shoved her feet into her boots. "Are you sure Line Security can't follow us here?"

"This is the only train on this line," Iain said. "One run a week in winter. Roads are closed. I suppose someone could come in a flyer. But no one knows we're here." His voice was even and patient. "Torin and Zhen aren't even expecting us. I didn't risk a message. But you know they can be trusted to help us."

She did not answer, only stood up, pulling on her coat, and looked out at the dazzle of sun on snow. Trust seemed far away. She'd met Torin Dimarco, and his partner, Zhen, a couple of times. Torin was a man like many she had known back home, with little to say in common conversation. And Zhen—Linnea remembered quick movements, bright eyes, a ready laugh, all masking a reserve Linnea felt unsure how to penetrate. She'd never learned the trick of making friends.

Linnea had seen messages between Iain and Torin, who knew many people in the workers' union movement in the capital and who had promised to prepare their way among the people there. Iain trusted him, and Zhen Kumar; but for Linnea, that was not enough. Now that she knew she could not trust Iain himself.

She looked around as they slogged through the snow toward the main buildings of the logging camp, which was empty in the winter except for the temporary caretakers. Heavy equipment loomed in sheds and open yards, silent, iced and snowed over. Wind whistled high above the treetops, the only sound.

They entered the lodge. Inside the main door was a shadowy refectory. At the table nearest the brightly lit kitchen, the three men of the train crew sat eating soup and drinking cups of steaming tea. A small, round-faced woman in her twenties looked up and spotted them. Zhen. Linnea saw the quick motion of her hands, meeting under the white apron she wore. But her cheerful face showed no recognition; she smiled brightly, as if to a stranger. "Torin," she called, "there's more company yet."

A tall, lean man, a little older than Zhen, joined her. "So I see." He addressed Iain. "On your way somewhere? Or looking for work? I've a little to spare at the moment, enough to last to the next train anyway. Starting with bringing in the new supplies from trackside."

Iain looked thoughtful. "Not in such a hurry, I guess. Could use a little coin to go on with. We're hard workers." Linnea suppressed a wince at his attempt at a common accent. It was a lucky thing that people did come to Terranova from other worlds; no one could know all their ways of talking.

"That's good to hear," Torin said in a dry voice. "We'll work it out, then."

The crew finished their meal quickly and boarded the train. As it rumbled slowly away, the four of them piled the stack of supplies—food and fuel—onto a small treaded flatloader, then Linnea and Iain trudged along in its tracks with Zhen as Torin drove it back to the storage shed behind the lodge.

Torin had been a union organizer at the shipyards, very much against the will of the owners, and he'd taken this job in the mountains with Zhen to get himself out of the spotlight for a few months. "Gives a chance for the owners to forget about me a bit, let some of the local workers step up and take over the work," Torin said, when they were finally inside, warming themselves by the iron woodstove in the corner of the kitchen. "That is, unless you two manage to get the Board of Control's attention here."

"We will not," Iain said. "Linnea needs a bit of rest. Then we'll move on again. Work to do."

Stretching her hands out toward the heat of the stove, Linnea hid a sigh. Iain assumed she would simply go on with him, continue the work. Not choose to stay here, safe for the moment. . . .

Linnea looked around. *Refuge.* Heat wavered from the woodstove. Beyond an archway, winter sunlight streamed brightly through the small windows of the main lodge, shining on the clean plastic floor and the spotless wood refectory tables, the ranked benches square and orderly. Order and safety, for now. A chance to rest, to think—to absorb the news that Rafael was alive and seeking them. To find a way to go on with her work, in spite of that. Because, of course, she must.

Torin, lean and mournful, never spoke much, though Linnea guessed that questions would come, and soon: why Iain and Linnea were on that train headed nowhere. What they were running from. "There's wood to cut," he said, and gathered Iain up with a glance. The two bundled into heavy snow gear, Iain's pulled from a storage closet, and vanished outside.

Zhen caught Linnea's eye and grinned. "That will keep them busy a while." She set the last of the clean plates onto their shelf and turned to Linnea. "Look. I'm glad you're here, but it's not without a risk, you know? So you need to earn your keep. It'll look better for Torin and me if anyone does come asking."

"Of course," Linnea said. "What do you need?"

"What do you know how to do? Besides that piloting thing."

"All kinds of jobs," Linnea said. "Maintaining machinery. General repairs. A little construction. At home we were on our own for most of that."

"Not much of that sort of work at this place in winter, with all the machinery shut down," Zhen said. "Building maintenance and monitoring, and repairs when things get frozen in or a tree falls. And only us to cook for." Zhen studied her. "How are you at wiring? There's a whole rack of lights gone dead in the main refectory, got to fix it before the workers come out in the spring."

Twenty minutes later Linnea stood on a ladder, testing slack old wires at a conduit junction along the wooden ceiling. "Still dead here," she said, and climbed down.

"I always liked your accent," Zhen said, taking one side of the ladder and moving it along toward the next junction.

"That's Santandru," Linnea said, answering the politely unspoken question. "I come from a fishing village there. Just a little place."

"Sounds nice," Zhen said. She steadied the ladder as Linnea climbed up and unlatched the next junction box. "Clean and quiet."

"It was nice," Linnea said, as she probed into the box. "Peaceful. People were settled." She touched a probe to the wire. "This one's live. So the break's between here and that last one. You want me to pull the wire?"

"No hurry," Zhen said. "Just tag it. We'll pull it tomorrow. I'm for some tea now, are you?"

In the kitchen, Zhen set the aluminum kettle on, then faced Linnea and went back to her earlier question. "So . . . people on Santandru are settled, are they?"

"We don't move around much," Linnea said. "Maybe to marry out, if everyone in your village is your cousin. Otherwise, your place is your place."

Zhen gave a gusty sigh, leaning against the clean wood of the kitchen wall. "So. Not this moving around, one job one year, somewhere else the next."

"No, it was never that."

"*You* moved pretty far."

"Because I had to," Linnea said steadily.

"And now here you are, got a man, got work to do—life's not like we plan it, is it?" Zhen sighed again. "I'd like to travel like you. Different worlds. . . ."

Linnea felt a flicker of surprise. "It's been . . . interesting," she managed.

Zhen looked at Linnea kindly. "But I'd miss home places. I guess you do, too."

Again that stab of regret and loss. "I miss my people," Linnea said. "I've not been home in—in a few years."

"That's hard." Zhen's dark eyes were warm with compassion.

"I lose count," Linnea said, her voice less steady than

she would have liked. She turned to the counter and
spooned tea into the waiting mugs. "All the jumps add up.
Weeks go by for me, but months back home. My sister's
children—they must be half-grown-up by now. They've
probably almost forgotten me." Or thought ill of her. She
knew how Marra would think: Better they should hate Linnea than be polluted by what she had done, going to Nexus
on a work contract, selling herself to the Pilot Masters.

Which was what she'd done, when it came to it.

Zhen shook her head with clear pity. "Me, I've got no
home place. Didn't get to finish school, my family broke
up and no one wanted to take me, so I've been working
since, working steady, on my own until Torin." She
straightened a little, proudly. "While we're here, rent-free,
we're squeezing out a little money every week. Going to
make a wedding next year, maybe the year after, be all
properly married like a couple of rich people. . . . And
Iain? He's made up his mind about you, I can tell by
looking at him. Won't you two marry when you can?"

"No," Linnea said, letting the edge show in her voice.
She did not need or want to be judged by anyone. At
home they claimed the right because they claimed her.
Here she belonged to herself.

Zhen took a breath as if to ask a question, then rose
quickly to fetch the kettle.

When Zhen had poured out the water, and they sat
across the table from each other, the mugs warm in their
fingers, Zhen spoke at last. "I wonder if I could do that.
Piloting."

So that was why she seemed nervous. "We can test
you," Linnea said. "When there's a chance." She sipped
the smoky tea. "But don't you have work here? And the,
the wedding."

"Why should a man own me, even if I marry him?"
Zhen grinned. "I'll learn what I want to learn. And if I'm
a pilot, well, that's good, honest work, isn't it?"

"Dangerous work," Linnea said. "The Cold Minds. . . ."

"Come for us all in the end, they will," Zhen said. "And you—you've seen them?"

Linnea nodded mutely, unwilling to speak.

"Terrible, I know," Zhen said softly. "That's why—well, it seems to me that the ones with the gift to fight should *fight*. The best they know how."

Linnea looked down at her hands, unable to answer.

To Iain's relief, Torin did not seem to believe in mixing talk and work. Iain dug gratefully into the hard physical labor. By midmorning, they had split enough wood for at least a couple of days, Iain guessed, and Torin had barely spoken at all other than to explain how to stack the wood. Iain's hands ached from wrenching and twisting the hatchet after misplaced blows. "Not much practice at this kind of thing," Torin said once, with a half smile.

"No," was all Iain said in answer, and they fell silently back into the rhythm of work.

They loaded some of the split wood into a lidded bin outside the kitchen door, then went in and stripped off their wet snow gear, hung it on pegs behind the stove. Linnea stood scrubbing potatoes at the big steel sink, while Zhen chopped onions. "Long time yet to dinner," Zhen said, as Torin leaned down to kiss her cheek. "Go hover somewhere else."

Iain studied Linnea, who seemed focused on her task, her eyes downcast. He knew that quietness—it meant she was thinking something over. But she seemed a bit more relaxed. She was all right, for now. He turned to Torin. "Do you have a comm panel here?"

"Company business only," Torin said.

"One message? And I need to check our incoming traffic."

"Couple of minutes, I suppose," Torin said. "Company snoops usually miss that." He shoved his hands comfortably into his pockets. "Oh, and first, I'll have to hear the whole story. Why you're here."

Iain looked at him.

"I always like to know what I'm being arrested for," Torin said, dry as ever.

By the time Iain had finished describing their run-in with Hakon sen Efrem, the potato soup was ready. Torin said nothing more about the matter while Zhen served up midday dinner on the kitchen's battered worktable, next to the stove. Iain tasted the soup cautiously, but it was excellent, as was the soft brown bread and the chewy slices of dried apple.

"So, Iain," Torin said, when they had all been served. "Your big talk about teaching us all to be pilots, how we're going to save everyone, that's not enough? You want to bring the Line back into it as well?"

"They'll just want to take over, they always do," Zhen said. "They've cost us one world already, from what you say."

Torin nodded. "It seems to me we're doing all right on Terranova. We can build ships, and you and Linnea can train up our own pilots. We can outmatch the Cold Minds, not like some farm outpost, like Freija, that you say they took so fast."

"There are more worlds than Terranova," Iain said.

"And you can't outmatch the Cold Minds," Linnea said. "You can't defend yourselves, not once they get loose in the world. I saw them. I got as close to some of them as you and me now." She shivered and cradled her soup bowl in her hands. "They get into you, and they take you over. You're dead, walking around dead. I saw them kill—" She broke off and looked away, toward the window. "They spread from person to person, in blood and spit and sweat. You can't tell they're there, not at first. I don't know. Maybe at first you don't even know you have them in you."

Zhen reached out and took Torin's hand, as if for comfort. "Then how can we fight them at all?"

"By not letting them get close enough to fight," Iain said. "Once they're loose on the surface, that world is contaminated forever, and it's always a defensive battle from that minute on. The trick is to keep them from ever landing."

"A blockade," Torin said. "Calls for a lot of ships."

"Yes, it does," Iain said. "We'll inspect all incoming ships—pass them through orbital stations, or through secure ground ports if there is no station. We'll find a way to test people's blood for bots, to know who's safe and who isn't."

"You mean there isn't a way yet?" Zhen demanded.

"The Line might have one," Linnea said. "But they don't share."

"So you don't even know whether you might have these things in you," Torin said.

"After all this time, we'd know," Linnea said.

Torin looked dubious. "And what if a ship dodges all this, lands anyway?"

"We destroy it," Iain said.

"You," Torin said. "With what? The Pilot Masters have the armed ships."

Iain lifted his chin. "And they're using them. I know you've picked up the patterns of jumpship traffic, you know Terranova orbit as well as I do. They don't want to cause panic. But the Line is already defending Terranova. And other 'valuable' worlds. All the new security procedures and monitoring that the shippers are complaining about, that's what it's for. It's nothing to do with the wage protests, or those slowdowns you've been involved with."

"Who said I was involved with any slowdowns?" Iain saw him exchange a grin with Zhen.

"But it's not enough, what the Line is doing," Iain said. "They've made no move to protect the little worlds such as Honua and Prairie."

"And Santandru," Linnea said in a soft voice. "There aren't enough pilots."

"That Selection thing," Torin said.

Iain got up abruptly and carried his plate to the sink. When he turned back, he felt more calm. "Yes. Selection. For generations now, the Line has not had enough sons. Being Selected to father them has become an honor so great that those who control it, who of course have received it themselves, don't wish it to be widely shared. When really all of them should be allowed to father as many sons as they can."

"And daughters, too, then," Zhen said. "As long as we're being practical." She lifted an eyebrow at Linnea, whose mouth twitched.

Caught by surprise, Iain snorted a laugh. "Impossible. You have no idea how strongly the Line would resist such an idea."

Zhen made a face. "What strange people they must be." She looked at Iain. "*You* must be."

"So how can you talk the Line into helping us?" Torin looked skeptical.

"The men on the Council care about power," Iain said. "They'll wonder why I refused their offer to reinstate me. What do I have, here, that could tempt me away from the Line? That's how they think." He quirked an eyebrow. "And so, I'll tell them. Try to make them see the profit in sharing the work of protecting the Hidden Worlds. That maybe they will even benefit from helping us." He saw Linnea's hard stare, and added, "Helping us, not taking over."

"Helping you how?" Zhen asked.

"Ships," Iain said. "Something we have to solve, with or without their help. We need a better ship for Linnea, a real pilot's ship. That old wreck we use for training—I don't trust it. With a proper ship Linnea could at least do screening runs more safely—and those are half of our traffic, finding out who can at least see otherspace."

"A top-line jumpship," Torin said. "A linker. That's aiming high. The Line has a few old ones in deep storage, but they're locked down pretty tight." He looked out the window, then back at Iain. "And yet there might be something I can do."

"I thought there might," Iain said with half a grin. "I'm thinking of those ships we talked about last time—the old ships in deep storage at a few of the orbital docks, and some of the skyports."

"I've seen one or two of them," Torin said. "Really old ships, they are. You think you could get one to work?"

Iain shrugged. "Why not? They were built to last centuries. Plenty of ships the same age are still in service."

"Not too many in storage, though," Torin said. "Ship gets taken out of commission, pretty often they break them down for parts, reuse what they can at the yards." He frowned in thought. "There's one I could maybe get you in to look at, though. For a few hours, at Port Marie Skyport." He settled back in his chair. "But that's one ship."

"We'll build more," Iain said, "in the shipyards here."

"That's quite a dream," Torin said. "How will you pay for them?"

"The Line," Iain said.

"The Line," Torin said, "won't pay for a thing they don't control completely. You know that. Remember it when they make you pretty promises. I always do." He shook his head. "You won't be able to get the yards to step up production, beyond what the Line requires, unless the Line agrees to it. And pays for it."

"We can change that," Iain said firmly. "With your help."

Zhen set down her mug with a thump and looked at Torin. "Remember three years ago? When you told me there were going to be organizers in all the yards, that the workers would have a voice? And I laughed, because the owners were against it. Well, it's been hard, but we got there, didn't we?"

"Yet here we all are, hiding in the mountains," Torin said. "Doesn't look promising for any of us."

"And that's why I need to use your comm," Iain said.

Torin sighed and rubbed his face. Then looked at Linnea, who sat resting her chin on her folded hands. "All right," he said. "I don't know anything. Fine. But if you bring in the Line, you set up a situation you no longer control." He spread his hands on the table. "Where you can't even keep yourselves safe anymore."

"If you see any other way," Iain said, letting his desperation show, "I wish you would tell me."

After lunch, Linnea worked with Zhen on replacing a rotted pillar on the porch, while Iain spent more than an hour in the tiny comm room off the deserted office of the site manager. He came out, looking tired, just as she was hanging up her borrowed coat. Zhen looked from Iain to Linnea and went silently off to the kitchen.

Iain took Linnea's hand and led her to a quiet corner of the main hall. Outside, the afternoon sun hung low, just above the tree line on the other side of an equipment shed. Linnea heard Torin and Zhen's murmuring voices in the kitchen. "How did it go?" she asked.

"Well enough," Iain said. In the shadows of the big room, his eyes looked remote. "Hakon *says* he will convey my message to the Council."

She caught the emphasis and nodded. "What comes next?"

"Hakon's leaving for Nexus tonight. Then we will see."

Linnea looked down at her hands, folded on the smooth boards of the table. She took a breath to steady her voice, and said, "And were there any messages for me? Any from offworld?"

"Nothing," Iain said.

She looked up at him. "You're sure."

His shoulders slumped a fraction: So she could hurt him, by reminding him of her distrust. Well, he had earned it.

"I can only say that I'm sorry," he said. "I can only promise never to lie to you again. But I've done that. The rest is up to you." His voice was gentle. "There was still no message from Santandru, from your sister."

Linnea looked back down at the table. She wished she could stop hoping. "And now?" she asked Iain at last.

"We keep working," Iain said. "And we wait." He looked deeply worried. "What else can we do?"

She felt cold. "You should have gone with Hakon."

"I can't leave you," he said. "And you can't go to Nexus."

"Then I'm a liability," she said bitterly. "The Line will use this against you, you know."

He reached across the table and took her hands in his. "The Line is our only hope, Linnea."

She pulled her hands out of his grip. Would he never understand? "The people I find are our hope," she said. "Look at Torin. He's helped organize the shipyard and port workers on half this coast. And Zhen, she's sharp. She's got that spark we look for. She wants to test for piloting, Iain. . . . There are more people like that, people who are willing to take a risk when it's important."

"But can we train them all?"

"You trained *me*," she said. She spoke quietly but fiercely. "You made a pilot out of *me*."

"The beginnings of a pilot," Iain said. "But we need dozens more. Trained men. We need ships. My broth—" He broke off. "Each Line pilot who helps us will bring us a ship. A jumpship, Linnea! Do you know the value of that?"

"I know the value," she said. "But you know what else they will bring. The old days, the old ways. Their ways. We have a chance here to make a new kind of pilot, a new kind of power, and you want to turn it all into what you understand. Hand control back to the men who have kept it to themselves for so long."

Iain jumped to his feet, turned his back to her. His tired voice was deep with anger. "You think it will change everything, what we've been doing for eight months now? The few people we find, and train, all on our own?" He swung to face her. "You know how hopeless it really is, no matter what we tell people, no matter what we tell ourselves."

"That is the only hope I see," she said. "Ask them to risk their lives for the Pilot Masters, and no one will come forward. Offer them freedom, the chance of controlling their own lives after all this is over—"

"They are strangers," Iain said. "The Line are my brothers—men I have known all my life."

"You have this dream," Linnea said, her voice shaking with frustration. "Going home, going back to your brothers. Making it all better again." She let her scorn show, for once. "They know that's what you want, that's why they offered it to you. But they will never accept you as a fellow pilot again. If they did, they would have to accept all of *us* as well. Me and the ones we'll train. And what would their Line mean then?"

"I don't expect to sway the Council," Iain said with obvious impatience. "I expect to sway Hakon, and men like him. If even some of the Line pilots join with us—"

"If they do," she spat. "If they don't just arrest us. Tidier, that would be." She was shivering. Her hand twitched toward the scar between her breasts, again.

Iain saw the gesture. His expression softened. "I won't let you be hurt again." He sighed. "I won't ask you to trust my former brothers. But surely you can trust *me*."

I can't, she wanted to say. *Not for this.* But she could not tell him that. He was so certain of his rightness. He would not hear her if she tried to tell him how desperately she longed for home. Of the fear for Marra, for Marra's children, that woke her in nightmare night after night. Things she had seen on Freija blended with the familiar places of her memory of home, blended with the fragments of the spiderweave overdose Rafael had given her, that had left its scars in her mind.

And there was only one way to protect her people: to make pilots of everyone they could find. To end the Line monopoly. To change everything. Yet even Iain did not see that.

She was alone.

FIVE

NEXUS: THE CITY
TWO MONTHS LATER

Fridric sen David slowed his steps as he entered the huge semicircular Hall of the Council, which crowned the tallest tower of the City on Nexus. No need for hurry. He was the Honored Voice. Everything waited for *him*. The men of the Council, gathered at the table, sat silent. Fridric's footsteps echoed from the high vault of the ceiling, the gleaming black veinstone walls.

Standing upright and stern beside Fridric's waiting chair, Honormaster sen Martin struck the stone floor a sharp crack with his cudgel-staff, and cried, "The Honored Voice is among us!"

Traitor, Fridric thought sourly. *I will have you, soon enough*. Soon he would have proof of the Honormaster's private attempt to offer pardon to Iain sen Paolo. The impending arrest of the messenger, Hakon sen Efrem—who was expected to arrive soon from Terranova—would provide all the evidence needed.

As the echoes of the Honormaster's strong old voice

died away, the twenty other Councilmen rose to their feet. They were correctly robed in the colors of their various offices, their long hair formally bound back with the colored silk cords that were their lineage-marks. All the real power of Nexus, and thus of the Hidden Worlds, was gathered in this one room. Fridric's weapon to wield.

Fridric reached his chair. At this moment he was conscious of the arrogant height of the tower, a reminder of the Line's centuries of power and wealth——and, far below, the Inmost Place, the meeting place of the ingathered Line for six hundred years. In the great underground chamber below the tower, the Tree that had grown on lost Earth stood white and bare: the place and symbol of each Pilot Master's oath.

Some of them had forgotten that oath. Empty words. . . .

Fridric gripped the high back of his chair with his left hand, and said, "We remember lost Earth."

"We remember," the Council said as one.

He raised his right hand, palm out, showing the old scar there. "We remember our oaths at the Tree."

Another rumbling assent. "We remember."

Fridric stepped forward to his place at the head of the long, oval table and stood with his fingers resting lightly on its surface, black stone shot through with flecks of brightness like stars. "My lord brothers," he said in acknowledgment, and sat. With a murmur and a shuffle, the Councilmen took their seats as well.

Another flutter in his chest. It was happening more often now. Nothing, of course. His physician would lecture him about stress, no doubt, as if Fridric sen David could simply set aside the burden of his office and rest.

He looked up at the expectant Councilmen. The new Dockmaster, a round-faced man of late middle age with dark-dyed hair and cold eyes, had a strange, strained expression, his hands folded tensely on the table before him.

Time to dispense with protocol. "Dockmaster sen Joen," Fridric said. "Have you something to report?"

The man's throat worked for a moment as he struggled for words. "There have been—shadows on the local-space scans," he said at last. "For at least the past week. They read as too small to be ships, but they move like ships."

Fridric leaned forward. "How many?"

Sen Joen glanced down at his palmscreen. "Five in the past eight days, Lord."

"Five? Why has this not been reported before now?"

"Central Orbital Control's relocation from Dock down to the City," the Dockmaster said, "has caused some difficulties in communication. And perhaps some inaccuracies in the systems because data must now be relayed so far."

That was it, then, as Fridric had suspected. Sen Joen had done a poor job hiding his bitterness when Orbital Control was moved from Dock, his jurisdiction, at Fridric's order. Yet Rafael's advice had been sound—Fridric was certain of that. So critical a system should not be run from an orbital facility, where it was vulnerable to attack. Here in the City their defenses were safe.

"I understand you," Fridric said dryly. "Is there any other cause for concern, anything besides these . . . shadows?"

Sen Joen looked sullen. "No, Lord."

"No missing ships? No delayed arrivals? No suspicious information from the outer worlds?"

"No, Lord."

"Then," Fridric said, "we shall continue to trust to our prudently designed defenses. Report any further shadows to me, and increase orbital patrols by fifty percent until further orders."

"Lord," sen Joen said, "it has occurred to me that—given how radically the Cold Minds modified the one pilot of theirs we have studied—"

"Out with it," Fridric said irritably.

Sen Joen licked his lips. "They need only the brain to pilot," he said. "The brain and enough organs to support it. It might be possible to, to—reduce a human to a size that . . . allows a jumpship much smaller than anything we think possible."

Fridric saw the revulsion on the faces around the table. Oh, this was absurd. Boys' tales told at night to frighten the little ones. "The Cold Minds," Fridric said, "will hardly choose *us* as the target of their first major assault. Attack the fortress of the Line! Only if they are determined to expend their forces on a pointless attempt."

Fridric looked around the table. "Our analysts' conclusion is clear, and our strategy has been perfectly in accord. Some of the minor worlds, the outposts, remain unpatrolled. Our enemies will take one of them, as they took Freija. There they imagine they will consolidate and grow to prepare for a more serious attack. One for which we will be ready."

The Honormaster half bowed, indicating a desire to speak. Fridric toyed with the thought of ignoring him, but that, of course, would ruin the surprise later. "Honormaster," he said flatly.

"Council Lord sen David," the Honormaster said, "it seems possible that the Cold Minds' initial priority will be not territory but obtaining new pilots for their ships. In which case—"

"In which case," Fridric said, "any of us, or any of our sons, could be mutilated and implanted in a Cold Minds ship, to serve their purposes until death." He smiled coldly. "But we are safe: Here, and on the major worlds, we have more than sufficient patrols to protect ourselves and any ships jumping in from otherspace. Or are you suggesting that the Council, that *I*, have been somehow negligent?"

"Not at all, Lord," the Honormaster said tonelessly.

"You are correct in one thing," Fridric said. "It is essential that no jump pilot fall alive into the power of the Cold Minds." He met the Honormaster's hard gaze with his own. "Let word be spread among the pilots. Any who fall captive must be prepared to choose death."

Silence fell. Beyond the men at the table Fridric saw, through the crystal inner wall of the chamber, the great central shaft of the tower, which rose from the Inmost Place; and just through the crystal, hanging invisibly suspended at the center of the shaft, at the level of this chamber, was Earth. The image of lost Earth, deep blue and dun, cloud-whorled, bathed in warm yellow light. Not dark and filthy with Cold Minds infestation, as it must be now; still free, still beautiful. *Forever lost.* The familiar, ritual grief stirred again in Fridric's heart.

The Line had saved humanity; and now Fridric would save the Line—for his son, and for the son soon to be born to Rafael. Fridric felt again the feathery flutter in his heart and dismissed it. He would live to win this fight. He *would*.

The Dockmaster cleared his throat. "Lord, we can order this among the pilots of the Line. But—your nephew Iain sen Paolo is teaching ordinary men to pilot. Or so he claims. If it is true, soon there may be dozens or hundreds of pilots we do not control, who do not understand a true pilot's high duty. We cannot keep these from the Cold Minds."

Fridric looked around the table, assessing the will of the men who sat listening. Rafael had suggested that he watch for an opportunity such as this, a moment of apparently increased threat. Abruptly, he knew that this was the moment. "We must end this now," Fridric said firmly. "We cannot let the knowledge spread further. Every captured pilot is another weapon against us."

The Honormaster looked down at the table, then up into Fridric's eyes. "What are you saying, Lord?"

Fridric did not waver. "My nephew is a liar, of course," he said. "He has yet to produce one properly trained pilot not born to the Line. He is scattering discontent and fear, and what is worse, false hope, to rouse the people against us—to weaken our control over the Hidden Worlds, and to exploit a time of danger for his own aggrandizement." He met the Honormaster's look with equal coldness. "My nephew is the greatest threat to our security that now exists." He turned toward the others. "I saw the rot in him, but I preserved his life out of sentiment—because of a promise I made to my brother, Paolo, before his tragic suicide. And now the boy repays me, repays us all, with a knife held to our throats." He let his voice break. "My son has urged me, again and again, to order the death of this Iain sen Paolo. And I—despite the cost to my honor, I find that I must now agree." His voice trembled.

The Honormaster stirred but did not speak. Beyond him Fridric saw slow nods around the table. No one spoke. *Good. They agree. Or at least will not speak against me.* Those dreams of his dead brother, Paolo, silent, eyes coldly accusing—they would surely stop, if he were only rid of the son. . . .

"Lord," the Dockmaster said. "Sen Paolo does appear to have trained one new pilot."

Fridric fixed sen Joen with a cold glare. But before he could speak, sen Joen went on. "The woman—the hired servant from Santandru, the one who seduced him into treason. It is known that she has made several independent flights."

Enough of this. "Lies and tricks," Fridric said forcefully. "We have known since the earliest days of the Line that no woman can pilot."

The Dockmaster cleared his throat.

Damn the man, would he ever simply bring out a point? "What now?"

The Dockmaster took a breath. "The second wrecked Cold Minds ship, the partial wreckage—as expected, we found fragmentary human remains in the portions of its piloting compartment that we were able to recover. Our analyses are now complete. This pilot, too, was not infested. And"—he looked away—"it was female."

Fridric made his way slowly through the maze of corridors and offices and control chambers that housed the secretive, efficient heart of the Council Tower: the headquarters of Line Security, the true strength of the Pilot Masters. He took this path at the end of every day, on his way to the car bay and home. It pleased him to pass the doorways to the rooms where workers for the Line sorted, sifted, and applied the information that was its real wealth, and those where tireless men kept watch over the safety of Nexus.

It comforted him to see that in a universe that was presenting him puzzle after puzzle, this place was as it had always been. That Cold Minds pilot could not have been truly female. Some genetic anomaly? Or perhaps there had been a woman in that part of the ship for some other reason, her flesh confused with the pilot's in the aftermath of the explosion.

As Fridric passed the door to Central Orbital Control, something caught the corner of his glance, and he stopped. A familiar profile, pale and chiseled as a cameo, there in the shadows just inside the door.

Rafael, his son. These days, to his immense satisfaction and relief, the man at his right hand. Fridric smiled and entered the room.

Ranked ahead of him in the blue dimness of the room,

a dozen security techs monitored near orbit on holoplates. Their murmuring voices identified ships, issued clearances for Dock and the skyport, authorized orbits. One of them glanced back at Fridric, or at Rafael. No doubt nervous at being observed by men so close to power.

Rafael only stood watching, his expression blank. The boy was tired, that was certain.

Fridric touched his arm. "Come away now, my boy," he said, keeping his voice low so the techs would not hear. "The day is long over."

Rafael looked at him. For an instant, Fridric would have sworn, the boy did not recognize him. Then he smiled, suddenly, warmly. "But I like it here, Father. I feel . . . close to my old work."

Fridric returned his son's smile. "It is hard to adjust to groundside life, I know. But one must keep a sense of proportion."

Rafael nodded respectfully and followed Fridric from the room.

"So, then," Fridric said, as they fell into step together. "Shall we share a car?" It had been so long since they'd spent any time talking together in private—almost never since Rafael's return from Freija. Since this new sense of duty had appeared, so welcome, so sudden. Fridric had never really known Rafael, not as a father should know his son. And now their time together was perhaps growing short. The fear of that caught at his throat. "Perhaps—you are free this evening?"

Rafael's expression conveyed polite regret. "I'm afraid I have some urgent projects to complete at my office here."

Fridric looked away to mask his disappointment. "Of course." They reached a junction of corridors, and Fridric hesitated. "How is—your woman?"

Rafael frowned slightly. "I saw her a few days ago. Her physicians assure me that the pregnancy is going well. The fetus is vigorous, they say, and perfectly formed."

"I receive the same reports," Fridric said. "I thought you might have more recent information. In a few months you will have—"

"*You* will have a grandson," Rafael said, staring off ahead, into a dark turn of the corridor.

"And you a son," Fridric said, and could not keep the sharpness from his voice. "Becoming a father changes everything. As you will find."

"Yes, Father," Rafael murmured. "Good night."

Fridric frowned after him. Perhaps he had given the boy too many responsibilities, too soon, at this stressful time in his personal life. Perhaps Rafael was feeling the strain of his new position. He had never taken on any responsibility before. It was a good sign, surely, that he was doing so with such eagerness now.

And yet something about his son made the back of Fridric's neck feel cold.

Well, Rafael would adapt. A man destined to rule—perhaps soon—must accept the burden of power. And Rafael was his father's son.

Fridric would think of it no longer. To do so would only increase his worry. He turned away and started toward the car bay, toward home and rest.

Rafael stopped as the door of his private office closed behind him. The dim lights burst into brightness, as they must when they detected human presence. With a clipped word, he shut them off entirely, leaving only the muted glow of the City through green-silk hangings that covered a wall of windows.

Rafael took a shaking breath and rubbed his eyes. He felt so strange. The pale, watery light hurt his eyes. So strange. His heart beat steadily, his breath came evenly, yet he felt . . . afraid. He had almost stopped his father, almost said—but what would he say? That his new position was driving him mad? That he had slipped into using spiderweave again, just a little, just now and then, to smooth over the fear, the feeling of hanging over an endless drop into darkness. . . .

The discontinuities, the times when he found himself in places to which he did not remember going. . . .

But he could not speak of it. He must not lose his position, must not lose Fridric's trust. It was important, it was vital, a need as unaccountable and almost as strong as—*almost* as strong as the 'weave.

The 'weave. *Now.* Risky, to indulge in it here, in a public building, with his father believing he had stopped entirely; but he could not go another moment without relief from the itch, the craving. His belly roiled unpleasantly, and he tasted metal in his throat. Ever since the wound on Freija, he had never felt healed, never felt entirely well. Never any rest, never free of strange thoughts, voices, impulses—A little quiet oblivion was what he needed.

He slid his fingertips into the inner pocket of his shirt, the pocket that always held a tiny osmotic capsule of 'weave. Felt around with increasing panic.

The pocket was empty.

Now that was strange. He had placed the capsule there this morning. Had he used it already? Used it and forgotten?

His stomach lurched again, and he gagged. He needed it, needed it now. A dry metallic whisper tugged at his mind, and he pushed it away. He flung back the lid of a box on his worktable. He had always kept—

There. The small enameled case opened to his thumbprint, and he caught up one of the iridescent capsules that lay inside. Swallowed it dry, against the rising nausea. Sank down on the resting-couch.

It would be better.

Coolness. His vision dimmed. It would be better soon.

Whispers, whispers—

The black tide rolled over him, and took him far, far down.

*H*e dreams. Content within the dream, he floats. Dreaming of walking the hallways of the Tower, men stepping aside for him; dreaming of a long descent into dark places, into narrow corridors that twist and coil. Then the dream changes; he sees his hands moving precisely, outside his control, opening a sealed access plate with his palmprint—and as his fear rises and begins to choke him, something presses down, down on his mind. Down. And he sleeps again.

Dreams again. He dreams that he is thirsty. Drinking with his hands. Plunging them deep into a dark place. Raising his hands to his mouth and drinking, drinking, easing himself with the thick, slimy liquid, the cool, sour tang of metal. Knowing it will help, it will make his mind more clear. Show him the way. . . .

*R*afael found himself standing in the Inmost Place. Dressed decently, hair neat enough, not drunk, not drugged—but what had brought him here? Brought him *here*? He had not come to this chamber since his Selection, more than two years before. Yet now, back from the 'weave, he was standing . . . here. At the center of the vast, echoing gathering place of the Line, the heart of its empty ceremonies.

Day or night, strong light always shone on this dais, beating straight down from around the crystal model of

Earth hanging in the shaft far above. The light stung Rafael's eyes, glinted harshly from the cold golden chain that hung down beside the Tree. The Tree: a chunk of dead wood, twisted, stained with age and the blood of hollow oaths. It could not really have come from Earth; that, like everything else, was surely a long-hallowed lie.

Rafael's hands felt strange. He looked down at them. They were dirty, blackened with something that felt slickly dry, like graphite lubricant. He brushed his hands together, and it drifted free, dust in the air.

His chin was cold. He touched it carefully with his ivory sleeve. More blackness. So he had been rubbing his face with dirty hands. That was all.

His head had begun to ache, and with it, as so often happened, a picture formed in his mind: This time it was his bed, high and soft and cool—safe inside the dark central cylinder of his flat.

He needed to go there, to rest alone, before anyone saw him in this place—saw him and wondered, spread questions. He knew what it would mean if he delayed, the nausea that would grow and grow.

He needed to wait. To wait until—

But there was no image in his mind. Only the beginnings of a trembling urgency, a need to act that would force him into motion again soon.

The 'weave would tell him, when the time came.

He started down the stairs that led to the depths below the platform, to the secret tunnels that would take him discreetly anywhere. The 'weave—it had never been like this before, never so demanding, seeming to guide his steps, seeming to urge him forward—

He set his palm on the latch of a security door, and it unsealed for him, as it must. Oh, he should have given up the drug, as he had claimed to his father he'd done. Given it up truly.

But it was far too late. He knew that as the door into darkness swung open before him—knew it with a sharp sting of regret that he had never felt before.

He was too far gone, down whatever road this was— wherever the 'weave was about to take him. Down, far down. In the end the last of his mind, the last of *himself*, would be gone.

For the first time in his life, that frightened him.

SIX

TERRANOVA

Iain shook his head impatiently in the light spring rain, trying to see where Torin Dimarco was leading him along the endless rows of darkened storage sheds. Torin strode on ahead, a tall, urgent shadow in the dimness of the huge storage-and-salvage lot at the back of Port Marie's skyport, the largest on Terranova. Iain shivered, partly from the predawn cold, partly from excitement. *No. Calm. See it first. Be sure.*

"Seventeen-L," Torin was muttering. "Seventeen-M. . . ."

They stopped in front of a metal building, ten meters high. It looked like all the others, cold corrugated metal shining slickly in the rain, lit from far off by a lamp on a high pole that served half a dozen of these storage units. A heavy, rusted chain, padlocked, held the door shut. Torin produced a key. "Now we see," he said, "if my friend got it right."

"If Line Security isn't waiting for us, you mean," Iain

said mildly. But he had to still himself consciously to hide the fine tremor of excitement.

"I've reason to trust my friend," Torin said flatly as he bent over the lock. He fumbled, fumbled. Overhead, a jumpship screamed toward orbit. Iain glanced up, watched it rise, a bright spark that faded fast against starless indigo, then abruptly vanished as it plunged into the cloud layer. *Going home.* Why was the pain just as sharp every time? He tore his eyes away and looked back at Torin, who had managed the lock. The chain slid loose with an echoing rattle. Torin gripped it and pushed, pushed again, leaning into it, and Iain moved forward and took hold below him. Their combined strength grated the door along its track just far enough. Iain smelled cold, still air, oil, dust.

Torin looked at him again, this time with silent warning, and slipped into the dark opening. Iain followed, and as he blinked in the chill, echoing darkness inside, Torin held up his handlight, played it around. Under the high ceiling, metal barrels, their blue paint flaking, lined the left wall, and racks of dusty machine parts the right. But in the middle, draped in thick sheets of yellowed plastic whose folds were marked with the dust of decades, loomed a huge shape—fifteen meters long, angular, narrow, but twice the height of a man. A familiar shape. Iain's heart leaped.

He kept his breathing slow and controlled as he reached out and took a fold of the plastic, tugged. It ripped, rottenly. Underneath he saw the gleam of metal, mirror-finish etched by years of flight into silvery mist streaked with black. With Torin's help, he stripped the covering away, tossed it aside in crumpled heaps.

A jumpship. Real. Iain stood among heaps of ripped plastic and stared at it. The details of its lines were unfamiliar, archaic, but he could no longer suppress a tremor of excitement.

"An old ship," Torin said. "As I warned you."

"Yes. Probably two centuries or more—that's why we lost track of it. Maybe the pilot died here, or deserted."

"Pilots desert?" Torin sounded disbelieving. "I thought all you Masters would rather die than leave the Line."

"Usually," Iain said flatly, and Torin snorted and looked away. Iain kept his focus on the ship. The etched decorative markings around the hatch showed that it had come from the old yards above N'Eire, long closed when the mines failed groundside. Fifth generation, maybe sixth—no, those rounded lines, it had to be fifth. So it would handle a bit choppily in an atmosphere landing—he would have to warn Linnea about that. . . . But the ship-mind would be a good one, attentive, responsive. They'd done superb work on N'Eire; many of the seventh- and eighth-generation ships made there were still in service.

Iain walked slowly back along the ship's flank, running his fingertips along the metal, learning its feel, its shape—trailing over the stubs that would grow out into airfoils for atmosphere landings, past the dark, sealed connectors for fuel, air, water, power on the ground. The protective lubricant on the skin of the ship, polymerized into sticky sheets years ago, was blistering and peeling away in yellow shreds, but the metal itself looked sound, felt faintly warm. It felt alive. "You were right, Torin," he said, his voice warm with relief. "They didn't pull the jump engine."

"Then you can make it work again?"

Iain stepped back and rubbed his face tiredly. "Oh—given time and tools. And we're in a shipyard—there will be tools. . . ." He grinned at Torin, letting himself feel a moment of triumph. "Linnea will have a proper ship, the same as a real pilot."

Iain saw Torin give him a quick glance, but the other man said nothing, only followed Iain for the rest of his circuit of the ship, stopped beside him in front of the oval entry hatch. "It's sealed," Torin said. "No one's ever cracked one of those, not without tearing the ship open."

"We route vital systems close to the hatch just for that reason," Iain said. "Forced entry wrecks the ship. But I can open it."

"You carry some kind of key?"

"In a way," Iain said. "The Line emergency codes should still work." He reached out and laid his palm on the pad beside the hatch, tapped his fingers in the quick, complex pattern that meant *Pilot seeks refuge.*

The pad flickered, lit. "It's still got power!" Torin marveled.

"A jump engine core never shuts down," Iain said. "It can't. The attosingularity sustains its own envelope as long as it's perfectly contained. It's what makes these ships dangerous to store groundside." He grinned at Torin as the hatch began to open. "We're doing this yard a favor, you see, by stealing it back."

L innea carefully set the last cooking pot, clean and dried, in its place on the shelf. Rain drummed against the window beside her. Behind her, Zhen Kumar slid two covered plates into the warm oven, showing a degree of faith in Iain and Torin's punctuality that Linnea knew she didn't really feel.

"Nasty night for a flight," Zhen said.

"He'll get through. Those ships are a lot more powerful than a commercial flyer." Linnea felt a twinge of worry all the same. The rain mattered nothing. What mattered, now, was Iain's deal with the master of Terranova's Orbital Station Six, an old friend of Iain's dead mentor and teacher Adan sen Kaleb. Nearspace flights based from Station Six had worked well so far, but could the stationmaster arrange clearance for a flight from point to point on the ground? The Line patrols were tracking uncleared flights, forcing them down. Arresting the pilots, right out from under Terranovan jurisdiction. So far, rumor said, all they'd caught was smugglers. But she knew they'd love to get their hands on Iain stealing a ship. Caught in the act, he would be in their power again. Not their brother then—he'd be their prisoner.

Rafael's prisoner.

Linnea picked up her cup of tea. Cold. She sipped it anyway. Of Iain's piloting skills she had no doubt at all. But trusting the stationmaster with Iain's life. . . .

"Torin's message said to expect them now," Zhen said. "A few minutes ago, in fact."

"They'll come," Linnea said. And at her words both women heard it, above the empty whistle of the wind and the rattle of rain on the windows. The high whine of a jumpship on approach, its landing jets on full.

"That'll be them," Zhen said, smiling.

Linnea was already pulling on her rain gear. "Let's go meet them. You said it's that clearing up the slope from here?"

"If that man of yours can find it in the dark." Zhen sealed her own shaggy coat and looked doubtfully at Linnea. "Are you sure it's safe? He won't land on top of us in the dark?"

"It isn't dark, to Iain," Linnea said. "The ship has better eyes than we do. Night vision looks like day."

"I keep forgetting you know these ships," Zhen said.

"A little."

"And this one will be your own!"

Linnea didn't answer, but she felt her mouth tighten at the thought. Her own ship—when the ones who needed ships were the trainees. Line pilots got ships of their own as soon as they could handle them, and it seemed Iain assumed they would follow the same plan in training here on Terranova. Which made no sense, with the numbers of people they had to train.

She and Zhen went out into the wild night. Cold wind and rain made talk impossible. The two women walked single file behind Zhen's handlight, up the wet, narrow path between clumps of leathery green ferns. Drops of water glittered on the lacy spikes of the leaves, and their feet crunched in sodden patches of still-unmelted snow.

As they walked, Linnea tried to keep her thoughts calm. But the old trapped feeling was stronger now. With this gift Iain was locking her at his side. As pilot of this ship, she could, theoretically, fly home to Santandru whenever she willed; but as pilot of this ship, she could never turn from her duty here. He was giving her choice, and taking choice away from her, in the same act.

Linnea stood with Zhen in the shelter of a clump of conifers and watched the ship settle, steaming faintly, in the middle of the little meadow. It looked to Linnea very much like the other such ships she had known, a knife shape of dark metal. The burned ground under the landing jets steamed in the rain.

The hatch irised open, and two figures emerged. First Torin, lanky and loose-limbed. The second was Iain. She knew the way he moved and the lift of his head as he turned to face the women, looking toward the beam of Zhen's handlight.

Then he ran forward and caught Linnea in his arms. She let him do it, tried to answer his obvious delight with a smile. "I was worried about you," she said, half-accusingly.

In answer he kissed her, then kissed her again. But just as her arms tightened around him, he turned away from her and swept a grand gesture toward the ship. "Look what I brought you. A real ship. Not like that wreck anyone can fly. This one will be yours and only yours."

"And that's better?" Her voice a little flat. "That still leaves us with only one ship for real training."

He did not seem to hear her tone. "A pilot needs a proper ship first. And you are just at the point in training where this is traditional. Look at it, Linnea! It's old tech, some of it, but it will work perfectly for you. We'll put you into it tomorrow, start the habituation." He kissed her yet again. "Tonight I could use a beer."

"Three beers," Torin said. "That was some ride."

"That's how these atmosphere hops are," Iain said. "Plenty of gees. I did warn you."

"Not enough," Torin said. "I thought my head was going to come off."

Zhen tugged at his arm. "Let's get out of this rain and put your head back on."

Zhen watched Iain and Linnea while the men ate their delayed dinner. Torin had been right when he and she talked in bed last night: There was something very wrong there. Here was Iain, smiling, his hair still in long, rain-damp strings down his back—so proud of this grand gift he had brought; and there was Linnea, like a trapped animal, smiling hard when Iain was looking, otherwise restrained, silent. Torin and Iain took turns telling the tale of their work on the ship, of the moment just at sundown tonight when they had rolled back the big doors at the front of the shed and Iain in the pilot shell had fired the jets, nudged the ship forward. How men had come running at the sound of the jets, how Torin had leaped through the hatch and flung himself into that box thing the passengers used, just as Iain took off—they'd had to rush the launch to get safely away before anyone got close enough to be hurt by the splash from the jets. Then a quick hop up through the winds and over the mountains, with Torin yelling and complaining the whole time and Iain laughing at him.

"I have sad news for you, Zhen," Iain said gravely. "I'm afraid that Torin will never be a pilot."

"Catch me in one of those things again," Torin said with emphasis, "and I'll never be a shipworker again, either. Or even a man. Zhen will have to keep me in a box and feed me through the lid."

Zhen laughed with the others, but it made her feel sad to see Linnea looking from one face to another with that quiet, forced smile. Why didn't she just tell Iain the truth? Why didn't she just tell him she needed, more than anything, to go home?

Iain woke with the unfamiliar warmth of Linnea's sleeping body against him. Most mornings, by the time he woke, she had worked her way to the edge of the bed and lay with her back to him.

He looked down at her sleeping face. There was so much anger in her—at Rafael, at the Cold Minds—and after he failed her, lied to her about Rafael, she'd swept him into that as well. Kept him well outside the tight, closed fortress of her heart.

But he had been patient for months, and almost against his will he was beginning, just beginning, to hope again.

He saw the gleam of her dark eyes under her lashes. "Good morning," he said gently. Green forest light washed the little wooden-walled room, but he saw that above the trees, the sun had returned. "Did you sleep well?"

She sat up, pulling the blanket around her as she did so—backworld modesty, old habit, or to shut him out? "Very well," she said mechanically. "So what is it we're to do today?"

Iain swallowed disappointment. *Patience.* "You need

to be installed in the ship," he said. "Don't eat breakfast. Some of the testing might make you dizzy."

She did not move. "I'll be all right," she said. "I always am."

Not yet, he thought sadly, and sat up. "We'll begin in an hour," he said.

L innea stood naked in front of the piloting pod, her black hair knotted back out of the way. She felt uneasy, undefended. Afraid. Iain, clothed, knelt half in the pod, his back to her, as he finished his final check of all the piloting connections. He had already attached a monitor lead to his temple; the silver wire seemed to have merged straight into his skin. "Any pilot can use any ship in orbit, or in atmosphere," he said. "And even for otherspace, a crude old ship like our trainer can be adjusted for a new pilot in a few minutes. But for a pilot's personal ship, the connection must be more intimate. Different for every man. I am telling the shipmind to prepare for a new pilot."

"Is it happy about that?"

He glanced back at her. "Even a shipmind this old is unintelligent, Linnea," he said. "Highly functional, but not sentient. It can talk, but there is no personality. No self."

"Is that why you don't name your ships? Back home—" She broke off. *Shut up.* She had almost broken her rule, almost talked about home again. It did no good.

"All according to interworld law," Iain said. "We can't repeat the mistake that created the Cold Minds— permitting independent thought in machines." He got to his feet. "Take your place." His voice was firm, sure—Iain the teacher.

She stepped forward reluctantly into the base of the pod, turned, and leaned back as he had instructed her.

The pod shaped itself around her into a piloting couch, smoothly and firmly supporting her body, and the lid hissed shut, sealed tight. She felt the tickle she had felt many times before, of life-support connections and waste connections sliding into place. Iain's voice from outside the pod reached her faintly. "We won't be going up today, of course," he said. "But every system has to learn you."

Now came the moment she dreaded most. The silver neural connections—many more of them than she had ever had to accept before—slid out from the inner walls of the pod. She heard the faint slithering sound they made. Something very cold touched her temples. She could not suppress a gasp.

Then, with a painless tingle, the same cold slid inside, inside, into her skin, into her brain. An invasion. She held her breath. When Iain spoke again his voice sounded naturally in her ears, as if they were standing in the same room. "The connections you've had before, with my ship, have been monitors," he said. "No control, just viewing and communication. And the training-ship interface—you mastered that very quickly, but you must realize it's crude, limited. That's why anyone can use it, why it can be adapted so quickly to different pilots. This is different, Linnea. It is very important that you keep still—your mind as well as your body. Do not even think about moving. All such thoughts can control aspects of this ship. I have instructed the shipmind not to respond to those impulses from you today, but you must begin to learn this discipline."

Linnea kept waiting for her eyes to come to life—for the world around the ship to spring into view as she saw through its monitors, as it always had when she traveled with Iain as pilot. But she saw nothing for a long, worrying time.

Then, abruptly, a pulsing, spinning gray fuzz filled her vision. She made a sound of protest, and nausea flooded her throat. A tingle in her arm, and she knew the ship had responded, medicating her. The nausea faded to numbness in her belly; the anger hidden in her heart dulled down, the same way it did when she worked herself to exhaustion.

"Why can't I see?" she muttered.

"Shhh. Hold still. These connections are deeper than the ones you've had before. Not just your vision centers; you'll have access to all the system readouts, using all your senses. Many channels of information. I will teach you how to check them and how to move from system to system. It's a lot to absorb."

She felt, again, that odd impulse to reach out toward him, feel some human touch. But as she had the thought, she also knew that at another time this mental motion— simply reaching forward—would have increased the ship's acceleration. She sensed a faint unspoken protest in her mind, and at the same time, Iain said, "Keep still, even in your mind, Linnea. The ship needs to form its connections while you are calm and still."

The gray fog was thinning, light and color beginning to leak through. With a sudden soundless *click*, she saw clearly. It was as if the piloting shell had vanished, though she knew it still held her cocooned in darkness. She saw Iain looking at, past, through her, a troubled expression on his tired face. With care, she subvocalized and heard her own voice: "That's better. I can see you now."

She saw his shoulders drop a little, some of the tension leaving him. "That's the first hurdle," he said. "Good work."

By the end of a few hours Linnea was exhausted. She had learned her way around the virtual monitoring systems, learned the most basic of the alarms she would feel as an itch in some part of her body, learned the simplest aspects of the piloting controls she would work with her mind. Much of her previous work had been with the monitoring system. The rest had been in the training ship, with its crude generic interface.

This ship was harder, much harder, to master, though Iain assured her that in time it would be as natural as breathing, swallowing, coughing.

"That's it," Iain said at last. "Your body readouts are beginning to look atypical. Fatigue chemicals building up. Anything the ship learns at this point won't fit right later." She saw him turn to a control board in the bulkhead. "Don't move."

For several minutes she held rigidly still as connection after connection pulled free of her body. Then, with a tingling sensation, she lost her ship vision, lay again in the tight blackness of the piloting shell. She felt small, alone, blind. A moment later Iain pulled the shell open, and she blinked in the relative brightness. "Well done," he said gently. "Soon you will be a real pilot. . . . Now come and rest."

Linnea kept silent as they started down through the woods toward the lodge. Late-afternoon sunlight slanted down through the trees, dappled the drifts of needles that covered the bare soil. She breathed in cold, fresh air, sharp with the green scent of conifers. So many trees. What a beautiful world this was, in its way. Worth fighting for. Just as Santandru was worth fighting for.

"Iain," she said abruptly. "How many more of these ships can we steal?"

He looked over at her, then shook his head. "I don't know. We can only try. But they are probably already locking them down tighter, after yesterday."

She looked down at her feet on the path, ahead at the mossy roof of the lodge below, just visible through the trees. "If you need to bring in the Line," she said, "if you can do it, I agree that we need their help. But *we* have to keep control of the training. You and I, personally." She stopped, and Iain stopped as well and faced her. She looked up into his eyes. "If you let them take you back, make you part of the Line again, then you have to obey them. Hand everything we've built over to their control. You can't let that happen."

He looked away. "I know, Linnea."

"Then keep that in the front of your mind. Sometimes I think you let your heart pull you into things." She felt herself flush. "Things you might be better off without. And this is something you want, just as much as I—" Her throat closed up, and after a moment, she went on, "As much as I wish I could go home."

He touched her shoulder gently, his eyes sad. "Your life has made you strong enough for this," he said.

She closed her eyes, willing the tears back. *But not strong enough to be who you need me to be. Not strong enough to give you any strength.*

They walked the rest of the way to the lodge in silence.

SEVEN

NEXUS: THE CITY
FIFTH DAY OF THE NEW YEAR

Fridric sen David woke with a gasp and sat up, scattering the rich silks, the embroidered quilt that had covered him. Lights sprang up in his bedchamber as he clutched at his chest. *Breathe. Breathe. Steady.* Only a dream. Already the details were fading from his mind. Rafael—Rafael falling free into space, his blank, pale face receding, vanishing. Fridric's house crumbling around him, rot sloughing the rich fabrics, metals corroding, wood splintering—a roiling sky, heavy and dark like a sandstorm, sinking down toward him through the holes in the roof. . . .

Breathe. His hammering heart paused, fluttering, for a sick, dizzy instant, then started again. The feeling of disaster still overwhelmed him. Something he had missed, not seen—but it had begun, he was too late, he could not stop it now. . . .

He stood up carefully and straightened his silk sleeping robe. The high, elegant room looked odd. Warm light gleamed on rich furnishings, but outside, through the great bank of arched windows that overlooked the eastern mountains, the first colorless glow of dawn was already creeping up the sky above the desert. The wash of light looked cold, sickly, strange. *Disaster.*

Fridric left his chamber and hurried, almost without willing it, down the broad granite stairs, down the hall to the back of the house, to the servants' wing. Empty now. He had sent them all away, all but the woman, dismissing even the ones who had been with him for many years. He could not risk having witnesses to his own weakness, to the strange spells that overcame him more and more often.

But Rafael's woman—the hired servant Yshana—was a different matter. He had brought her here weeks ago, driven by his obscure worry about Rafael, unsure that Rafael would properly protect her and the unborn boy inside her: Fridric's grandson. His heir. Fridric would make no mistakes with *this* boy. No mistakes at all.

Fridric's palm opened Yshana's door, stood in the doorway. Faint light from the window across the small room washed over the woman in the bed. All her former beauty had long since gone. She lay knotted on her side, her belly seeming to weight her in place, her dull, pale hair tumbled on the pillow. As he watched, her eyes opened and she raised an arm to shield them from the light. "Lord sen David," she mumbled.

"Go to sleep," he said. "Everything is all right, Yshana."

She nodded and burrowed back down into her pillow. Behind her, in the rising light, the lamps of the City began to go out.

All is well. Fridric turned away, let the door close gently behind him. Chanted the words in his mind, as he had been doing so often of late. *All is most certainly well.*

He stopped in the hall and pressed his fingers against

the side of his neck. His heart beat steadily. These fleeting episodes were nothing to be concerned about.

It was time to begin another day.

*R*afael cannot sleep. Helpless in the shrinking pool of
light at the center of his mind, he knows that he will
never sleep again. He cannot close his eyes; he no longer
controls them. He does not know who he is. Four times,
five times, as his will has slowly faded, he has gone to the
place where he hid that thing. Under the Inmost
Place—even now a ghost of pain begins. Four times, five
times he has opened the small panel. Reached in. Tasted
what waited there.

Carried it to the places commanded to him, by the
voices he cannot hear, but whose meaning he understands.

And every time, after that there has been less of him
left. The light is smaller—he is alone with the voices,
quick chittering voices without words. . . .

He can see, if he concentrates his mind, but what he
sees fills him with horror. A room now, a high, dimly lit
room full of men at holoplates, he knows this room. But
now as Rafael's body walks along behind them, the men
are slumping forward into the glowing images before
them. As Rafael's hand—*there*, he sees it—his hand
holding a neural fuser touches each of their skulls in
turn. Congealing their brains, killing them. The men try
to escape, but trapped, wired into their stations they cannot, and so they die—

Now the room is burning, chemical smoke, a harsh electrical smell, braided with the stink of burning cloth, hair,
flesh. And Rafael's body walks away from the flickering
redness, past other men running toward the room shouting,
their mouths opening and closing, but his hearing is going
now, he cannot hear, he cannot see—

This is not the 'weave. He knows this, with complete simplicity. He has been wrong, wrong from the start. He shrinks into the center of the circle of light and begins to howl.

The circle of light flickers, narrows.

He is alone.

NEXUS: DOCK

Hakon sen Efrem's first hint of trouble was a rough docking: The arm was wrongly positioned, and instead of the smooth, accustomed joining maneuver, his jumpship ground against it with a screech of metal. Hakon felt in his pilot's body the momentum of the mass of his ship, unbalanced against the docking arm, trying to tip over it—he fired the attitude jets rapidly, percussive *chuffs*, and shuddered as the fabric of his ship creaked and scraped against the arm.

He should be able to control the docking process from his own ship, but it had been years since his last drill in the technique. After a few moments of struggle, though, he felt control slide into his hands. He settled the ship into place on the arm, felt the clamps lock on and the faint jolt as the arm began to draw the ship into its bay inside the station. A moment later, the gentle tug of the station pseudograv pushed him down into his piloting shell, and he heard a faint hiss rising to a roar as atmosphere returned to the bay.

He waited impatiently for the ship connections to withdraw from his body, then burst out of the shell, ignoring the ache in his muscles left by twelve subjective days in the jump. He did not bother with clothing, but slapped the comm switch. "Dock," he said. "This is Hakon sen Efrem. What just happened?"

Silence.

He opened to all channels. "Dock! Respond!"

Still silence, though he caught a quick gabble of chatter that broke off, not anything responding to him. It sounded almost panicked.

He dressed quickly and left the ship. His private docking bay was cold and dark; the lights did not come up, as they should have.

The reception room at the hub connecting the docking bays on this level stood silent, deserted. No attendant greeted him with offers of refreshment and rest; no tech stood at the diagnostic station, running checks on his ship. Hakon strode out into the gleaming central space, looked up and down the shining metal corridors at the other docking bays. All empty. At a cross corridor far away someone ran past, vanishing before Hakon could call to him.

Hakon hurried into the main body of the station. He saw no one. Well, there was always an attendant at the trainees' dormitory, and he knew that part of the station well from the years he had spent in training there as a boy. He ran toward a lift that would carry him there.

After two minutes no lift had come. Hakon slung his traveling bag over his shoulder and turned toward the emergency gangways, steep stairs almost like ladders, easily manageable in the low pseudograv. As he started to climb, an alarm began to sound in the distance. Not the insistent whoop of pressure failure, as, of course, with his long training, he instinctively feared. This buzzing meant security failure. Intrusion.

Intrusion? Here?

Hakon felt it more than heard it, then—a sharp, metallic *clunk*, enormously loud, followed by a rumbling groan of stressed metal. Clutching the rails of the gangway, he felt the rippling shock of that impact in his hands and feet, through the metal mass of the station. Then came another shock, and another. Then a series of small explosions. Sometimes in an emergency, a ship docking to the skin of another, or to an orbital station outside a docking area, would seal itself on with metal bolts shot into the skin of the station. Damaging and dangerous, but in an emergency—

Hakon was already scrambling up the ladder, then the next, the next, six decks up, seven, *there*. Racing down the corridor toward the training area, he passed breathless boys pelting the other way, fright plain on their faces, but he did not want to stop them or slow himself by asking questions.

Here came one of the instructors, a recently retired pilot, a friend of Hakon's father. "What is it?" Hakon called.

The man slowed. "Ships," he tossed back. "Dozens of ships jumped in. Some locking on here, some landing at the City. Orbital defenses down. They say—Cold Minds—"

Crystals of ice crawled up Hakon's back. "Cold Minds! How could they—"

"Get to your ship, brother! Jump away, jump anywhere!" And he was gone.

Those *things* had locked on to the station—if he tried to return to his own ship, they would catch him. But—

The trainees' ship bay. Full of jumpships set up with general interfaces for training, any jump pilot could link into one and use it if he had to. He would escape that way, with as many trainees as he could jam into the ship. Down that next corridor to the left—

Hakon burst out into the control room overlooking the ship bay, and lurched to a stop, his fists tight against the heavy plast of the room's port. He was too late.

Something had cut or torn a hole in the door of the bay below. A hole three meters high, two meters wide. Through it Hakon saw only dimness, faintly blue-lit. Shapes moving. A ship had latched on there, torn its way in. There were *men* coming out of that ship.

No, not men—things that had been men, once. Figures dressed in gray padded rags, their motions oddly jerky, like puppets on strings, their faces slack and dead.

And then Hakon saw them, backed into a corner of the bay, with no escape possible: a small group of boys, trainees. His breath caught. Their instructors must have run. No, one at least had fought—his corpse lay sprawled on the deck near the blasted hole, blood pooled around the shattered head. Hakon heard no sound through the thick vacuum-proof port overlooking the bay, but he saw the boys clearly. Some of the younger ones, children of twelve and thirteen, wept in terror as the things approached them.

Hakon threw himself at the hatch leading down into the bay, but it did not open. When the Cold Minds ship had broken through the bay door, some atmosphere must have vented from the bay. Now the pressure differential held the door tightly closed. He could not get down to the floor of the bay. He could not help them.

He leaned against the window, watching, shaking. There, not twenty meters away, not five meters down, stood the boys. At their head stood a boy Hakon knew: Reiven, the younger brother of a man he had lived with for a while last year. The boy's face was set, impassive, staring at the figures approaching them. Hakon felt sick with horror. Though Reiven did not know it, the Cold Minds would not kill him, or even infest him—not with their need for human pilots. They would simply implant all these boys into their ships. Into those seven training ships, perhaps, left as a gift to the invaders—

Then Hakon saw what the boy held in his hands.

A fueling hose in one. A cutting torch in the other. The fuel for ships' attitude jets was dangerously explosive—

So—Reiven did understand. Helpless rage took Hakon then, and he slammed his hands against the thick plast of the port. He could barely see through his tears. He dragged his sleeve across his eyes and saw that Reiven had spotted him.

Meeting Hakon's eyes, the boy's face crumpled, and he looked even younger than he was. Sixteen? He would have been sixteen by now.

The things had nearly reached the huddle of boys. The others clutched each other. Across the distance between them, Hakon saw Reiven master himself. Saw the boy look toward him, his expression urgent.

He would not act until Hakon was safe.

Hakon turned away, sick with grief, and plunged into the corridor, heard the hatch slide shut behind him.

Then came the muffled *thump* of an explosion, the roar of venting atmosphere. He hoped Reiven had taken that ship with him.

No time to grieve. Shaking, Hakon struggled to his feet, fought to focus his thoughts. There were lives he could save, men he could lead, something still to salvage from this.

Terranova. They would rally at Terranova.

Then turn and fight. And wipe those *things* from the Hidden Worlds forever.

Weeping, the air tearing his throat, Hakon ran for the jumpship bays.

THE CITY

By the time Fridric had bundled Yshana, some portable valuables, and a neural fuser into a bubble car, the ships of the Cold Minds had begun to land on the desert floor outside the City. He could hear the rumble of their engines even inside the car, even under his house. He set the car in motion with a shaking hand. If the transit system shut down while they were still in the car, in one of the tubes, well, they would have a more merciful death than they could expect otherwise. The fuser would see to that.

And he had sent one carefully coded message.

The woman Yshana slumped in her seat, arms wrapped around her belly, sobbing. Surely not for Rafael. Fridric had heard wild reports of Rafael, his actions this morning—

But if the reports were true, then Rafael must be dead. By now some man of courage must surely have crushed out his life.

As the rings of light flashed past in the tunnel, Fridric fought back grief. Let anger burn his heart to flint. He would be strong. Rafael was dead, but there was work to be done. The unborn baby this woman carried was the last thread, the last hope of Fridric's line. And that line *must* continue.

At the skyport station he half dragged the woman from the car, up the moving ramp, out onto the smooth poreless black surface of the field. All around ships were rising skyward on hissing jets—the few jumpships that were kept here rather than at Dock; with luck they would break through the Cold Minds' orbital pickets and jump to freedom.

As he would. As he would. Here was a trainee ship, down from Dock for atmosphere-landing practice. An instructor and a boy ran toward it, shouting, as Fridric forced the hatch with his Council override code, shoved the woman inside. The hatch irised shut, cutting off the anguished shouts of the unlucky former pilots. Fridric bundled Yshana into one of the passenger shells, skipping most of the hookups—they would jump out-orbit, just a skip, and he would redo the connections properly for the long jump once they were safe. . . . She was still crying, useless thing. He slapped her into silence, then stripped down. Years, decades since he had piloted, but he remembered the stiff, awkward feeling of flying a ship through one of these training interfaces.

It would do. It would save them. The two luckless pilots were still pounding on the hatch when Fridric cut in the launch engines. The bloom of fire gave them a more merciful death than they would likely have found otherwise. The ship rose into the sky, where strange, dark enemy ships blossomed and floated down over the world that Fridric had loved and defended. Ships bringing death, ending everything. Jouncing, shuddering, Fridric and his cargo ascended, the old skills slow to come back under his hands, his hands stiff with age as they had not been, all those years ago.

DOCK

By the time Hakon reached the jumpship docking bays, by a twisting route through maintenance and service corridors, his ears ached from the constant slight shifts in pressure. The Cold Minds were tearing their way in, crudely cutting and patching, venting air that the station's systems then labored to replenish. The emergency hatches that should have slid shut every hundred meters or so had not done so; and Hakon was grateful, it would have trapped him, trapped them all for the Cold Minds' convenience.

A light shone just ahead, and he heard a voice. He rounded the last bend in the corridor and came out into a small room, an auxiliary control. Its panel, still active, swirled with light. As Hakon moved to look more closely at it another man appeared, a tech in blue, his iron-gray hair clipped short. "Pilot," he said. "Get to your ship, or it will be too late."

Hakon looked up at him. "How do I cut docking control? If that's in place, the Cold Minds will be able to latch us all down from Central."

"Didn't you notice that the pressure hatches aren't working?" The tech shook his head, a jerky motion. "Central Control is gone."

"Gone!"

"We shot the control boards," the man said, his voice strangely calm. "Blew the main power conduit." He looked hard at Hakon. "Killed the techs. No use to the Cold Minds, any of it. Any of us, either. Orders." He raised his hand and Hakon saw the welding torch it held—crude, as a weapon, but it would do. With a cold certainty Hakon knew who had killed those techs.

"Now you go," the tech said. "While I finish here."

"Finish!"

The man's eyes looked abstracted. "The main power plant . . . They've almost all gone now, the ones who got to ships. They'll need you, they'll need all the ships they can get. Go! You need to jump out of range in the next two minutes."

Hakon hesitated, then bowed to the tech, the full bow of respect to an elder. The tech did not seem to see it.

Hakon ran for his ship.

NEXUS NEARSPACE

Accelerating, still accelerating. Out of the atmosphere, still accelerating. Fridric's ship showed him the incoming invaders, not visible by eye but circled in orange in his inner sight. More acceleration. The woman must have passed out by now; he could only hope the fetus would survive this. He saw a few green circles, flashing out one by one—jumps, he hoped, not destruction. Some of the Line would survive this. Some of them at least.

As his ship flung itself on toward the minimum distance for jump, Fridric saw the death of Dock: an immense white flash, quickly masked black by his shipmind. Hundreds of ships, hundreds of men, gone in an instant. He wondered how many had escaped. What had been salvaged. Where the survivors would go.

Not his concern. He had stopped being the Honored Voice when the first Cold Minds ship entered atmosphere. He had lost the right to be Honored Voice, failing as he had with Rafael.

But he could still save something that mattered. Rafael's son would redeem his line, redeem his name. If the baby survived to be born. . . .

Fridric knew where he would go. A distant, out-of-the-way world, worthless to the Line and so possessing no ships or resources the Cold Minds would covet. A world where a neural fuser and a little wealth would buy safety, and silence, for as long as he needed. A world where he could ensure the future of the baby yet to be born.

Fridric would jump for Santandru.

EIGHT

TERRANOVA
TWO MONTHS LATER

Atmospheric descent. As the ship shuddered, buffeted by the thin, fierce winds high above Terranova, Linnea fought to keep her body relaxed, motionless, to control the landing with her mind as Iain had trained her to do. Worry pulsed behind her thoughts. She had carefully planned their approach to avoid drawing the attention of the Line patrol ships, and Station Six had granted her clearance at the start of her flight this morning—but now, back from the short training jump, she had not been able to raise them at all. Maybe a comm problem, with this old ship. Yet she had to land; the fuel allowance for this flight was about used up. She only hoped that a patrol ship would ask questions before shooting her down.

And Zhen worried her, Zhen who lay sealed into the instructor's mat beside Linnea's shell. Through the ship's eyes Linnea saw her, stiff, blanched, terrified in the feeble-seeming hold of the fabric cocoon. "Zhen," Linnea subvocalized. "Zhen, you're safe, the mat will hold you down. Don't be afraid." But she felt the other woman's fear, wordless, through their mutual connection to Linnea's ship.

This had been Zhen's piloting test run—two short in-system jumps, to see whether Zhen had the ability to perceive otherspace and thus to be trained as a pilot. She'd done well, surprisingly well, but now—Zhen's eyes half closed, rolled back into her head. Linnea reached out, reached into herself, and now she could not sense Zhen, who had lost consciousness. It happened sometimes, even to pilots. . . .

No more time for that. Final approach. The forested mountainside, sharp-shadowed in the near-level light of the sinking sun, seemed to leap up toward Linnea. Snow still covered the trees at this altitude even in late spring. In Linnea's virtual perception, a blue light pulsed at the landing site she and Iain had chosen, a small, snowy clearing on a nearly level shoulder of the mountainside. No light was actually there, of course; the ship had placed it in her vision to guide her. She checked her descent again, decelerating just within the limits of safety. Patiently, she watched the approach, and at ten meters she gave the landing jets a little more fuel. Setdown was gentle, perfect.

As soon as the shipmind reported stable ground position, Linnea disconnected herself from the ship and scrambled free of her piloting shell. She dropped to her knees beside Zhen's cocooned body. "Zhen! Zhenevra, wake up!" The other woman's eyes stared unseeing. *Readouts.* Heart good, breathing good, stimulants going in. . . . Linnea waved her hand in front of Zhen's face. After a moment Zhen's eyes widened, and she gasped.

"We're down," Linnea said, weak with relief. "And you did well. Very well."

"I'm—" Zhen swallowed hard. "Sick."

"You're getting a drug to help that," Linnea said, touching a control. "When you can, I'll help you sit up."

"I'm one of them," Zhen mumbled.

Linnea met her eyes. "Yes. You are one of us."

"Oh, good," Zhen said thinly, then turned her head and threw up.

"I told you not to drink any water this morning," Linnea said irritably as she swabbed up the mess with a rag, tossed it in the cycler. She got to her feet and reached for her clothes. "Come. We need to get the ship covered and get moving."

The sun had gone down in this short time, so Linnea doused the lights in the ship before opening the hatch. Snow had begun to fall. Big flakes swirled into the lock on a gust of chill air. The world glowed deep blue, only a few lights visible high on a ridge far away. "We'll have a long hike to the station," she told Zhen. "Are you strong enough?"

"Yes." Zhen's nerves seemed to have calmed. She helped Linnea drag the big bundle of thin camouflage cloth out of its locker, then spread it over the ship from nose to tail. Snow was already sticking to it as they lashed it in place.

Linnea hoisted her small pack onto her back. "Come, then. We've got about five kilometers to cover."

The soft, unpacked snow made for hard going. Zhen kept quiet for a while, then, as they were climbing down into a gully across their path, she said, "How do we fight them—the Cold Minds? With little ships like that one?"

"We protect ourselves, first," Linnea said. "Protect our people. Then we contain them. Then, when we're strong enough, we go after them, wherever they are."

"How long will that take?"

Linnea looked up and down the gully, trying to find

the best way up the other side. "Better not to ask," she said finally.

"I know we have to try," Zhen said. "I'm—I'm glad I'll be able to help, I really am. But I don't see how it's possible. I don't."

Linnea knew the questions in Zhen's mind. *How can we ever win, against something that can hide anywhere, that can hide inside us?* Linnea shivered, remembering, again, the lost world Freija: her friend and protector Omoi shot dead in a cave on a night of bitter rain. Old Kwela's rigid face as she leaped into emptiness. The slack, blank faces of the infested. "Maybe we can't win, but we can't lose, either," she said flatly. "Better to be dead."

They trudged on in silence—climbing down onto a mountain road, skirting a brightly lit fuel station, scurrying out of sight of the occasional traffic. When they finally neared the mountain village of Cormontayne, Linnea stopped in puzzlement. The train must have come in early, and the station was jammed with people, more pouring off every minute, carrying sacks and bags and bulging luggage. At the terminus of the line! Where had they come from? And where in this small village did they all expect to find shelter?

As she and Zhen started across the last open space toward the station, a shadow stepped forward from behind a commnet kiosk, into weak light from the distant station doorway.

Linnea stopped Zhen with a touch. Iain. But the look on his face—

Zhen spoke first, her voice trembling. "What? What is it?"

"Something is happening," he said. His voice sounded strained, strange. "The orbital-raid alarms went off down in the city about two hours ago, then stopped. There's no news. Commnet's jammed with people asking what,

what? Nobody's got any *facts*." He ran his fingers through his hair. His hands were shaking.

Linnea gripped Zhen's arm fiercely and faced Iain. "You think it's the Cold Minds?"

"I don't know," he said again. "But those alarms are meant to react to a lot of ships jumping in at once, unauthorized."

"We didn't see anything up there," Zhen said.

"We were coming into atmosphere two hours ago," Linnea said. "We wouldn't have."

"So it's them," Zhen said in small voice. "Where are the others?"

"Scattered." Iain met Linnea's eyes. "Hidden. We'll reconnect by commnet when things settle down. If they do."

"Torin?" Zhen gasped.

Iain barely hesitated. "I don't know. He was out, in the city. He must have run like the rest of us. I came up on the train, had to fight my way on. But I had to find you." He turned to Linnea. "I need you to take me up to Station Six. To my ship."

Of course Iain would want to face this attack from his ship. What an unarmed jumpship could do, Linnea could not guess. But she realized with a shiver of strangeness that she had the same thought in the back of her mind. Safety, mobility, the ability to really *see* what was happening up there. Being enclosed, where those things could not touch her. "Of course," she said. Snow fell thickly now from a dark sky, but the nav chip in the palmscreen in her pocket would guide them back to her ship as surely as any map or beacon. "Let's go."

Zhen pulled away, her eyes dark with distress. "You go. Torin's down in the city. I have to find him."

For a moment, Linnea saw, words failed Iain. "He's— the city's in confusion," he began.

"He's my man," she said stubbornly. "We'll find each other. And then find you."

Iain turned to Linnea. "Is she a pilot?" he demanded. Behind his shoulder Zhen watched Linnea, her face a tight mask of controlled anguish.

"I—" Linnea swallowed hard. "I don't know."

His brows lifted. "You don't *know*?"

Linnea planted her feet. "Even if she is, she's still a free person. Don't go on about high destinies, not now. Let her go find Torin." She looked into Iain's eyes, spoke with all the urgency she could muster.

Finally, he looked away. "All right. Zhen, go. Watch for a message in the next couple of days—if the commnet is still up then."

But Zhen had already gone.

I ain settled himself in the passenger shell of Linnea's ship. He dreaded the ride up to Station Six in this thing, joined to the old ship by a passive link without control or volition. But Linnea insisted that he use the shell, with its better protection against acceleration; she didn't yet trust herself completely. And, keeping to tradition, he would obey. This was her ship. She was Pilot.

She had allowed him to calculate the flight parameters, and as a result it was as hard a launch as he had ever made from a planet surface, higher acceleration even than their last-minute escape from Freija. Reckless of fuel. They only had to reach Station Six.

The old ship did not cut engine noise as efficiently as Iain's own did, and he heard nothing but the crackling roar of the launch engine and the scream of atmosphere over the skin of the ship. Acceleration crushed him into the padding of the shell. He struggled for each breath. Through their mutual connection to the ship, Linnea's voice spoke in his inner ear, perhaps reflexively praying—words he didn't understand out of context, a constant ragged chant.

Then, cutoff—silence that roared in his ears and the
welcome lift and lurch of zero gee. He took deep gulping
breaths of free air. They were falling—falling up in a
long arc that would intersect Station Six in a matter of
minutes.

She was doing everything right; he must not interfere.
After a few minutes Linnea spoke. "Let's look ahead."

Iain had been waiting tensely for this, unwilling to jog
her elbow. In a moment Iain's shell seemed to vanish, and
he saw with the eyes of Linnea's ship. In this low orbit,
the dazzling pure curve of the limb of Terranova still hid
Station Six from their view. "Try long-range readouts,"
he said. "Look for anomalous ships. Anything not in the
traffic system will be flagged—"

"—orange," Linnea finished, as space ahead of them
and out-orbit sprang into crowded life. A cloud of flagged
symbols, all orange. There must be a hundred or more.
Iain felt his hands, his physical hands, gripping the soft
lining of his shell as his staggered mind struggled for
words.

"The Cold Minds can't have that many ships," Linnea
breathed. "They *can't*."

He must set aside fear. No time for that. Quick thinking, quick action might still save them.

He made himself look closely, look carefully, at the
flags attached to some of the nearer ships. Vectors—all
the nearest ones seemed to be converging on Station Six.
Probably every station had its nimbus of ships. Almost
all of the ships looked small, powerful, maneuverable,
there were only a few the size of a passenger carrier—but
if the Cold Minds were invading Terranova, why were
they stopping in orbit, why not penetrate the defenses and
land near the population centers, that would—

"Iain," Linnea said sharply. "They're Line-flagged.
There's traffic on the private Line channels."

Iain wanted to tear himself free from the useless passenger connection, get to the instructor's links, see what Linnea could see, hear the channels. But he would be blind, locked into his body, for almost a minute while the new connections formed.

Then abruptly he did hear the channels. She had sorted out the comm system, routed it to him. A chatter of voices, men all talking at once, no way to cut into that or make sense of it. He could make out one thing: panic. His heart went cold.

Iain held himself still, his heart thumping, as they approached the station. The jumpship landing pads bristled with ships, full beyond capacity. Jumpships hung everywhere in holding positions up-orbit and down-orbit; others were maneuvering in toward open spaces on the skin of the station. Linnea was evidently learning how to pick out snatches of chatter on the station control frequencies, and once a woman's angry voice stood out from the rest: "Stand off! All ships, stand off! If you are not in distress, hold until we can assign you docking. That's an order! The emergency docks are restricted to—" Her voice vanished again in the sea of chatter.

"I have to know what happened," Iain said flatly. "We have to get aboard the station."

"I know." Linnea's voice was calm in his ears. "Just a moment. . . . Station Control. This is Kiaho—" She gave her call sign and her ship's registration number. "Station Control, I am a trainee pilot. Repeat, I am a trainee pilot. Request approach assistance on a single control channel." She repeated it several times.

Abruptly the chaos of voices vanished and only a single voice spoke. "There are trainees all over the place out there," the man's voice said. "No women, though. Who are you, Kiaho?"

"I'm from Terranova. A, a pilot from Terranova. I've got—"

"There aren't any pilots from Terranova!"

"There are now," Linnea said firmly. "I also have a Pilot Master aboard—he needs to know the situation."

"No one has told us the three-times-damned situation," the man said. "And I've got Pilot Masters up to my back teeth, already aboard the station. More every minute. Anytime now they'll be trying to break in here. . . . Look, if the one who's with you can make some sense of this, talk sense to these men, you bring that ship in. There's a refueling slot for unmanned tugs, ten-seventeen in the lower southeast quadrant. It's got an emergency air-lock tube. Best I can do."

And then, of course, Iain had to wait, struggling to hide his impatience, as Linnea spent long minutes edging her ship into position, then locking it down into the slot, which was designed for one of the big, bare-bones orbital tugs. It took longer still for the glass-fiber accordion tube to seal itself tightly enough to the access lock of Linnea's ship that pressure could equalize.

Then Iain was free, and he ran through the station in the light pseudograv, taking the steep metal-grid gangways two steps at a time, with Linnea close behind him. He heard the confused roar of men's voices from the jumpship reception area long before he reached it. The corridor opened out into a wide, high space, a passenger waiting area crowded with Line pilots—some he knew, some strangers to him. Some younger ones huddled together, trainees and boys too young to be trainees; here was an older man carrying a crying toddler boy; there was a silent clump of old men. All were randomly dressed in anything from piloting clothes to feasting robes. Some talked, some stared emptily at nothing. Some wept. A few recognized Iain, fell silent, nudged each other.

Iain stopped in the center of the room, and the silence spread. He felt Linnea take her place at his side, not touching him, but offering a presence that calmed him. Iain spoke into the near quiet. "What has happened?"

Confused words burst out as a dozen men tried to answer him at once, and then at his side Linnea shouted *"Quiet!"* The sharp, strong female voice shocked them into silence.

All but one. A man came forward, a pilot like the rest of them, but not dressed as one, his fine black tunic torn and stained with what must be blood, his brown hair hanging half out of its braid. With a shock Iain recognized Hakon sen Efrem. Who had left Terranova four months ago, barely enough time to travel to Nexus and return.

But that Hakon had been calm, contained. This one—his face was dirty, lined, his eyes haunted.

"What has happened?" Iain asked again, and against his will his voice shook.

Hakon's voice was hoarse. "The Cold Minds have taken Nexus."

Iain felt Linnea move closer to him. He made no move to touch her, all his mind and thought on Hakon. "That can't be," he said. *Not the center. Not the heart and fortress of the Line.*

"It fell," Hakon said. Tears stood in his eyes. "It is gone, and hundreds of our—our brothers—" His voice broke. "All dead." He took a breath that was half a sob, and said, "We were betrayed."

"Tell me," Iain said quietly, his heart pounding.

Hakon's gaze hardened. "We were betrayed by your cousin. Rafael sen Fridric. He was infested by the Cold Minds." His voice was even, level. "He has destroyed us all."

NINE

In the jammed passenger lounge, surrounded by weary, frightened men, Linnea crouched next to a sleeping boy of two or three. He lay curled up under an old shirt, his back to the bulkhead. She envied him his sound sleep, at the edge of this room with its confused jumble of voices, men coming and going. She looked up at the pilot sitting beside the boy. In spite of his long, yellow braid, he looked very young, barely more than a boy himself. "He's not yours?" she asked.

"Not mine," the man said. "I was at the field, and the Cold Minds were landing. They were *landing*. And the boy was calling for his father, but no one came, and I knew I would be one of the last ships out, if I even made it. So I took him."

Linnea reached for her palmscreen. "What's his name?"

"He says it's Kini. That's probably not his real name. And he doesn't know his patronym yet." He touched the boy's smooth cheek. "He was afraid, in the jump. He'd never been out before. My ship kept him sedated most of the time. I hope he's all right."

"The medtech will be right along," Linnea said, trying to put a soothing note into her voice. "Let's keep him here for a bit, ask new men coming in if they know him. We'll get him back together with his father."

She straightened wearily. Hours, she had been here, helping station personnel sort things out, collecting names and stories. Iain came and went, guiding pilots to the beds that were being found for them. Ships were still trickling in, some of them bringing people who were in bad shape. Someone had to sort out where each one should go, what each one needed. She and Iain had stepped up to help.

At least she'd gotten the stationmaster to lend her the medtech, who could spot the ones who needed to go to the infirmary rather than just be sent off to rest. Always in the back of her mind was the thought that any of these men might be contaminated with nanobots, maybe even in the early stages of infestation. The stationmaster's first act had been to lock down all outgoing traffic, stranding passengers headed outsystem and others headed home, but protecting Terranova, for now. And locking them all in with—whatever was here. She looked around uneasily at the crowd. Watching people's eyes.

The other orbital stations had these same problems, she'd heard. Maybe the boy's father was on one of those. In that case, they might be apart for a long time. Quarantines everywhere, uncertainty everywhere.

Though most likely the boy's father was dead. Most people who'd been caught on the ground on Nexus, in the City, must be dead or worse. That much was beginning to be clear. And many more who didn't have ships, or couldn't get to them, had died when the orbital dock blew.

Linnea stopped and listened, for a moment, to the talk

all around her. "No," one man was saying firmly, "there was no landing until after Dock exploded. There can't have been. Our orbital defenses—"

"—were wrecked, I told you that. Wrecked from groundside," a small, dark man, a tech judging by his short hair, said with anger she guessed he would not have shown to a pilot if he weren't so tired. "They had all the time they needed to set it up, to attack groundside and Dockside at the same moment. And they did."

Beyond those two, another pilot squatted in the middle of the floor, his face in his hands, sobbing helplessly. That one needed a look from the medtech, she decided.

Just then the medtech made his way to her side. "That's it, Lin," he said. "The infirmary's full. If we want more beds, we'd better lock down some of the transit dormitories before *they* fill up."

Linnea made a note on her palmscreen. "What about pilot territory?" She'd never seen the part of the station set aside for Pilot Masters in transit, but word was it was spacious and comfortable compared to the rest.

"Full," the medtech said. "Taken up by the old men and boys, mostly. That's all they'll tell me. They've got a physician of their own on staff up there—he's seeing to them, I guess."

No doubt in the best private clinic money could buy. "I'll talk to the stationmaster," Linnea said. "Maybe he can get them to share resources."

The medtech only snorted and moved away before she could point out the crying man. Well, there was plenty to do. Some of the ships that escaped Nexus and the destruction of Dock had been piloted by trainees, or retired men—their passengers had not all been properly prepared for the jump, and some had arrived feverish and dehydrated. One or two had died in transit.

Before she could turn toward the weeping man, who now crouched silently with his hands still covering his face, she saw the men in the big room—those who could stand—rise to their feet. A hush fell. Linnea turned as a wiry old man, a newcomer, strode out of a doorway to the center of the room. Even dressed in what were obviously borrowed and ill-fitting clothes, with his thin white hair loose on his shoulders, he dominated the younger men and pilots around him.

Iain appeared beside her, tired and rumpled but watchful. "That's Honormaster sen Martin," he said in her ear. "High on the Inner Council. He might know something."

The silence was almost complete now, except for a crying child somewhere. The old man, the Honormaster, looked around at the men standing around him. "Brothers," he said heavily. "We have suffered a terrible loss. Immeasurable. We will not know the final toll of the attack for many days or even months. We will mourn, but that time is not now."

"We'll take back Nexus!" someone shouted, his voice raw with tears—Linnea recognized him as a man who had arrived with a dead passenger. His father, it might have been. There were so many, she could not remember.

"We will act," the Honormaster said, "in accordance with honor and custom. We will be avenged. In time." He lifted a hand to quell the murmur of protest. "In time. We cannot launch our counterattack until we know what resources we have. Until we know who else has survived. Until we find the Honored Voice and re-form the Council." He looked around at all of them. "For now, tonight, brothers, we must rest, all of us. Tomorrow we will speak of this, but with clear heads. I am told that this station is under quarantine, so we certainly have time." His voice rasped. "Who is in charge here?"

Linnea looked around, but could not see Stationmaster Segura in the room at the moment. Gone off to deal with some crisis elsewhere, no doubt. She stepped forward.

"I am not in charge," she said. "But I know the arrangements that are being made for your people."

The Honormaster looked at her sharply, then at Iain beside her, and his eyebrows went up. "So? What arrangements?" He seemed to be addressing Iain.

Iain only looked at Linnea, and she said, "The old men and the youngest boys have taken up all the Line facilities. There are some transit barracks, several travelers' hostels. But with passenger transport suspended, many spaces are already occupied."

"Turn them out, then," the Honormaster said with a shrug. "Pilots cannot sleep in corridors when beds are available."

Linnea set her hands on her hips. "It is the middle of the night, station time," she said, as calmly as she could. "We can talk about how to redistribute people in the morning. Surely your pilots can manage on benches and such until then. The ones who are sick are being seen to. The rest will have to manage as best they can."

"You are refusing my instruction?" The old man seemed puzzled.

At that moment someone behind her cried out in fear, and she saw the young blond pilot on his feet, staggering backward, clutching the sleeping boy. She turned. The man who had been weeping now stood swaying on his feet, reaching out uncertainly as if he could not see clearly. He coughed, a weird retching bark. An older man moved forward to take hold of his arm, and Linnea shouted in sudden panic, "Stay back!"

The men nearby froze, staring at her. The man in the center turned his head slowly from side to side, as if trying to place her voice. Tears ran down his dirty cheeks. Black tears.

"Stay back," she said again in a thin voice. "No one touch him. Iain! Call security."

The Honormaster was beside her. "He can't be infested, not—"

"He *can* be infested," she said, not taking her eyes off the sick man. "It could have happened on Dock, or groundside. It only takes a few bots, only a moment to pass them. And they had all that time in transit to grow."

Security arrived, and sensibly, Iain had told them what to be ready for. They wore hazard-protective gear. One with a stunrod knocked the man unconscious. When he was down, they bound his hands behind him, bound his legs at ankles and knees. Then they unfolded a loose, crackling plastic isolation bag, sealed him inside it, and lifted him onto a stretcher. The bag would hold nanobots inside its seal as easily as it held in microbes.

One of Stationmaster Segura's deputies, looking terrified, touched Linnea's arm. "What do we do now?"

Linnea shook her head. "I'm no expert on these things."

"You're the closest we have," Iain said, setting a firm hand on her shoulder.

Linnea closed her eyes. He was right, of course. "All right." She shook her head to clear it. "All right. That floor has to be cleaned. Burned clean. And anyone who might have touched that man needs to undress, take a shower. A good one. Burn the clothes."

The deputy sighed. "Decontam showers we have." He looked at the long dark shape on the stretcher. "Do we shove that out an air-lock?"

The Honormaster stepped forward. "That man is a Line pilot. Our brother Raheer sen Petrus. This is a Line matter."

"The safety of our station—"

"Will be preserved," the Honormaster said. He turned to the security men. "Put this man in isolation.

Treat his body with respect, but see that there is no threat to the station." He turned to Linnea. "We don't know anything about this . . . process. We must understand it better. Whatever the cost. Even if our brother must suffer."

Linnea felt sick. "Watch if you like," she said hollowly. "Just don't make *me* do it."

"But you must help us," the Honormaster said. He turned to Iain. "Sen Paolo, of course she must. Our only . . . expert. I know you have seen them; but I'm told that this woman lived among them, on an infested world, for months. Surely you will consent to lend us her services?"

Linnea bit back an angry interjection; Iain had as much as told her they needed this man's goodwill.

Iain looked at Linnea, then back at the Honormaster. "It's Miss Kiaho's decision, not mine," he said quietly. "Or yours. She is not my servant or anyone's. And I am not of the Line." She heard the bitter weight he gave those last words, and hoped the Honormaster had not.

The Honormaster turned to Linnea, seemed to gather himself, and said, "Please—Miss Kiaho. For all our sakes. Help us study this man."

Iain, too, was looking at her, his dark face urgent.

She sighed. "I'll do it, then."

FOUR DAYS LATER

Early morning. Linnea dropped her empty coffee cup in the cycler and got to her feet to pace, again, the length of the bleak waiting room. The walls of the cramped space seemed close, grim, the paint fading with years from green to the color of lichen back home. She had come to know this little detention facility, at the center of the station, far too well in just a few days. She felt queasy already, and she had not even seen—*it*, not since last night.

Iain was here, too, as he had insisted from the start. He got to his feet and stopped her with a touch. His hand on her arm brought her back to reality, warmed her a little, but that did not change the fact that in a few moments she would be looking into those eyes again: the blind eyes of infestation.

A brisk, brown-skinned young woman, a Terranovan physician, appeared in the doorway of the waiting room. "It's ready."

Iain's hand dropped to Linnea's arm, and they followed the physician down a narrow corridor, into a darkened room. The top half of one wall was a pane of thick unbreakable plastic. On the other side was—the enemy.

The body of the infested jump pilot lay, tightly restrained, on a gurney. It was naked. To Linnea's eyes, it seemed still human, even this far into the process. Then it turned its head and looked toward the plastic barrier. Linnea knew it could not see her through the reflective half-coated plastic, but cold fingers still traced down her spine. The eyes were too dark, unfocused. Something not human looked out from them. Something not human had finished building its structure in the brain of the pilot.

She shivered. "I think—I think it's over."

Iain slid his arm around her. The physician kept her eyes on the infested man. "I was able to scan it again this morning, with the portable unit," she said. "There's clearly some kind of regularized metallic network, very fine, very intricate, inside the skull. And it's interlinked with much greater complexity even than yesterday. The areas of concentration in the abdomen have grown, too." She frowned at the thing. "But it still hasn't shown any sign of speech or cognition. You appear to be right."

"Yes," Linnea said. Her voice rasped in her dry throat. "These things, the bodies with bot networks inside, they're mostly just tools. Tools the Cold Minds use to spread their bots, and to build what they need to protect themselves. These things can't do much without direction from outside. When the controlling Minds don't need them anymore, they let the bodies die."

Iain's arm tightened around Linnea. "Rafael must have brought a controlling Mind to Nexus with him," he said. "He couldn't have been fully infested if he could still pilot. It must have happened after he arrived on Nexus."

"I cannot see how," the physician said. "Nexus security was very careful with your cousin's ship. Isolated it, hit it inside and out with hard radiation—nothing should have been alive or functioning in there. And he did not have access to it."

"Maybe he carried it inside his body," Linnea said. "Not an infestation. Something like a parasite."

The doctor looked disturbed. "That's another scan we need to do, then, on all the incoming pilots."

Linnea shivered, still staring at the thing on the gurney. "Can this one—is it possible that something is left of his mind?" She took a shuddering breath. "Is he conscious in there, still?"

"I don't see how," the physician said bluntly. "That network must disrupt the electrical processes of his brain almost completely. I doubt that he is conscious. Or if he is, that he understands where he is and what has happened to him."

"Kill him," Linnea said in a shaking voice. "You can't keep a human being alive just to study—this." She stood rigid in Iain's half embrace. "It's wrong."

The physician looked down at her notes, then up at the body on the gurney. "I'll bring it up with the Line representative, but I provisionally agree. The new blood test will be up and running soon. So we don't need this thing. We can irradiate it and burn what's left."

Linnea looked into the empty eyes of the thing. Into the blackness where the lost soul howled. "That would be a mercy," she said in a thin voice.

•   •   •

THE NEXT DAY

Hakon sen Efrem stood alone in the cramped meeting room, waiting for the others, brooding over the flatscreen image of space just outside the station. In rooms like this one on all the stations, he knew, the Line had gathered to witness the final disposition of Raheer sen Petrus: His ashes would be given to time.

Hakon had known Raheer, known him well; they'd moved in the same circle in the City, among other politically interested younger pilots who sought opportunities to distinguish themselves to Council members and elders. Hakon remembered him, a quiet and dignified presence at many dinners and gatherings, a man whose judgment he had learned to observe and even to emulate. Raheer would have gone far.

Now he was gone. The first of the Line to fall under infestation.

The first after Rafael sen Fridric.

But Raheer would certainly not be the last. Hakon shuddered. The blood tests would begin tomorrow. Hakon had elected not to be among the first tested; all those who passed were to be sequestered from the rest of the station, and Hakon had work to do.

Again his impatience surged. The old men were already creeping back into control, the few surviving bureaucrats and senior men on all seven orbital stations linked in by comm—shutting out the heart of the Line, the working pilots. By their oaths they would have to obey this makeshift Council. As the Honormaster's new liaison with the pilots, it would be Hakon's task to see that this happened.

His fists tightened. He had another task, one that burned in his heart: to ensure the counterattack on Nexus, as soon as it could possibly be launched. He owed this to the memory of the boy who had died so bravely in the training bay; he owed it to hundreds of his brothers. But first he must gather ships and pilots from the rest of the Hidden Worlds, as many as could be spared.

The grim numbers were beginning to emerge already. About five hundred of the Line's two thousand active pilots had been on Nexus, or on its orbital dock, when the Cold Minds struck; and only about two hundred had escaped. Of those not on Nexus, any who were in transit homeward at the time of the attack would probably be intercepted and captured by Cold Minds ships when they emerged from otherspace near the planet. Nothing could be done about that: There was no way to reach a ship in otherspace. A warning beacon placed anywhere near Nexus, to catch them on emergence, would be traced and eliminated at once by Cold Minds patrols.

What Hakon had to work with, now, was grief-stricken pilots, both those from Terranova and those who would arrive from the rest of the Hidden Worlds. Most of the population of the City itself, their home on Nexus, had not escaped: fathers and grandfathers, lovers and brothers and sons of the surviving pilots. All dead now—or worse. And so were almost all the men of the other class: men born on Nexus who had not tested out as pilots and took jobs as bureaucrats, Line Security men, skyport workers, minor functionaries. The Line had probably lost a fifth of its pilots—and nearly all its old men. Nearly all its leaders and teachers.

And nearly all its young sons. The past, and the future. The knowledge, and the hope. All cut off, leaving—what?

The strength, the determination of those who survived. And Hakon to lead them into battle, if no one else would.

The door slid aside, and Hakon turned as Master sen Martin entered, then stood regarding him mildly. "Pilot sen Efrem? Are you well?"

"Honormaster." Hakon bowed, the full formal bow due to the head of the interim Council. "A sad occasion."

"We cannot properly honor them all," the Honormaster said, inclining his head in response. Hakon caught the catch in his voice. Like so many, the Honormaster was in mourning: His lifelong lover, Isak sen Semyon, was one of the confirmed dead in the City. "When the Line can truly gather, we will do so. But this man's sacrifice has earned this honor."

The ones who had been chosen to witness this event at the Honormaster's side began to filter in quietly, take their places. Those not of the Line stood to the rear of the room, and Hakon wondered who had known Line ways well enough to arrange this; then he saw Iain sen Paolo. So *he* had found his way onto the list. Working his way up into a position of influence, of course. A woman attended him, the same one Hakon always saw with sen Paolo. An unusually faithful servant, that one. Plainly dressed in men's clothes, with a strong-boned face and sharp eyes, she had no beauty that was to his taste; but Hakon supposed loyalty counted for much in times like these.

Hakon looked around at the other men of the Line. Not proper honors, indeed: No one of the Line wore mourning white; some were in worker's coveralls or worse. Hakon fought back his anguish: They were so near to losing six hundred years of honor and tradition. Outward things, the Honormaster called them, as if they were unimportant. But outward things could build inward unity. Build strength. Help ensure that the old ways would return when they could.

The Honormaster stepped forward from Hakon's side and bowed slightly to a tall, heavy Terranovan in station coveralls. "Stationmaster Segura. Thank you for coming."

The stationmaster nodded, looking a little disgruntled, perhaps, at being welcomed to a room on his own station.

Hakon approved of him in general; he seemed efficient enough at his duties, though quite out of his depth now, with so many great names of the Line all around him.

The Honormaster stepped into pickup for the comm that would send his image to holoplates on every station: For the first time, he addressed the ingathered Line. He stood very straight, his head thrown back. "We remember lost Earth," he said. "We remember our oaths at the Tree. . . ."

Hakon fell into ritual, letting his mind wander elsewhere. The funeral ceremony passed as they always did, brief, meaningless to most who stood witness.

In a few days, once everyone had been tested, it would be possible to travel groundside again. Hakon was certain that the old men would choose to establish themselves there, probably in the capital, Port Marie; after recent events they would not feel safe in orbit, and he could not blame them.

As the Honormaster's assistant and liaison with the pilots, Hakon would be there. And so, he was sure, would Iain sen Paolo. That would be no problem if sen Paolo knew his place, if he valued the honor of the Line and joined in the call for retaking Nexus. But there were whispers already that sen Paolo did not favor the idea. Certainly the woman with him and her allies among the common workers did not. Time, they wanted time; they wanted to be defended. They did not understand that the Line, cut off from its soul, from its home, would quickly wither. And then where would they be, any of them?

Silence fell, and Hakon brought his attention back to the flatscreen display in front of them. A dazzling blue-white arc of Terranova sliced into one corner of the screen; the rest was black, the stars and nebulae invisible to the camera in the blaze of the planet's light.

But something moved. Silently, a small golden yellow spark drifted into view, receding slowly. At the proper moment, the Honormaster spoke, his voice rough with grief. "We give our brother to that which is unending, and will endure beyond our own ending. Farewell, Raheer." He touched a control.

A brief flash, and once again the black blankness of space hung undisturbed.

The Honormaster covered his face with both hands, a slow ritual gesture. Hakon and the other men of the Line did the same.

And, he saw, from the corner of his eye, so did sen Paolo.

Interesting.

Late that night, Linnea looked up from her commscreen in the improvised office she and Iain shared. She rubbed her aching neck. Trying to arrange for the blood tests to be administered, and to plan how to share out the supplies among all seven stations when she still didn't know how fast they could be manufactured—enough, that was it for tonight. She'd know more in the morning.

She flexed her shoulders and looked over at Iain's workstation. He was still not back yet.

So she knew where he must have gone. She locked her screen and got up. Why did he do this? Why was he so drawn to the places where pilots gathered? They treated him like an exile, an outsider, and she saw how it hurt him. Yet still his old life called to him. She went out into the dim corridor and started for the place where she knew she would find him.

A few of the quarantined pilots had gotten in the habit of meeting in the same passenger lounge where they'd gathered when they had first arrived. Hakon sen Efrem was always there, talking up his idea of immediate counterattack. Taking back Nexus. Cleaning it out, rebuilding it. He seemed to think it would be possible merely because he wanted it to be possible.

She clattered down a set of metal stairs and turned left down a wide corridor marked with signs pointing toward various passenger bays. The old men on the new Council that was forming—they would never allow a hotheaded attack, they were deliberate. They understood what she was arguing for, the need for more pilots, more ships, more resources, and to make the Hidden Worlds secure before stripping away pilots for an invasion.

Iain had said he was sure of the Council's support. But if that was true, why was a smart man like Hakon sen Efrem continuing to push the matter? When it could only hurt his long-term ambitions?

She turned a bend in the corridor, and here was the archway she wanted. Sen Efrem was there, of course, in full flow. "The sooner we decide on attack, the sooner we will be ready to strike," he was saying, as she reached the archway leading into the room. "The Cold Minds on Nexus will never be weaker than they are this moment. We can take back what is ours and avenge our brothers, all of them. Including Raheer sen Petrus."

Iain looked up and saw Linnea standing in the archway, and his eyes lit. When she reached his side, he gave her a half smile, and murmured, "Not much longer tonight. They're tired, too."

She shook her head, irritated. "Come home. Please."

He glanced back at the others, and dropped his voice to a whisper. "The linkers did go out today."

So that was why he'd come here: to be sure of that. Commnet linker ships had been held up like all other traffic, and she knew the demand that had been building up groundside. Information was still coming in, ships that had jumped toward Terranova long before all this happened; but they were locked down in quarantine as soon as they arrived. Nothing was going out again.

Until today. Today the ships had gone out at last, all piloted by men who'd had no contact with anyone from

Nexus. News of the fall of Nexus, the exile of the Line, would spread from world to world, and every pilot who could free himself to come here would do so. Dangerous, Iain said; so many of them would be thinking only of revenge.

At that moment she realized that the voices had stopped, and men were looking at Iain. She stepped back from him, and he turned to face them. "Forgive me. I did not hear the question."

"Fuel," sen Efrem said. "What inventories are immediately available groundside? And what regular supply can the refineries reliably produce?"

"Having only two or three ships," Iain said mildly, "it never occurred to me to worry about running out of fuel. But there has always been enough for normal traffic."

Sensing the circling hostility behind sen Efrem's polite request, Linnea moved to stand beside Iain. He did not appear to notice.

Sen Efrem ignored her as well, his brown eyes cold. "You know we are not discussing normal traffic, Iain," he said. "Our fleet will require a significantly larger supply of fuel, with full auxiliary tanks for maneuvers and landing."

Iain's voice was still mild. "*Our fleet* will require an achievable mission."

Linnea glanced over at Iain. He stood politely, hands clasped behind his back, chin high. So it was coming at last: the open challenge to sen Efrem. She schooled herself to an appearance of calm.

"We cannot abandon Nexus to the Cold Minds," sen Efrem said, as if speaking to a boy.

"It is already too late," Iain said evenly. "Once truly infested, a world will never be clean again. Nexus will never again be a safe home for the Line."

"We do not know that this is true," sen Efrem said.

"Common sense—" Iain began.

"Common sense tells us," sen Efrem said, "that we must strike while they are still concentrated on one world and before they have constructed more ships. This is when they are most vulnerable."

Iain shook his head. "The Cold Minds know this. They may already be outflanking us, moving against other targets now, while we are in disarray. *We* are the ones who will never be more vulnerable."

"You appear to know a great deal about their strategy," sen Efrem said scornfully.

"I remind you," Iain said, "that I spent days on Freija. Linnea, months. We saw how they work, once they possess a world. They protect themselves first." He shook his head. "The secure bunkers far below the City—that's where they will have placed their controlling Minds. Those bunkers were designed to withstand any attack we could muster now." He looked around at the other men. "We have better uses for our strength than to throw away lives on an act of revenge."

Sen Efrem's eyes narrowed. "And what . . . safer course of action do you suggest for us, Iain?"

"I have outlined it for the Council already," he said. "You were there, Pilot sen Efrem. We need to monitor Nexus. We must build up the defenses around the shipyards on Ishtar and Kattayar. And"—he set his hand on Linnea's shoulder—"we do not yet know the full toll, but certainly the Line lost hundreds of pilots. We need to replace them, and more. We need to replace the trainees who died, and the boys who would have been trainees. Linnea and people like her are the answer."

Linnea saw the disbelief on a dozen faces, heard a rising mutter. She stepped forward, out from under his hand. "We have already found many possible pilots on Terranova," she said. "We will find others, here and on other worlds. With your help, we can train them quickly."

"Useless," an old man said. "What can we teach a man, a groundsider man, about piloting in time to be of any help?"

Linnea bristled. "We need pickets," she said. "Orbital guard ships, to jump out with warnings at the first sign of Cold Minds activity near any of the Hidden Worlds. We need more commnet ships—the little worlds need the same protection as Terranova, the same access to information. None of that takes more than basic jump navigation."

"All this may be true," sen Efrem said, and all eyes turned toward him. "It may be that these . . . other pilots will help us in our work, someday. But understand that we cannot hold back this counterstrike to wait for that. We cannot hold back out of fear." He looked at Linnea. "The woman's fear is understandable." His voice was gentle, and he smiled at Linnea. "You saw them, you were in danger from them, and you are still afraid now. What you do not understand is that they murdered our brothers, and we—"

She could not bear it. "You'd have murdered *my* brothers just like that," she said tightly. "You Pilot Masters wanted to cut off my whole world, all my family and people, leave us to the Cold Minds. You never tried to defend Freija. You killed it instead, and all its people. And now with this attack you would do the same again. Abandon us."

"We are the Pilot Masters," sen Efrem said. "We have always protected you as best we can. But retaking Nexus—"

She cut him off. "Mounting this attack will receive no support from the dockworkers' union, I can promise you that." She saw Iain's startled look. So he had not been talking to Torin, groundside. Well, she had.

"An illegal union," sen Efrem said, "that—"

"A real one, and stronger every day," she said hotly.

"I've talked to their leadership. I've talked to the pilots of the orbital lifters. No fuel will come up from groundside. No new ships."

Sen Efrem shook his head, dismissing her words. "We can negotiate with these workers ourselves. If we pay them enough, they will agree to help us."

And now Iain spoke. "May I remind you, Pilot sen Efrem, that the Line has nothing to pay them with?" Linnea saw sen Efrem flinch. Iain continued, "Nexus is gone. The Line has some assets among the Hidden Worlds, but with the commnet half-crippled, it will take weeks or months to gain access to them." He looked around at the listening pilots. "Linnea is right. You need the help the Terranovans can give you." He met sen Efrem's angry gaze. "They will help you if you continue to protect them—as your oaths already require."

Linnea faced sen Efrem. "We won't trade our worlds, our homes, to try to win back yours. We won't trade our children for the tombs of your fathers." She heard the rising rumble of objection, but pushed on. "I know about all your oaths and promises. They were made to *us*, to all the Worlds. Keep them!"

"We will keep them," sen Efrem said, "in time, and in the manner that seems right to us. But the question of attack is not open to any dictation from groundsiders—even groundsiders who think they are pilots."

"That will be for the Council to decide," Iain said. Linnea heard the anger under his words, anger he would not be able to contain much longer.

"Then I will see you before the Council," sen Efrem said.

Iain stood looking into the other man's eyes for a long moment.

"You are dismissed," sen Efrem said coldly. "You have other responsibilities, I am sure. The Line does not require anything further from you this evening."

Linnea touched Iain's arm. "Let them talk to each other," she said. "It's only talk."

After a moment, he nodded, and they left the room. As they turned the corner she heard a murmur in sen Efrem's voice, followed by a shout of laughter from the men in the room. She kept a tight hold on Iain's arm. *He is trying to drive you to folly, Iain,* she wanted to say. *He wants you to weaken yourself.* But she knew that, at this moment, he would not hear her.

TEN

Linnea sighed with relief as Iain sealed the hatch of their temporary quarters behind them. The message light on the comm panel blinked softly blue; before Iain could spot it, she set her palmscreen down on top of it.

Barely two meters in any dimension, home was a transient cubicle three levels below the main docking level—a cubicle that had been meant to put up one person for no more than a day. They had been lucky to get it, with the station jammed as it was. The small space held only a narrow bed, a stool, and a triangular desk-table tucked in the corner; the dull green paint on the metal walls was scratched and peeling.

Iain had a mat for himself on the deck beside the bed. He kept it rolled up except when it was time to sleep, because there was no other floor space. Linnea folded herself cross-legged onto the bunk, and Iain began to unroll the mat. "That was well done up there." He looked at her. "Time they learned to listen to *your* people."

Linnea sighed. Her people? They were Iain's as well. His grandfather, his real grandfather, had been a contract servant from Santandru, not the revered pilot whose name Iain's father had borne. "It won't make any difference whether they listen or not," she said, and pulled a blanket over her legs. The cubicle, against the outer skin of the station, was too chilly when darkside, too hot when sunside. "They are who they are. They'll fall in line behind Hakon sen Efrem, in the end."

Iain dropped onto the mat and studied her. "I think they will not," he said. "And Torin and Zhen and you will have a great deal to do with that."

"The Line will never accept someone like me or Zhen as a pilot, with the same rights they claim," she said bitterly.

Iain got up on his knees in front of her, and she let him take her hands in his. "In a generation," he said. "if we all live, piloting will be just another profession—an important duty, yes, but nothing more. The Line's old links to history are lost. The Tree is gone beyond reach. Their oaths stand only in their hearts. Their sons will make none." His hands tightened over hers.

That is no bad thing, she wanted to say, but pity for him silenced her. It was a moment before he could go on. "You will help this change to happen. You saw the pilots tonight—they did listen to you. You know Torin listens to you. You are the first of many, will be the teacher of many like yourself."

No. Her heart lurched. She looked down at their clasped hands. "I didn't ask for this."

"I know," he said. "I know where you want to be."

Of course he knew. He slept beside her. He had certainly heard her, some of these nights, dreaming of disaster at home on Santandru—dreams made worse by the faint echoes of the spiderweave overdose Rafael had once given her, that ever since had made her nightmares so much more vivid, all her fears more real. She could not meet his eyes. "And you—I know you would rather be fighting for *your* home. Just as sen Efrem wants. But—" She could not continue.

"But we are both called elsewhere," he said. "Called to be more than we were. More than we want to be, perhaps."

She leaned forward and kissed him. She had begun to love him in those brief, tumultuous days when she first knew him, when he had been one of the masters of the Hidden Worlds—prideful and confident. . . . But this quiet, grieving, serious man moved her more deeply still. Could still wake her heart to pain.

Iain leaned against her, into her embrace, and rested his head on her shoulder. "Tired," he muttered.

Linnea knew at that moment, with complete clarity, that the task Iain had set for them was impossible. It would break them both. She sighed, a deep sigh that ended in a shudder of weariness. "So am I."

Iain straightened, let go of her. "Messages. Then bed."

But when he called up the queue of messages on the little flatscreen comm, he exclaimed in surprise. Linnea saw one of them outlined in red. "What's that?"

"Family code," Iain said. "But it can't be. I have no family."

Linnea moved over to look more closely. "Open it."

Iain took a deep breath, then pressed his palm against the ID pad, tapped out a code with his fingers.

She saw him go still. "It's—it's from Rafael. Sent out ten days after the invasion."

"That can't be," she said numbly. "It must be a fake. A trap." She could read the words:

Come and save them.
They are afraid.

She frowned. "Who does he mean? '*They* are afraid—'" She shook her head firmly. "I don't believe it."

"The message is real," Iain said, a little sharply.

"How do you know?"

"Our family's private code crystal is implanted in Rafael's right hand," Iain said, "just as it is in mine. He used it to encode the message."

She sat rigidly straight. "They *have* him, Iain! They control him. They've infested his brain."

"The comm code has two parts," Iain said. "The implant is scanned, but then a complicated confirmation pattern must be tapped with the fingers. No. I am certain that this message was from—whatever is left of Rafael."

"Nothing can be left of Rafael!" She remembered Freija: Infested humans were totally controlled, their minds gone, once the bots had had a chance to build their internal networks.

"I wonder," Iain said. "Remember—Rafael took spiderweave, took it for years. That would get him used to confusion, fragmented thoughts—it's probably why the bots could occupy him for so long without his knowing it. He would have thought episodes where they controlled him were just the memory loss from the drug."

"But what difference would that make, once the bots were all through his brain?" She felt sick.

Iain leaned forward, resting his elbows on his knees. "Maybe the changes, the damage the drug caused, have allowed a part of Rafael's personality to adapt, and persist. To control again, sometimes, for a few seconds or minutes." He frowned. "Maybe he wants to tell us—that some of us are still alive there. . . ."

She lifted her chin. "Or," she said, "there is a much simpler explanation. That this is a trap. You know what will happen if the Line believes there are Line prisoners alive on Nexus. The Council won't be able to hold them back." She glanced at the comm. "Does anyone else know he's communicating with you?"

"No." He sounded certain. "No one without my family code implant could read that message."

"But Line Security might be able to trace it back to Nexus, which would be enough," she said. "What if Hakon sen Efrem learns about this? He'd get his invasion. And he'd discredit you with the Council. Iain, they would arrest you."

"Or worse," Iain said steadily. "If they had any evidence that could be twisted into a hint that I was part of my cousin's treason, the Line would execute me."

"There is no death penalty on Terranova," she said.

"They would execute me anyway," Iain said. He frowned down at his interlaced fingers. "I agree. We will not tell them. For now." He looked up at her. "But if there is any other indication that some of our people are alive on Nexus—then I will come forward with this. I must."

"No matter the risk?" she asked quietly.

She saw the raw pain in his eyes. "I have no other choice."

Seven days later, Iain returned to their cubicle to find all Linnea's few possessions gathered into her old travel bag, lying firmly strapped shut on the neatly made bunk. That was quick—the decision to allow travel to Terranova had only been announced an hour ago.

The first rounds of blood testing had taken some time to accomplish. Men who had been cleared needed to be separated completely from those still untested. Stationmaster Segura was tearing out his sparse hair trying to manage the logistics in a station crowded to capacity, with new ships arriving daily from the rest of the Hidden Worlds. The first few days had gone smoothly, until tests discovered a second infested man—a very young, newly passed pilot, in whom the nanobots had barely begun to take hold. He was put in confinement, weeping with terror, and managed to hang himself the first night.

Now, at last, men were being tested, cleared, and allowed to take up their piloting duties again. The station was beginning to clear out at last. And early this morning the Board of Control on Terranova had announced that it would permit tested individuals to land on the surface in approved shuttles.

So, at last, the stranded passengers could go home. The old men and boys of the Line could go groundside, to take up a strange new existence far from the wealth and security of the City on Nexus.

And Linnea would return groundside as well, to work beside Torin and Zhen. Iain touched her travel bag gently. She had taken steely hold of her duties, insisting on taking the first shuttle down. He touched the commscreen, called up the shuttle schedule. Less than an hour before Linnea would have to be aboard. He wondered if she had intended to say good-bye, or to evade it.

He found her, at last, in one of the workers' refectories, one that had been set up as a comm center for use by the Line. From the corridor outside he saw Linnea at a table in a corner of the small, crowded room, leaning with her chin on her palm, talking crossly to someone—Iain could not tell who it was. A blurry image, the back of someone's head, hung over the holoplate.

She was as busy as he was, her days taken up by messages from Torin, from the unions, and from businesses and information services and anyone who used the commnet demanding to know when proper circulation of linker ships would be fully restored. The Line helped in none of this work; dealing with groundsiders was groundsider's work.

Iain finally caught Linnea's eye, and she nodded once in acknowledgment, still talking to the person in the comm. Finally, she closed her conversation, shut off the comm, and began gathering her palmscreen and papers. Notes for training schedules, he knew, using the few pilot volunteers Iain had found—younger men, mostly, barely passed as pilots themselves, and willing to believe that the world had changed.

Linnea joined him in the corridor, with a brief quick smile that lit her dark eyes. She was neatly dressed, as always, in a tunic, trousers, and gripsole shoes all of dull gray. Always she effaced herself; her black hair hung straight to her shoulders, clean and combed, but she made no other effort to be attractive. Perhaps it made sense, given whom she was dealing with on a daily basis: If she did not present herself as ornamental, a Line man might be slightly less inclined to discount her.

"Not half my list done yet," she said, looking down at her palmscreen as they walked back toward their room. "Oh. I need to ask. Have you gotten any of the pilots to agree to recruit new trainees on other worlds?"

"A few," he said. "A few say they'll try."

"And test them? People can't travel all the way to Terranova for that."

He sighed. "I will bring it up with the Council."

Linnea gave a brittle laugh. "They don't want this, none of them. And one thing I can't get them to understand is that they should be testing women, too."

"It does go against everything they've been taught—"

"Then they should set aside what they've been taught," she said sharply. "We can't afford to waste half the human race."

Iain suppressed a sigh. Even after all this time, she would not try to understand how deep the customary Line beliefs went, or how hard the men would cling to them now that everything else was lost. Her own world had been no paradise for women, judging from what she had told him of her life. But she did not feel the pull of old customs; she had broken free.

The Line took a stronger hold on its sons. Always, now, Iain felt a deep visceral pull toward home, familiarity, the outward appearance of honor. . . .

They collected Linnea's travel bag, and, feeling strangely lost, he followed her to the shuttle's boarding bay. She seemed to sense his mood as they reached the bay, and she took her place in line. "I'll be back now and then, you know," she said, smiling. "Training runs with Zhen—she asked me to do it, not to hand her over to your Line pilots. It will keep my hand in."

"It will bring you here for a couple of hours before the run, and a couple of hours after," Iain said. "Not much."

Her smile faded. "That's the best I can do. It will have to be enough, until you are ready to come groundside."

Iain felt a vague anger that troubled him. Of course there was no choice: She must go.

But as he watched her disappear into the shuttle's boarding tube, he could not shake the feeling of wrongness. The feeling that he had made a wrong choice. That he had lost her.

ELEVEN

L innea held her battered travel bag tightly against her in the hot, crowded passenger compartment of the shuttle, her eyes on the viewscreen on the front wall. The view, ahead and down, was dizzying. Glittering blue ocean flashed past, looking flat and hard from this altitude. Most of the people around her kept their eyes elsewhere, or closed them tightly. The shuttle shuddered and bounced, buffeted by the atmosphere as it continued to brake. Somewhere, a baby cried hysterically, and the man in the couch beside hers was praying or swearing in a thin, strained voice, in some language she did not know.

Slower, slower. Slower still. At three kilometers of altitude, the roar suddenly increased—flaps on the shuttle's stubby wings, she knew. Presently, the deceleration that had made it hard to breathe began to ease. The water was much closer, finely wrinkled with waves, and then, with breathtaking abruptness, they were over land, close over land, landing with a sharp jolt. The screen went blank.

The braking jets roared, tossing Linnea forward against her restraints again.

Then they were trundling toward the terminal. The air in the compartment, thick with sweat and the faint acid stink of vomit from some unlucky newcomer to free fall, felt sticky on her skin. Linnea breathed a shallow sigh of relief as the shuttle lurched to a stop. She let the first rush of desperate passengers clear the compartment before she began to release her straps. The shuttle had been jammed with passengers: some incoming from other worlds, some who had planned to travel outward—travel that was now indefinitely suspended. There were a few Pilot Masters among them, pushing disdainfully through the mass of sweaty groundsiders.

The pull of real gravity felt oddly light after the rough landing. Linnea had to place her feet carefully as she descended the steps from the hatch. Always before, she'd stepped straight into the open, onto the pavement, but no more. A metal tube lined with sheets of plastic, strung with glaring lights, stretched out ahead of her. "Please keep moving," a recorded voice was saying from somewhere, over and over again. "Final screening is located in the terminal building."

Linnea shuffled along the crowded tube. Over the smell of the other passengers, the air stank of plastic and the recycling scrubbers it had probably been through about a hundred times. Just like Station Six. She might never have left.

The tube led into the terminal, into a room that was entirely lined with the same sealed plastic. It looked like a room carved from a glacier, but it was fiercely hot and humid. There she waited with the rest while medtechs in isolation suits drew blood and checked it. It made sense, with so much at stake.

At long last, Linnea was cleared and allowed to pass through a temporary air-lock to the terminal itself.

Straight ahead was a wall of glass open on the shuttle field: late afternoon, late spring, a bright sunlit day.

A short, dark-haired woman slammed into her, and she almost stumbled, then caught herself. "Zhen," she said, grinning. "You didn't have to come!"

"I had to see for myself," Zhen said, and took Linnea's bag. "I thought you would never come groundside again. I had a bet with Torin." They started through the crowd toward the bright entrance and the promise of fresh air outside.

"Where *is* Torin?"

Zhen sighed dramatically. "Working, still, of course. You know what he's like now. You talked to him yesterday."

"I haven't talked to you in longer," Linnea said. "How's your work?"

"Well, you know," Zhen said. "Waiting tables, it's the same everywhere. Sore feet all the time. But it keeps us. Torin and his union work, that doesn't cover a thing until there's a contract."

"Once you're back in pilot training, you'll be paid. Iain's working it out."

"I hope so," Zhen said, sounding a little doubtful. "Torin's—not pleased that I'm going to be away so much, though." She looked away, and went on, "Anyway, I wasn't expecting any training for quite a while." Linnea couldn't blame her; everything in chaos, what were the chances of things ever getting that organized?

Well, that was Linnea's job. One of them. She and Zhen pushed through a heavy glass door, out of the terminal into vivid light and the steady rumble of traffic. A cool breeze ruffled Linnea's hair. She had forgotten the fresh salt scent of sea air.

They started toward a cab stand. "What's going on with the fuel contract?" Linnea brushed her hair out of her eyes. "I couldn't get a straight story out of the Line men up there."

"Torin says the owners don't believe the interim Line Council has the power to sign a new agreement," Zhen said. "The old Council, that's who the owners are used to negotiating with. The owners are afraid that anything the Line agrees to now, the real Council will step away from later. When there is one."

That explained the Pilot Masters' evasiveness with Linnea, then: None would care to admit to being dismissed like that. Keeping their pride all clean and unpunctured was more than a full-time job; maybe it was time to stop worrying about it. "We'll settle that," she said firmly. "Who else are the refineries going to sell to? And who's going to protect their big investments if all the jumpships are stuck on the ground?" They reached the taxi stand, empty at the moment. "How about recruiting for pilots? How is that going?"

Zhen's face went wooden. "Stopped. Didn't seem the right time to try."

Linnea frowned. "You don't mean that. Offering people the chance to fight—"

"It was Iain," Zhen said reluctantly. "He said to leave off for now. He didn't say why."

Linnea took a breath to swear, then let it out. Of course he'd said that—he wouldn't want to provoke the Line just now. He treated them as if they were made of glass.

Well, she had no problem with provoking them. She'd get things moving again. Another job.

They rode to Zhen and Torin's house in an open motorized pedicab. The blond teenaged girl guiding it wore a garish purple silk jacket embroidered with green palm trees, and loose green shorts. Linnea had never been to Port Marie before, Terranova's capital: a subtropical sea- and skyport with a deep central harbor, an ancient volcanic crater. The steep, rocky outer slope over-looked broad black-sand ocean beaches and had filled in almost solidly with hotels and little houses. Terranovans came here from other places to vacation, it seemed, and so even services like this cab had a touch of gaudy extravagance.

At a busy corner, Zhen stopped the cab and paid, and they climbed out. Zhen led the way up a narrow side street, its name painted on every corner: SUNROSE. Two- and three-storied houses leaned over the pavement, jammed side by side and painted in a shivering rainbow of colors. Flowers hung from balconies. Windows stood open, and bursts of music and voices caught Linnea's ear. Port Marie was a big city, the biggest Linnea had seen since the City on Nexus. But unlike that insular, almost silent place, this was alive, filled with people, bright colors, the smell of cooking. On one corner a fiddler stood playing a tune Linnea almost, almost knew; the sweet sad sound of it tugged at her as they passed. There were fiddles back home, though no one in Moraine had owned one.

Half a block farther on, Zhen led her aside through a yellow-painted gate and up some narrow brick stairs. A tall blue door halfway up had been painted with a gaudy blue bird, its huge fan of tail feathers dotted with blue and green eyes. Zhen touched the door with pride. "I just painted that two days ago."

"That's not a real bird!"

Zhen laughed. "A peacock. They really had them, back on Old Earth. I had a book with a picture of one, when I was little."

Linnea peered at it. "Those can't really be eyes on its tail? On those feathers?"

"Nobody knows anymore," Zhen said, then pushed the door open and swept a Line pilot's ornate full bow. "Welcome!"

The doorway opened into a long, airy room with tall

windows at the front and rear of the building. A kitchen occupied one corner, and a bed the opposite one. "This is home," Zhen said. "We took a room for you upstairs. Just a little bedroom, but it looks over the courtyard in back. Quiet, for here. And there's room for Iain if he visits, a nice big bed for you both." Zhen stepped out of her sandals and gestured toward a set of cushioned chairs. "Sit. Let me get you some wine."

Linnea sat down gratefully and accepted the cool straw-colored wine with pleasure. After weeks in the bleak, white-lit station, the vividness and richness of Port Marie had tightened her nerves. Maybe the wine would dull the overload.

"You've settled in quickly," she said after her first sip.

"Used to moving," Zhen said from the kitchen. "One contract to the next. This is the next, only there's no contract just yet." She arranged some slices of fruit and cheese on a blue-painted platter and carried it over to a table between her chair and Linnea's.

Best to start clearing the air. Linnea set down her glass. "How are you and Torin really managing here? Since everything."

Zhen gave her an oblique glance. "Oh, well, you know. With Nexus gone, the owners've lost their grip on us a bit, and Torin's had plenty to do with the unions and, and just sorting out what comes next. I help when I can."

Linnea nodded. "It's an opportunity for Torin," she said. "But I think your gift is for piloting."

Zhen picked a slice of plum from the platter, then looked up and met Linnea's eyes. "I wish Torin thought so."

Linnea waited.

"If the union takes, if we can get a decent contract to continue that work, Torin and I will have enough money to make a wedding." Zhen flushed. "We've been saving for that for years. Now it's, it's not out of reach anymore. A wedding, and babies. He, he doesn't want to wait."

Linnea clasped her fingers together and sighed. "Do you?"

Zhen looked frustrated. "I don't know! If I thought it might really happen, maybe I wouldn't. But—this war. Torin keeps talking about a permanent contract. But—"

"But there won't *be* a permanent contract," Linnea said.

Zhen nodded. "It's what he's hoped for so long, and now it seems almost in reach, and I think he wants everything to come true at once."

"Not until the Cold Minds are dealt with somehow." Linnea looked up at Zhen. "It hasn't soaked in yet, down here. People here haven't seen them." She shivered. "Once it's clear what the risks are, everything will go on a war footing, and the Board of Control will lock everyone into their jobs for the duration."

"I'd best quit at the restaurant, then." Zhen sat down and leaned back with a sigh. "If the danger is so much, why are *you* still on Terranova? Why haven't you gone home to Santandru, to your family, to protect them?"

"I'm working to get them better protection than I could give if I was there," Linnea said sharply. "Real protection. Commnet updates, guard ships. That takes more pilots than we've got now."

"Back to pilots," Zhen said.

Linnea sighed in annoyance. "Yes. That's the key. That and ships. We've found maybe a thousand old ones put by here and there on different worlds. Not enough even if all of them function. We need to build a whole lot more, and the shipyards here are the best. Terranova will be the new center. For everything."

Zhen nodded. "Money to be made. Good for the workers. That's why Torin's here."

"That's what I'm working for, too. In a different way." Linnea leaned forward. "The Line, what's left of it, is going to settle here. And I know them. They'll want to rebuild everything they had before—have all the power they had before. And people like us can't stop them unless there are as many of us as there are of them—as many of our pilots as theirs."

"They can't fly without our fuel," Zhen said. "And the ships we can build."

"We can't live without their protection," Linnea said. "That gives them power over us. They'll use it the way they always did before, to divide us and make us afraid, to keep us quiet and obedient. They haven't tried it yet, but they will. Unless we're ready for them. Unless we change them."

"We?" Zhen shook her head, smiling. "What, the four of us?"

Linnea straightened in her chair. "You, and me, and Torin, and Iain, and anyone with sense and heart. Those Pilot Masters, they see that they will never be half so powerful and rich again, not if people like us can also pilot jumpships." She looked at Zhen. "People like you and me. You're key. You're one of the first. We need you."

"I wish Torin was sure of that," Zhen said. "He says—he said once, it's easy for you. After all, Iain's a pilot, too. You don't have to choose."

"I—" Linnea said. She picked up her glass of wine and half drained it. "We all have to choose. We've got to fight them in the best way we can. And for you, that means piloting."

"And stopping our lives, Torin's and mine, until this is over," Zhen said.

"We all have to do that," Linnea said bleakly. "Let go of what matters to us, for now. Or we'll lose it forever."

After two more weeks of training, Zhen was ready for her first solo jump through otherspace. She dreaded it. She would make it from Station Six, in one of the small passenger jumpships, now unused, that were docked there. Unlike a commnet linker ship, fitted and adapted to a single pilot, these ships could be piloted by anyone with the gift and the training. With passenger travel suspended, the pilot instructors were using them for their trainees. Linnea had agreed to train Zhen rather than handing her off to some Pilot Master; that was some comfort.

It would be a short jump, Linnea told Zhen—out to the edge of the system, then back again. Less than an hour, subjective, and entirely routine for training.

Zhen had her doubts. She had made that jump twice, but with Linnea on the instructor's pad beside her, linked in with her, ready to take over if Zhen blanked. Everything had gone perfectly. But this time she'd be alone.

Zhen climbed the stairs to Linnea's little room to say an early good night; they'd be getting up before dawn to catch the shuttle. But Linnea didn't answer Zhen's knock, and she sighed and kept climbing, up to the roof. There, of course, was Linnea, a dark figure sitting folded into herself in the corner where two angles of the roof met, arms clasped around her knees, her feet bare to hold herself in place on the corrugated metal, the cool breeze ruffling her thick black hair. Out over the round harbor, calm as glass, the last pale green light faded to the misty horizon. The crescent moon hung just above the mists, a pale yellow paring—smaller than Earth's moon had been. Overhead, glowing eerily in sunlight against the plum-colored sky, the thready plumes of cloud left by shuttles climbing toward orbit made a tangled web of light.

Zhen coughed, and Linnea turned and saw her, then sighed and leaned the side of her face on her folded arms. "You should be in bed," she said indistinctly, and Zhen knew with an odd certainty that Linnea had been crying. Well, damn. So she wasn't made of ice like she pretended.

Zhen picked her way carefully along the slope of the

roof, sat down beside Linnea, and looked out at the view. The yellow-gold lights of a few cargo vessels, scattered over the dark surface of the harbor, looked motionless from this height.

After a moment, Zhen said quietly, "I know you miss Iain."

"Ah." Linnea laughed a little. "Used to him, after all this time. But I'll see him tomorrow. No, I was looking at the sea."

Zhen took a deep breath of the fresh salt air. "It's pretty, I guess."

"At home—on Santandru—we live from the sea," Linnea said in a remote voice. "My da was a fisherman, and his da before him, and his before him—it's how we kept alive. Then my village lost our boat, some kind of failure, an explosion, and we had to evacuate. And I had to take a work contract on Nexus."

"And you saved them," Zhen said. "Iain told us so. Even your village, Iain said you sent them what they needed to get another fishing boat."

"But I don't know if they ever got it," Linnea said. She rested her chin on her folded arms and sighed. "No way to know. My sister's never messaged me, she was so angry at me for going to Nexus; and she hasn't answered any that I've sent since then. So I don't know if she's even alive, or the children. I don't know anything. It may be years before I know."

"You're a pilot," Zhen said. "You've got your own ship now. Can't you just go?"

"You know I can't." Linnea's voice was low and bitter. "I'm the one who can talk to both sides, to both kinds of pilots. And—" Zhen heard her take a shaking breath. "And I've seen more of the Cold Minds, close up, than anyone else alive. So they tell me I'm a, a strategic asset—I have to stay near the center of command. They can't spare me. Not ever."

"Would it take that long, just to go and come back?"

Linnea raised her head and gazed out over the darkening sea. "Santandru's too far. If I jumped home, then jumped right back, it would take more than half a standard year, objective time. I can't be gone for that long." She closed her eyes. "And what worries me is—I'm not sure I *would* come back."

Zhen touched Linnea's shoulder, lightly. "That's rough," she said. "To be stuck here, not knowing."

Linnea was silent.

Out over the bay, as the light faded from the sky, the faint cloudy traces of nebulae began to appear. Shapes with names Zhen had known from childhood—the Old Man's Eye, the Two Brothers, the Rabbit—all dimly colored and flecked with the first stars of evening. The shapes of home, the familiar sky of spring-into-summer.

And out there, up there among the stars, those *things* were hiding, moving. Zhen knew Linnea was sure of it. And what else were they doing, maybe right now, maybe to Linnea's people?

"Let me go for you," she said abruptly.

Linnea raised her head and stared at Zhen. "You can't."

"Why not?" Zhen shrugged. "I'm ready to make jumps on my own. I could get word of your family. You know the Line's not going to send any ships there, they don't care. But we need to know what's happening everywhere."

"We will send a ship," Linnea said, "with an experienced pilot, as soon as we can spare one. Iain has promised me that much."

"And when will that be? Send me. I'm good at it. You said so yourself."

"It's too far," Linnea said firmly. "Put it out of your mind, Zhen."

"You made long jumps almost right away, and you—"

"No." Linnea got carefully to her feet, stood balanced on the slope of the roof. "Don't even think about it anymore. Plenty of people have family they're worried about and can't get to. That's just how things are now." She shivered. "It's getting cold. I'm going in."

STATION SIX

I ain found Linnea leaning against the bulkhead in the dark passageway outside the traffic control center. Her arms were folded, her head down. He went to her and set his hands gently on her shoulders. She did not look up.

"Come and rest," he said. "It's been twenty hours now, Linnea. They'll notify us if—when there's any signal.

She didn't move. "I can't believe she did it," she said hoarsely. "Tried the long jump. There's so much she hadn't learned yet. She wasn't ready."

Iain steadied himself. "The risk is—not as bad as you think," he said. "People in training, they become too confident, they overreach." Iain tightened his grip on her shoulders. "But they make it. They find their way back. Most of the time."

"Some of the time," Linnea said remotely. "I know the statistics. . . . And if they never come out of otherspace? They just go flying on until they starve, or freeze—"

"There's no way to know what happened until she comes back," Iain said. Her shoulders were rigid under his hands, and he tightened his hold. "All we can do is trust Zhen. She's bright. She's gifted. She'll find her way home."

"I'm not good at this," Linnea said. "Maybe you're right. Maybe the Line *should* take over."

Iain suppressed a sigh. He had begun to wonder, in recent weeks, whether a vital attribute of jump piloting was complete, supreme confidence—whether in fact it was the arrogance of the Line that made its pilots succeed. And if so, could that arrogance ever be taught to people like Linnea? "Of course you will continue to teach," he said quietly. "We need you. This happens to every teacher, sooner or later. Trainees—misjudge. They always have."

"But this is *Zhen*." Linnea's voice shook. "Our friend. How am I going to tell Torin what happened?" She closed her eyes, and the tears spilled over.

Iain pulled her into an embrace. "We'll tell him together," he said, cold with dread.

TWELVE

TERRANOVA

Iain reached Sunrose Street near the middle of the long Terranovan night. He had not been here since the grim day a month ago when he and Linnea brought Torin the news that Zhen was missing. A bad memory. He had seen neither of them since. Setting up pilot training schedules, with his Line trainers sometimes pulling out without warning, had kept him on the station. But now he'd been called groundside, presumably to report to the Council. And he'd come a day early, of course, to see Linnea. Now—when it was too late—he wondered whether she would be glad of it.

The rain had stopped when the tram reached Sunrose. Iain set off up the narrow street, hearing rainwater trickling in the gutters, seeing an occasional window still lit yellow. His eagerness to see Linnea, which had carried him through the long flight, dissipated a little as he approached the house where she lived. She'd been remote, lately, when they commed; tired, he'd thought, but was that true? He shouldn't have presumed she would welcome him. He did not know, anymore, what she wanted from him.

Yet he'd be seeing more of her, soon enough. The Council was about to decide whether to attack Nexus with the resources they could gather quickly or to move to protect the Hidden Worlds first. She'd been working to build a case for patrols, and he could help prove the plan was possible. Maybe simply working together would bring them closer again.

At least he would see her.

The street was deserted, this late. Shallow puddles shimmered under the streetlamps. The familiar yellow gate glistened slickly as he pushed through it. He climbed past the blue door that had been Zhen and Torin's. Torin had moved out the second week, Linnea had told him, to a tiny back room at the union offices. Now a FOR RENT sign had been tacked to the door, half-covering Zhen's peacock. At the top of the stairs, light glimmered from the small window next to Linnea's door.

He tapped on the door, and after a moment it opened. She looked up at him and seemed for an instant not to know him. Then she stepped back, wordless, and let him come in. It cut at his heart to see how sallow, strained, and tired she looked.

He closed the door and set down his travel bag. He knew better than to touch her. He'd hoped, after all this time, that she'd at last overcome her memories of the bad times, but now—"Linnea? Are you all right?"

Abruptly she turned away and began straightening papers on the small worktable. The little room held a wide mattress on the floor, the worktable with a comm setup, and two stacked crates piled with more papers; that was all. "I'm sorry," she said. "I've been working since dawn, my head's in a fog."

Reluctantly, he asked her, "Should I go somewhere else for the night?"

She set down the papers, and her head drooped. "I don't think so." She looked at him, her face colorless, dark shadows under her eyes. "I'm glad to see you. I am. It's been so—quiet. Even when I go to a meeting, Torin is there, and he—I just can't—he won't talk to me, Iain. Not outside of business."

With a soundless sigh, he gathered her into his arms, rested his cheek against the top of her head. "You're doing good work," he said. "Important work. And Torin will forgive us."

Abruptly, she stiffened. "Stop soothing me down," she said sharply, pushing him away. She dropped into the chair at the worktable. "I'm sorry, Iain. It's just—" She broke off.

So she still couldn't talk to him. Best to sit down, not stand over her. . . . He looked around the little room. He did not want to sit on the bed—to seem to presume anything, or invite anything—but there was no other place. He lowered himself down onto the clean, worn yellow blanket and leaned back against the wall, trying to hide the sadness that ached in his throat.

She stared at him, and finally said, "What?"

"I miss you," he said quietly. "I care about you. I don't want to lose you."

He saw the words strike her, saw her shoulders drop with tiredness. Watched as her pride gathered itself again, as he had known it would. She lifted her chin and met his eyes. "I know, Iain. You came to Freija for me. You landed on an infested world and searched for me. You saved my life."

He nodded.

"And if I told you—that more than my own life, I need to go home," she said slowly, "you would say that I should do it."

His heart went cold. But he could not lie to her. "If you needed it that much, I would."

She rose, and came to him, and sat beside him on the bed. "Then—I'd better not tell you," she said simply. She leaned her head against his shoulder, and they sat in silence. There were no words safe to speak.

TEMPORARY COUNCIL HEADQUARTERS, PORT MARIE

Concealing his tension with the ease of long practice, Hakon sen Efrem entered the office of the provisional head of the new Council and made a carefully correct bow. By the end of this meeting, Hakon knew, he would have swept Iain sen Paolo aside, clearing the road for his ambition to lead the assault on Nexus. Or Hakon would be headed for obscurity, his hopes dismissed.

Council Lord sen Martin, the Honormaster, nodded an expressionless acknowledgment of the bow. The room, in a rented building near one of the bayfront parks, was small and plain by Line standards, but early morning sunlight streamed through broad windows behind the Honormaster, bringing the colors of the room's simple rugs and hangings to warm life. "Sit, Pilot sen Efrem."

"Thank you, Master sen Martin." Hakon obeyed, taking a chair opposite the Honormaster. *Calm. Patience.* Empty courtesies first, then minor matters, then—"Do you find these new offices adequate, Honormaster?"

"I enjoy being groundside again, much though it pains me to admit it," the Honormaster said. "And I enjoy seeing the gardens from here. In the Council Tower I never saw flowers from one month's end to the next." Sen Martin was dressed in noncommittal black, not yet claiming the amethyst robes of the chairmanship of the Council. *Or perhaps his tailor hasn't finished them,* Hakon thought wryly. The old man's thin white hair was tied loosely back with a white cord—mourning, still, for his dead partner. "And you," he said. "How do you find your new duties?"

"Challenging, Honormaster." Hakon felt a moment of pride, again, at the thought of his recent election as Council voice for the active pilots. It had taken him away from the Honormaster's side, but he'd had good reason: it prepared his next move. "I believe it suits me."

"You do the post honor, Pilot sen Efrem." Master sen Martin gestured toward a carved wooden tray, with a coffeepot and cups, set out on a side table. "Please."

Hakon half bowed politely and began to serve them both. It was not a proper coffee service; the cups were brightly painted, heavy. But Hakon poured with care, every gesture correct. The Honormaster was still the most senior Line Council member known to have survived the disaster, and the only one from the Inner Council itself. His voice carried weight. He had been a friend of Iain sen Paolo's father, before the old man's disgrace and suicide two years ago; but Master sen Martin had then managed to survive the rise to sole power of Paolo's enemy and brother, Fridric sen David. He was a man to be reckoned with: a man who understood that even the most principled goals required flexibility in a man, if they were ever to be achieved.

Hakon set the cup of fragrant, steaming coffee before the Honormaster. The issue of reconstituting the Inner Council still dangled, and Master sen Martin seemed content that it should. Perhaps he was hoping for Council Lord sen David's return, to reassume the burden of decision. Hakon had long ago decided that Fridric was dead. It was as well. That whole family shamed the Line that had nurtured it. Most of the working pilots agreed with him on that.

When Hakon had poured for himself, he settled back in his chair and waited while the Honormaster drank first. Master sen Martin sighed in contentment and set down his cup. "You may begin," the Honormaster said, "with the most recent count of Line survivors."

Hakon set down his cup and gathered himself. "The news is not good, Honormaster. Reports have now reached us from four of the five major worlds and sixteen of the minor ones."

"Then we now have something approaching the final numbers." The Honormaster's voice was flat.

"Yes, Master sen Martin." Hakon's voice was toneless. "The count of surviving pilots remains just above sixteen hundred. More than three hundred are known to be dead or taken by the Cold Minds, and another ninety-four are unaccounted for." He consulted his palmscreen. "It grieves me to report—we now must conclude that the losses in the invasion appear to have included most of the population of the City. Our scouting missions have detected no sign of organized survivors, picked up no transmissions."

The Honormaster closed his eyes. "Go on," he said.

Hakon sat silent for a moment, looking down at his palmscreen. The horror of the loss still burned in his mind. What he'd seen the day of the invasion, the tales he'd heard from other men. . . . At last, he cleared his throat and continued, "Almost all of the contract servants and support workers are presumed killed or taken. We lost—we lost at least twenty thousand men of the other class, of our Line-descended cousins who were not pilots and lived in the City or on Dock. The Cold Minds killed or captured thousands of senior men of the Line, almost all those who were on the surface at the time of the attack. And we—we lost most of the thousand trainees." His voice was husky. "And almost all of the young sons of the Line."

The Honormaster's face went gray. "No word, then, of any other ships that escaped with children?"

"None beyond those we already know of," Hakon said.

"Slightly more than three thousand men and boys of the Line are known to have survived, and we will find a few more refugees on outlying worlds. But—"

"But we have lost a generation." The Honormaster looked shrunken and old.

"We will rebuild, Master," Hakon said quietly. "We'll have other sons."

"Certainly. Certainly." The Honormaster sat silent, gazing down into his cup as if some answer, some hope could be found there.

Then he seemed to gather himself; his haggard expression smoothed over. "Let us turn to the question of your request for a voting position on the Council rather than the traditional observer's role."

"My brother pilots urged it, Master," Hakon said. "I agreed to request it only because, as never before, working pilots are now a majority of the Line. It seemed to us that—"

"The request has been denied."

Hakon controlled his expression. This startling abruptness was not a good sign. "I hope I have not offended you."

"No. No. I like drive in a young man. But what you ask is out of the question. We have never offered a working pilot a seat on the Inner Council."

"The Council is not at full strength—"

"Other Council members may have escaped Nexus," the Honormaster said.

"Pardon, Master, but a final census will take something close to a standard year to achieve."

The Honormaster sighed. "I will tell you then, Pilot sen Efrem—and this is for you alone, not to be discussed with your hotheaded friends."

Suppressing a wince at the pointed term, Hakon bowed agreement.

"Council Lord sen David, the Honored Voice, did

escape the fall of the City," the Honormaster said. "He sent a message in the Council's highest code, requesting that we conceal both his escape and his destination—a private family issue. But he intends to return to his position as soon as it proves to be possible."

Hakon stared out at the bright garden beyond the Honormaster. This put all his calculations in disarray. "He intends to return to his position? Even after his son—"

"Lord sen David has always been a powerful man. Such men are not always accustomed to considering political repercussions. Or the fact that the ground can change." The Master's sharp gaze met Hakon's. "Nevertheless, I am sure that you are as prepared as I am to serve him loyally, in accordance with our oaths at the Tree."

"Of course," Hakon said.

"We will not speak further of this," the Honormaster said. "We expect his return before the year is out. So you see that now is hardly the time to introduce radical innovations such as seating a working pilot on the Council."

Hakon knew he must not simply agree, or the Master's probing would have exposed a weakness. "May I say," Hakon said carefully, "that Iain sen Paolo's ideas certainly constitute radical innovations, and yet the Council has listened to them." There—that served two purposes.

"There is innovation and innovation," the Master said. "We must acknowledge this new reality—some of these groundsiders may be useful, trained as pilots of sorts, to take on tedious patrol duties and free true pilots, *Line* pilots, for more important missions." He sipped his coffee again. "But, Pilot sen Efrem, our central customs must not change. Not now."

Hakon felt his fingers tighten on his cup with trembling tension, and he schooled himself back to outward calm. Time to abandon this point and come at last to the real reason he had requested this meeting. "Honormaster, that brings forward another issue. A disturbing discovery." He reached into the pocket of his black tunic and found the data crystal, set it on the worktable before the Honormaster.

Master sen Martin pushed the crystal into a slot on the worktable and watched as an image formed over the holoplate. His brows lifted. "A set of message headers?"

"Messages that, over the past month, we have intercepted on their way to Iain sen Paolo." Hakon took a breath and plunged on. "We have traced their source. They come from outside the commnet."

The Master's gaze sharpened. "Outside?"

"Dropped in from unauthorized ships," Hakon said.

"The Cold Minds," the Master said. "The Cold Minds are sending messages to Iain sen Paolo?" He looked back at the headers.

"He has not received these—I ordered them held," Hakon said. "But I have reason to believe at least one earlier message went through."

"These are marked as coded. A closed code. Has it been broken?"

"It cannot be broken, Honormaster," Hakon said. "It is a family code." He met the Honormaster's eyes. "Sen Paolo's family code."

"These cannot have come from Council Lord sen David," the Honormaster said slowly. "He is still in transit to his destination. So—"

Hakon swallowed in a dry throat. "So Rafael sen Fridric, the traitor himself, is sending messages to Iain sen Paolo."

The Honormaster sat back slowly, his expression stunned.

"And sen Paolo is here, in the city, this morning," Hakon said carefully. "Expecting to make a routine report to the Council. To answer any questions you may have."

"And he will," Master sen Martin breathed, staring at the image over the holoplate. "He will."

Early in the morning Iain took his turn in the ground-floor shower, wishing he could carry the chill from its cold spray through the rest of the day. The rain had drawn off again, and Port Marie sweltered in humid gray murk, already nearly unbearable at only the start of a long day.

When he came back to the room in his dark blue formal tunic and trousers, Linnea was nearly ready. She wore a dress, Terranovan professional wear for women: a neatly cut bodice flaring out to a flowing calf-length skirt. Its deep wine color suited her. "I like that," Iain said.

"I wish you would wear pilot black." She sounded irritated. "I know they've offered it to you."

"Until the Inner Council declares that it has re-formed, no one on Terranova has the power to reinstate me," Iain said. "And I can be more effective as an outsider."

"Why? It means the Line men don't listen to you."

"It means the Terranovans do," he said, and saw her ironic almost-smile.

To spare their good clothes from dust and sweat, Iain paid for a pedicab to get them the kilometer downhill to the meeting place at the Line's new quarters. When they arrived, as he climbed down from the cab, he saw with dismay two men in brick red Line Security uniforms manning the entrance door. Linnea followed him, and he saw her eyes widen slightly—she had been in the hands of Line Security almost three years before, on Nexus. He moved closer to her. "We've come for the Council meeting this morning," he said to the men. "You'll find we're on the list." He gave their names.

The senior man checked a palmscreen, scanned their

identity papers. "You're cleared," he said to Iain, "but we are to further verify Miss Kiaho's identity."

Iain clamped his jaw against protest as the other guard ran a small scanner over Linnea's right palm and right eye. Iain saw her fright, the pulse jumping in the side of her neck, during the wait while the scans were compared with a central database. He schooled his expression, hiding his anger and impatience.

At last the senior guard pronounced that Linnea, too, was cleared, and the heavy etched glass of the door slid aside. Iain and Linnea entered, and Iain saw Linnea shiver in the first chill burst of cooled indoor air.

Hakon sen Efrem stood waiting to greet them in the empty lobby—no doubt he had arranged for the gate guard to call him, hence the delay. Hakon wore pilot black of the finest quality, clothes he must have had made for him in the city. His brown hair shone, pulled back into a severely correct pilot's braid.

And two men in the uniform of Line Security flanked him.

Hakon nodded politely. "Iain."

Hakon ought to have used Iain's patronym in this setting. Iain merely said, "Hakon." *Calm. This man is dangerous.*

Hakon's eyes narrowed and he glanced at Linnea. "And your staff," he said, flashing a cold smile.

"Linnea Kiaho," she offered. "I wouldn't expect you to remember."

Hakon turned back to Iain without replying. "I've received some new information. I must speak with you." He glanced again at Linnea. "Privately."

"The Council is expecting me," Iain said, smiling steadily. "And I'm sure you have many pressing responsibilities today."

"The first being this matter," Hakon said. "I must

insist." His expression hardened. "I must insist in the name of the Council."

So that was how it was. An arrest, or near to one. Iain half bowed polite acceptance. "Then I am at the your disposal, of course." As he straightened, Linnea's eyes, dark with concern, met his.

Hakon followed Iain's glance. "Your staff is welcome to—"

"I think Miss Kiaho should wait for me somewhere else," Iain said, his voice edged with urgency. "At, say, our old friend's new residence?" Torin's office. He saw understanding in her eyes. Now if they would just let her leave—

Iain saw Hakon's contemptuous shrug with relief. She nodded to Iain, her expression troubled. But she left.

When Iain saw her climb into a pedicab outside, saw it roll off, he turned back to Hakon. "What is this, Pilot sen Efrem?"

Hakon only turned and started down a dim corridor. Iain could do nothing but follow, the security men walking close behind.

A neat trap, Iain thought with despair. He only hoped Linnea had truly escaped it.

THIRTEEN

A few minutes later, Linnea pushed through the door of the shipyard workers' union offices, already looking around for Torin. A man at a worktable looked up from the newsfeed he was reading, leaned back in his chair, and called, "Dimarco! Someone to see you." Linnea nodded her thanks.

After a moment, Torin Dimarco appeared from a back room. He looked thin, and his gray-green work coveralls had obviously not been washed in a while. His eyes were tired. He'd been working much too hard since Zhen's disappearance.

"Lin," he said with a nod. "What's the bother?"

"I think the Council has arrested Iain," she said.

"Wait," Torin said. "Arrested? For what?"

"Because Hakon sen Efrem wants it, Torin," she said angrily. "Why do you think they would arrest him? Iain's been a thorn in Hakon's side since the Council moved down here."

Torin folded his arms across his chest. "What happened?"

She told the story quickly, and when she finished, Torin nodded again. "What do they have on him?"

Linnea only shook her head, and Torin sighed. "Come on back."

Linnea stood tensely until the door of his room had closed behind them. "I think it's Rafael," she said. "He s-sent Iain a message a few weeks ago. I think the Council knows about it."

"A message?" He stared at her. "A message from the Cold Minds?"

"It didn't make much sense." She shivered. "Something about, 'help them.' 'Help them, they're afraid.'"

Torin leaned on the edge of his worktable and scratched his chin. "Help who? Who's afraid?"

"I think Iain believed there might be—survivors," she said.

"Line survivors, still on Nexus," Torin said. "Why would Rafael tell us that? He's one of *them*."

"He, he took a drug. Rafael did." She clenched her jaw to keep her voice steady. "It's called spiderweave."

Torin's eyebrows went up. "High-class stuff."

"It—he took it for so long, Iain thinks it means Rafael might—still be alive inside his mind," she said.

A spatter of rain struck the window, and Torin turned to look at it. When he looked back at Linnea, his expression was faintly amused. "So tell me what *you* think it meant."

"I think it's a trap," she said whitely. "For the Line. And Hakon sen Efrem wants to lead them into it."

"Him again," Torin said, his voice remote. He rubbed forehead wearily, then looked straight into her eyes. "Lin, I was planning to warn you about Hakon sen Efrem."

She stood very still. "So tell me now."

Torin looked grim. "The pilots pulling out of the training program lately? That's sen Efrem's work, directly his work. He's been doing it to keep pressure on Iain. To keep Iain busy up in orbit, distracted, while sen Efrem lobbies the new Inner Council and preaches to all the off-duty pilots who will listen to him. He's tired of waiting for his attack on Nexus. He's got the younger pilots lined up with him. Now he's trying for all of them."

She dropped her face into her hands. "That—" She struggled for a word. "That *mucksucker*. Slimy, blind—" Linnea stopped. "What do we do, Torin? I don't know the laws here. Iain's got rights, doesn't he?"

"If he was a citizen here, he might," Torin said. "We could get a lawyer, go to the Council, and demand to talk to him, and if they refused, there might"—he lifted a finger—"*might* be some kind of trouble for them. Inconvenience anyway."

Linnea looked out at the rain. "But as things are—"

"Exactly." Torin rubbed his face again, yawned into his cupped hands. "Let me get on the comm. See what I can find out."

Linnea clenched her fists. "I'd like to have a few words with Pilot Master sen Efrem. If you can arrange it."

Torin's mouth twitched, the hint of a grin. "I thought you might."

She smiled back thinly.

As Torin had told her she would, Linnea found Hakon sen Efrem at the Port Marie skyport. One of Torin's men had passed her through the gate into the storage yards. Once she was inside, no one took a second glance at her in her worker's coveralls, carrying a canvas bag of tools, with the useless but real-looking ID card dangling from a pocket.

She stopped outside the Line storage facility for dead ships and spare parts. The tangerine sunlight of late afternoon slanted along dusty concrete outside; inside the chilly hangar, everything was brilliantly lit, blue-white and clean. Linnea walked in, looking around with curiosity that soon became disbelief.

At least a dozen ships were being repaired and re-worked here, brought back to life and function. And Iain had been made to beg for two, and to agree to do the necessary work himself. Hakon had whole crews at work on every ship. Anger boiled up inside her, and she pushed it back. No time to be distracted by that.

She spotted sen Efrem in a clump of techs, studying the mounting on a maneuvering jet. He wore blue-cloth coveralls, smeared with the fine oil used to preserve the metal surfaces of ships in storage. "No, see," he was saying, "it's a nonstandard unit. The pilot must have had it replaced in some backworld port, look at those welds. I'm betting it's out of some other yard entirely, and probably a hundred years older than the ship."

"Then how are we supposed to—"

But sen Efrem had raised his head and spotted Linnea. "Improvise, gentlemen," he said. "Please excuse me."

He walked toward her, wiping his hands carefully on a gray cloth, then stuffing it in a pocket. But he did not extend a hand to her. "Interesting to see you again. Dressed like that. Have you taken a new job?"

"By all means let's talk out here," she said coolly, "if you want half of Port Marie to hear what the Council's been up to."

He looked amused and pointed toward a glass-enclosed office, and they entered. He closed the door and turned to face her. Beyond him she saw men out on the work floor, watching curiously. "I'm busy," he said shortly. "You want to know where sen Paolo is. I won't tell you. You want to know when you'll see him again. That's not my decision. You want to know why we arrested him—"

He broke off, and studied her. "Or do you already know?" He stood incongruously straight in the coveralls. "What can you tell me about this?"

"Nothing." She focused on his face. "When will Pilot sen Paolo be free?"

"First," sen Efrem said, "don't call him 'Pilot.' That's for honorable men. And second—" He smiled at her. "That's all I will tell you."

She took a breath. "Lot of ships here. More than Iain knew were this close to ready." She looked at sen Efrem. "Planning something?"

"Just replacements," sen Efrem said easily. "You know how many Line pilots lost their ships in the confusion, or when Dock blew."

"It's a convenient way to buy their support for your attack, certainly," she said. "Like arresting Iain. Will you let him go after the attack is launched?" She felt cold. "Or are you going to kill him?"

"That would be dramatic," sen Efrem said, "but there's no need to go so far. You'll see him again. When things are in motion."

"The attack on Nexus, you mean," she said. "The attack Iain was trying to stop because—"

"Because he is a coward," sen Efrem said.

"Because it can't be done." Linnea lifted her chin. "Even if you can uproot the Cold Minds, you'll scatter them to all the other worlds, which you'll have to leave unprotected."

"Not the ones that matter," sen Efrem said. "Those little worlds are irrelevant to the future of humanity. As Nexus is not. As Terranova is not. Should we wait here playing sen Paolo's games until the Cold Minds come here, in force?" He shook his head contemptuously. "You claim to be a pilot. Think like one, if you can."

"Just one man," Linnea said, "Rafael working alone, was able to bring down your defenses. Orbital control at

Nexus was centralized, because that was *tradition*. If that is thinking like a pilot, well, I would rather not."

He stood a little taller. "What did you intend to accomplish by coming here?"

"To insist that you free Iain sen Paolo," she said. "And that you stop interfering with our work."

"To insist?" sen Efrem looked disgusted. "You do not insist anything, here. It is the Line that decides."

She kept her voice steady. "Then you underestimate Iain. You certainly underestimate me. And what's worse, you underestimate our people, the Terranovans and the others on other worlds. You and your friends think you can impose your will on forty-six worlds because that is tradition."

"No," sen Efrem said in a reasonable voice, "it's because we *can*."

"You think," she said, "that when this is over, if it ever is, we will all bow to your wishes as we did six hundred years ago. When you had ships and we were just a few miserable refugees you saved from a dying world."

"We still have the ships," he said coldly. "And only we can protect your little worlds."

"Not for long," she said. "You can't take back piloting now, make it your guild secret again. The knowledge has spread too far. And to the right people at last. For six hundred years while you followed your customs and swore your oaths and held up all your traditions, *we* were out here building worlds. New worlds."

"Scrabbling to survive," sen Efrem said. "Still."

"Some of us, maybe," she said. "No fault of ours, that we got set down on poor thin little worlds. . . . But look at Terranova. Do you really believe your world of pilots outweighed what Terranova's people have built? And do you really believe they won't fight to protect it? Make *you* fight to protect it?" She leaned against the worktable again. "Nexus is dead. Even if you get it back, it's dead, because the idea of your power is dead."

"You are wrong," he said. "We'll rise again."

"*I* am not blind," she said. "It comes down to a question, and I hope you will think about it. In a few years we'll outnumber you, we pilots from the other worlds. That is a fact. You cannot prevent it. Do you want to be our teachers and our partners? Or do you want to be simply"—she swept her hand in a flicking gesture—"irrelevant?"

His face reddened with obvious anger at her echoing of his own words, but he smiled tightly. "Well spoken! And most persuasive. But I'm not convinced."

"It's not your choice," she said. "You took an oath to protect us."

"Sen Paolo abandoned his oath," sen Efrem said, "quite lightly, when it inconvenienced him. When you urged him to. And you have the impudence to tell *me* what it means!"

She bit back an angry reply. "Forty-six worlds of innocent people depend on your oath," she said.

"I will not be lectured by a servingwoman." He straightened. "I have a message you can carry to the *real* yard workers and dockworkers. To those unions you talk of."

She waited.

"Work quietly," sen Efrem said. "Under Line direction. Help prepare the invasion fleet."

"And why should they do this?"

"Because if they do," sen Efrem said, "then after our victory, we will consider offering them our renewed protection."

She stood very straight. "I want to talk to Iain."

"No," sen Efrem said. "Sen Paolo has dealt with the Council before. He knows from his own experience—an incident involving you, I believe—that with the Council, one's reputation can be as badly hurt by the appearance of a crime as by the crime itself." He smiled.

"You denounced him," she said slowly. "You brought false evidence against Iain in Council."

"You and he are so alike," sen Efrem said. "You think one person, or two people, can accomplish anything they wish through sheer stupid stubbornness. You both underestimate the Line. And me." He brushed a streak of dust from the sleeve of his coverall. "This is the last warning you'll receive. The new Inner Council listens to *me*."

She stared at him, itching to strike him in the face; then saw the many watching men out in the hangar. He would probably welcome a reason to arrest her for assault. Finally, she said in a soft voice, "You made an important enemy today, Hakon sen Efrem."

He only laughed and opened the door for her. "Goodbye, Miss Kiaho."

She did not look back at him. But she did not forget his smile.

FOURTEEN

Iain stood again before the Council, still wearing the formal tunic and trousers he had put on this morning, but rumpled and sweaty from his confinement since noon in a small, hot room below ground level. His hands bound behind him, he stood with his head high. Weavings drawn over the windows of the chamber shut out the night, but he heard rain drumming against the thick glass.

Hakon sen Efrem, in his pilot's black tunic, sat far down the table, at Iain's left, a glowering presence.

"We have considered," the Honormaster said. "We have deliberated." Iain caught his sidelong glance toward Hakon. "It is the conclusion of the voting members of this Council that the messages you have unlocked for us are nothing but the mutterings of a fading mind, pleas for help and rescue as Rafael sen Fridric sank under the influence of the Cold Minds." He set his hands on the table. "However, this does not excuse your concealment of the first message. And it does not remove all cause for suspicion."

Iain waited, patiently, for the words that would tell him his fate.

"Therefore," the Honormaster said, "you are ordered to return to Station Six. Your work will be restricted to training new groundsider pilots, freeing more true Line pilots for the work of forming the attack force for Nexus. You are physically confined to Station Six and will not return groundside before the attack is launched. I have an order to that effect from a Terranovan magistrate."

Master sen Martin glanced at the notes on the screen in the tabletop before him. "Finally, all your communications will be intercepted and monitored by Line Security. You will open any family-code messages in the presence of Line Security. If they have reason to suspect that you are receiving meaningful communication from Nexus, you will be placed in the detention facility on Station Six, indefinitely.

"Have you anything to say before you are returned to Station Six?"

Only one question was worth asking. "May I speak with Linnea Kiaho, as I requested this morning? I am told that she's waiting outside."

"Time is of the essence," the Honormaster said. "Five minutes only, in the presence and hearing of Line Security." Again the flick of a glance toward Hakon sen Efrem. "After today, you will not communicate with her again, directly or indirectly; if we discover that you have attempted it, we will arrest her."

That had to be Hakon's work. It was vicious enough. Iain felt numb. Five minutes.

He had five minutes to tell Linnea that he would never see her again.

L innea jumped to her feet as the heavy doors to the Council chamber swung open at last. Two Line Security men armed with stunrods brought Iain out to her, then took one step back and stood watching.

So they were to talk in a public lobby, in front of guards. She felt a rush of rage at the sight of Iain's bound hands. Then raised her eyes to his face. And went cold.

He was looking at her as if—as if the sentence had been death.

"Tell me what happened," she rasped.

"House arrest," he said, "on Station Six. Pilot training. They won't let me come groundside, at all, before they launch the attack on Nexus." He sounded empty.

Relief flooded her. "That's not so bad," she said. "I can come up and see—"

"No," he said. "They want you where you are, Linnea. I won't be in contact with you. They'll monitor everything I send, everything I receive. If I try to speak to you, if you try to see me, they'll arrest you." He tilted his head toward the Council chamber. "*His* work."

She shook her head. "But only until the attack," she said. "Then you can—"

"Linnea." His face changed, hardened. "There's something I must tell you."

She clenched her fists at her sides, waiting.

"When the attack is launched," Iain said, "I will go with it. I must be with my brothers."

"No," she whispered. She swallowed tears, her throat aching. "No, you can't. You'll die. You know the Cold Minds will be ready—"

"My brothers have elected to attempt this," Iain said. "And I never left them, Linnea. Not truly. You know that I am still—what I always was."

"Yes," she said, anger straightening her spine. "Still what you always were. *Not of the Line.* You broke your oath. The Tree is gone. Can't you set this aside?"

"I don't want to," he said simply. "If I let them go, even into a trap, and remain behind—no matter the reason—I will be false to, to the center of myself. False to my father's memory. False to the tradition that made me what I am."

"You'll be a fool," she said hotly.

"I'll be a pilot," he said. "I am sorry, Linnea."

The guards stepped forward and took hold of his arms again. She could not speak, could hardly see him for the tears burning in her eyes. "Good-bye, Linnea," he said.

And he was gone.

NEXUS

*H*e *was once Rafael.* Mostly when that thought comes to him he digs down further into the bright circle in the center of his mind, into the place where they cannot come, the spider-thoughts, the chittering voices.

The spiderweave has taken his mind, and he is mad—

The Cold Minds have taken his body, and he is dead—

One, two. One sickening truth or the other. His body walks, he knows that, acts, even speaks sometimes—words, so there are people to hear—but he has learned not to look out through his eyes, to see what can be seen.

The City, dark under the cold stars.

The Inmost Place, stinking, slimed with bots.

His home, its green-glass windows cracked, its stone floor silted with dust. The climate shield is gone. He knows because when he looks out through his eyes, he also senses his own breathing—hot, scraping breaths of air dry beyond bearing and thick with dust. Nothing to stop the storms now.

His voice is speaking now. Slow and strange, not his voice, dust-raw but also not his, not his—*Do this again and we will take three of the little ones and feed on them.*

He must look. He edges, edges, to the corner of his mind where his eyes still work, peers out—

Filthy little boys, cowering in a dark, cavernous room,

squinting against the light from behind him, the flickering light from his eyes. Dozens of dirty children, crying and snotty and shivering. Cowering away from—him.

From what walks in his body.

No more resistance, the not-his voice says, and a door closes between his body and the dark room beyond.

Though he dives at once back into the safety of the inner place in his mind, he hears the children's hopeless crying for a long time after.

FIFTEEN

SANTANDRU
FIVE MONTHS AFTER THE FALL OF NEXUS

Fridric sen David settled the jumpship carefully into its landing cradle, one of only three in this miserable excuse for a skyport. He had done it. He had gotten them here alive. Years, decades after his last flight as a jump pilot, he had brought himself and his heir safely to refuge on Santandru—a backwater where the boy could be born, safe from the Cold Minds for at least a few months. Then, when the baby could travel, Fridric would make his triumphant return to retake the reins of power and lead the counterattack on Nexus. . . .

With shaking hands, he stripped the monitors, the food and medical and waste connections from his gaunt body. A long jump, more than a subjective month, had taken its toll on him. His whole body ached. He stank.

He straightened his spine, wincing. The status board showed the necessary refueling and ground-power connections being made outside the ship. Probably by hand, judging from this world's tech rating. But fuel was fuel.

He moved to the passenger shell. The medical monitors had kept him apprised of the woman's health, the progress of the pregnancy. All the same, he felt a shiver of relief when he threw back the lid of the shell and saw her with his own eyes: the woman breathing quietly, the shipmind-interface mask still hiding her face, her gravid body still safely restrained and safely connected to the systems that fed her and kept her and the fetus healthy. He'd had the shipmind sedate her for landing, not wishing fright to induce early labor. But she would have to walk on her own from here; he could hardly carry her. He tapped a code for a stimulant, then carefully removed the interface mask from her face.

Her face, glistening with sweat, made her look nine days drowned, but that was only the effect of her pale skin in the weak greenish light. Her hair, ash-blond when clean, made a gray-brown, greasy frame for her face. After a moment her eyes opened, and he saw again the icy blue of Rafael's eyes—his son who was almost certainly dead. The eyes had been the reason he had chosen her for Rafael.

A new beginning. Fridric would be an attentive father this time, guide his grandson down all the right paths. The boy would be disciplined, dutiful, worthy, as Rafael had not been.

Yshana tried to speak but could not seem to coordinate. He shook his head at her. "Don't bother. We're landed. I'll help you climb out." She was a heavy burden even half-supporting herself, but at last he got her on her feet. This training ship had none of the amenities of a Line pilot's personal commnet linker ship; there was no refresher closet, merely a toilet, and not much in the way of shipboard stores. But in half an hour or so they were both dressed, as neatly as they could manage, and had eaten some dry emergency rations. No doubt the Santandru port control officer was pacing the pavement outside.

When the hatch irised open, Fridric shrank back from a gust of icy air. An hour before local sunset, it was almost as dark as night outside. A cold wind whined. Heavy clouds scudded past, low overhead.

There was no officer waiting on the pavement. There was no pavement, or not much of one—some cracked fragments, some rutted mud. Frozen now. The lights of the landing field glared on the miry ground, rimed with ice and as rough as if it had been plowed.

Well, there was no help for it. They both needed a safe place to sleep, as soon as possible. He would find Asper Cogorth in the morning, after rest and food for them both.

And he would say nothing of the Cold Minds. That would only cause uproar, suspicion. He had come straight from Nexus, left the day it fell—no ship could have arrived earlier with the news. This backwater might get no message traffic for several more months; that would be enough time to get the child safely born and arrange their journey back to civilized worlds—to Terranova, the logical choice for the temporary home of the Line.

He helped the woman step down onto the ground and guided her away from the ship. As they left its shelter, the wind met them like a cold wall, pressing Fridric's clothes against him, seeking out every opening and seam. Chips of ice snapped against his face. Yshana leaned against his shoulder, and they pushed forward toward the low, dark outline of the control shed.

The bitter air smelled of spoiled fish, of the nearby sea. Another world—light gravity, thin air, the scent of salt. Fridric had forgotten the odd, disconnected *difference* of being on another world. He had not left Nexus since Rafael's birth.

With an effort, Fridric tugged open the door of the control shed and half dragged Yshana through. The wind tried to snatch the door from him, but he jerked it closed.

Yshana walked, swaying, to the heatbox that crouched in one corner and stretched out her swollen hands in front of it.

The attendant rose from his chair at the status panel. He was a man almost Fridric's age, tall and bulky, with a squint. He peered at them both: the heavily pregnant woman in a black cloak over black-silk nightclothes, feet jammed into men's boots; and Fridric in a rich overrobe of amethyst velvet with gray tunic and trousers, the first thing that had come to hand in his hasty departure from his house. "Where's the download?" the attendant asked. "I should have been able to——"

"This is not a linker ship," Fridric said. "We are private travelers."

The man pursed his lips. "I'll need to see your papers, then."

"We have none," Fridric said. "Nor are we obliged to furnish them to you."

"That may be, for pilots and such," the man said. "But not private travelers. We have rules, on Santandru."

Fridric planted his feet. "I am a senior official of the Line. Traveling with my servant."

The man frowned. "Where is your pilot?"

"I was pilot," Fridric said, and heard the note of pride in his voice. "Extraordinary circumstances. We require decent accommodations. How far is the nearest city?"

"Middlehaven's the *only* city," the attendant said. "Two kilometers, about. Your woman had best not walk it in this weather, this near to her time."

Fridric gave him a cold stare. "Walk? Of course not. I presume you have transport? You will drive us."

"Can't," the man said. "Not until my relief comes. Half an hour, maybe. He'll be early, he'll have seen your ship come in, and he'll think there's news. But I can give you some good hot tea. Your—she should sit down. My wife never used to——"

"No matter," Fridric said. "You may serve us tea."

Yshana sank gratefully into a chair. The attendant turned to a small, cluttered alcove, where he opened a metal box, dropped a pinch of some powder into each of three chipped black mugs, and poured hot water into them from a dented kettle. "This will pot you up good and warm," he said, handing Yshana the first cup. She sipped it and smiled tremulously.

Fridric took the tea and tasted it. Bitter and stale. The taste, he knew, of his exile.

His temporary exile.

The port attendant's relief did not arrive until full dark, by which time it had begun to snow hard. Fridric wedged himself into the tiny backseat of the attendant's battered old bubble car, a free-driving model—the "road" was nothing but a slightly smoothed ribbon of gravel and mud, with no vehicle guidance or even any lights. The woman took the passenger seat in front and promptly fell asleep despite the cold, her head lolling against the door frame. Clutching the bag that held his valuables, Fridric could not take his eyes off the road—what he could see of it. The narrow beams of the car's headlamps vanished in swirling snow. He could only trust that the man driving knew the way by touch.

They were in the town before he realized it. A few weak streetlamps shed a yellow glow on the thick flakes falling past them and not much else. Light gleamed from a few windows, but the streets were empty and no shops were open. In fact, he saw no shops at all. As the car ground its way up another steep and snowy hill, the man turned, and said quietly, "I'm taking you to a decent rooming house I know of. My cousin runs it. Heat in the bedrooms, and the woman is a good cook."

Fridric shuddered at the thought of what the woman would probably be cooking, but he nodded. Just for tonight. Tomorrow he would set about finding Cogorth, the man he had dealt with long ago in the matter of the family scandal—arrangements that had brought the woman Linnea to Nexus, but not, alas, the evidence Fridric must find and destroy before his return to the Line. This world was a convenient refuge for more than one reason.

The car lurched to halt in front of a low house like any other—no sign, no light by the door. "This is it," the driver said, gently shaking Yshana's shoulder.

Fridric sighed. Tomorrow he would certainly have this Asper Cogorth make more comfortable arrangements. A quiet cottage on an isolated country lane, with a reliable servant to see to the work of the house—

Pain lanced through his head. Too long since he'd eaten properly, slept properly. But perhaps it would be sensible to settle in town instead. It would be good to have people about, plenty of people. Yes. The pain eased. He winced a little as the car lurched—Yshana had finally come unwedged from her seat. Now she stood looking down at him, a puzzled expression on her face.

Fridric groaned and leaned forward to climb out of the car, knock on the door of the mean little house, face the primitive horrors that certainly waited within.

As he was dropping off to sleep that night, a bowl of potato soup slimy with leeks churning in his stomach, the coarse bedding clutched close around him (this was a heated room?), he thought with all the pleasure he could muster of his real purpose in choosing this world as his refuge. He knew from Line Security's extended interrogation of the woman Linnea that her sister lived in this town as well. And that the sister possessed that elusive piece of evidence, the only existing physical proof that he, and thus his grandson, were not descended from the legendary pilot David sen Elkander—that this hero of the Line had chosen to pollute the Line with outsider blood rather than admit his own sterility.

Find that evidence, destroy it, silence the woman who knew about it—and his nephew Iain's widely broadcast claims could be dismissed. For where was his proof?

And the baby boy to be born, Fridric's heir, would be safe. And he, Fridric, could bring the boy with him in triumph as he returned to restore the Line to greater wealth and power than ever—

His heart lurched once, then settled into a regular rhythm again. His health would improve, certainly, away from the pressures of Nexus politics. Perhaps the symptoms would leave him entirely. He would gain strength while his grandson did. . . .

Fridric slept, dreaming of light. The whispers in the back of his mind barely disturbed him at all.

He had to walk more than a hundred meters to a public comm the next morning, in bitter stillness unwarmed by the watery light of the distant sun. His finely made boots, thin and slick-soled, kept slipping on the snow and ice. He'd never thought that snow could get him so wet—wasn't it frozen water, after all?

When he found the comm, standing on a stone pillar in the open on a street corner, he had to brush the snow away even to see the front panel. He studied it, blowing on his cold fingers to warm them. There appeared to be no way for it to read his credit chit, let alone the palm of his hand, and so he had no way to pay for the call. A couple of shabby people passed him, then a third, a birdlike old woman swaddled in black wool, who stopped. "Out of coin?"

Fridric swung and stared at her, then said, "Yes. Please lend me some."

Her eyes were strangely cloudy, and she did not seem to be focusing on him. "It's only a penny," she said, holding out a disc of dull metal. "Do the same for someone else later. That will pay me." When he had taken it, she hobbled away. Only then did he realize that she must be nearly blind.

Fridric finally found the slot in the side of the comm and fed in the coin. A voice recording, so old and degraded that it sounded like the screech of a bird, said "Input number, please."

Number? There was a square array of buttons on the front of the thing, but the markings, the numbers, had been worn to unreadability. He tried saying, "Asper Cogorth," but the thing did not seem to be able to understand words. It just burped and rasped, again, "Input number, please."

A fourth passerby showed him the little touchscreen that let him search the listings, and a fifth punched in the number for him, with a wondering stare at his gray braid, his pale purple robe.

Rattles and buzzes while Fridric stood there shivering, his feet getting colder and colder in the thin, sodden boots. And it was beginning to snow again.

At last a distorted voice said, "Cogorth."

Finally. Fridric sighed, and said, "I must meet with you."

"Who is this?"

"Someone important to your future," Fridric said.

Silence. Then the voice came again, cautiously. "Your accent—"

"From Nexus," Fridric said. "That is all you need to know."

Another pause. Then the voice said, "Where are you?"

"How should I know?" Fridric asked, irritated. He looked around. "I'm on the edge of a square. There is a gray building on the other side with a tall spike on top of it. The roof is stone."

"I'll be there in fifteen minutes," the voice said.

Fifteen! Fridric took a breath to protest just as the comm made a chunking sound and went dead. "Time expired," the fuzzy rasp said.

Fridric groaned and rubbed his aching head. How he hated this miserable world.

Asper Cogorth stopped the bubble car at the edge of Simon's Square and peered through the whirling snow at the dim figure standing by the public comm: a tall man, his heavy-browed face lean and saturnine, his iron-gray hair braided back. He looked cold and angry. And he had the air, certainly, of one of *them*. Of a Pilot Master. Asper's heart sank. What could one of them want here? Bad news, it had to be bad news. Danger.

But Asper had to face it. It was his fault, the agreement that had brought this man here, for which Asper had been paid, because of which he had let Linnea Kiaho go to Nexus and probably to her death. If anyone was to suffer as a result, it had to be Asper. No one else.

He took a breath, then let the car roll forward and brought it to a stop near the man. He turned, glared down at Asper through the scratched plastic of the roof, and opened the door. "Cogorth?"

"Yes."

With a grunt, the man lowered himself into the passenger seat and pulled the door shut. "Take me to your house. I require a hot meal."

His heart beating hard, Asper said, "I'll take you to your own house when we're finished talking." He pulled away from the curb and started slowly up the road to the ridgetop. "What is this all about? Who are you?"

"I am one of the men you dealt with before," the man

said. "In the matter of the work contract that Linnea Kiaho accepted."

"I guessed that," Asper said flatly. "Listen to me. I did what you paid me to do. I watched for someone to come forward with the thing you described. I gave her the contract. She went to Nexus." His hands tightened on the control bar. "And you paid me. There is no longer any obligation between us."

"That will be true when I say it is," the man said. His voice was deep, with a cold note to it that made Asper's skin prickle.

But there was a question he had to ask. "Linnea Kiaho. She—is she well?"

"I wouldn't know." He seemed uninterested. "She was alive on Terranova a few months before I left Nexus."

Asper knew he must not let this man see his worry, or sense that he was protecting anyone. "Why are you here?"

"To find safety and privacy for the birth of my heir," the man said, his voice quiet.

"Your *heir*." Asper stared at the man, whose name he had never known. "Who are you?"

The man drew himself up. "Fridric sen David. The Honored Voice of the Inner Council."

The most powerful of the Line lords. Here, demanding Asper's service. Asper's hands tightened on the control bar. *Think.*

"And, once the child is born, to retrieve my personal property from the thief's descendants. Because you chose to disobey my clear instructions to send the thing to Nexus with Linnea Kiaho, I have been forced to the trouble of coming here myself and clearing up the matter. Secrecy is imperative."

Asper closed his eyes. He would not act again to betray his own people.

"I will, of course, pay you," sen David said, touching a

bag hanging at his waist. "I require only a few months of refuge and will travel back to the central worlds as soon as I know my grandson is strong enough to withstand the voyage. I had thought to have agents of my own on this world by now, but that matter was not arranged in time. So you must assist me instead."

Asper said carefully, "What are your specific needs, Lord sen David?"

"*Council* Lord sen David," the man said. "We require a comfortable private house near medical facilities. My womanservant must be attended by a physician, today. We will need a woman to cook and clean—you have a wife?"

"She has no time for outside work," Asper said. "I can find you a house near the clinic. A woman to work for you. But the cost—"

Sen David held out a credit chit. Asper looked down at it but did not move his hands from the control bar. "I'll tell you tonight what the charge was, and you can transfer the funds to my account."

"As you wish," sen David said coldly. "And you will tell me where I can find the woman who holds my property."

Asper's mind raced. Was Linnea still in danger from this man? How could he protect her *and* his family? "Remind me of her name."

Sen David faced him. "Her name is Marra Saldanha. I am very eager to talk to her." His smile was like the smile on a skull.

"Ah," Asper said, his voice bleak. "I remember Marra Saldanha. I'm afraid I can be of no help to you—I believe she is dead." His hands ached. "Now I need to be about your business. Where are you staying?"

Asper let his passenger out near the boardinghouse, with a promise to return in the evening with word of the arrangements he had been able to make. As he watched sen David walk to the door, his calm slipped for a moment, and he bared his teeth in rage and fear.

Time. *Time*. It was agony to drive away sedately and slowly, in the direction of his office, in case sen David was watching. Eight blocks away he parked the bubble car, leaped out, and ran left down an unevenly stepped alleyway between a jumble of sagging back stoops, now snowed over thickly. Three blocks down he stopped, looking back—the snow, thicker than ever, completely hid him from uphill. He ran up a set of snow-drifted brick steps and let himself in through a neatly painted white door. "Marra!" He was calling her name before he saw her, standing wide-eyed in the doorway to the main room of the house. "Marra," he said, "pack."

Her eyes widened. "What?"

His voice shook with urgency. "I'm sending you away, now, on the next flatloader to Moraine. You and the children. Pack."

She came to him and took him by the arms. "Asper! What in God's name?"

He stopped, his mind frozen. He did not know what to tell her. Their marriage a few months after Linnea's departure had brought life and joy into his plain, solitary world, and now they had a daughter together, a child, he had never thought he would be a father. Now he had put her in danger as well. . . .

Marra's patience finally snapped. "The boys are still at school. Rosa and the baby are asleep. Tell me straight, Asper."

He took a breath. "A man from Nexus is here."

Marra's hands went to her mouth. "Linny! Linny's not—dead?"

"No, no. As far as this man knows, she was well only months ago. No. This is—it's safer for you and the children to be elsewhere, hidden, until this man leaves Santandru. Just a few months."

"I don't like this," she said. "I won't go hide in Moraine for months and leave you here, with a man from Nexus around."

"I have business here I can't step away from," he said steadily.

She planted her fists on her hips. "The Vital Records Office! Would the world end if papers didn't get filed in the right place for a while? Can't some other man cover for you?" She spoke angrily, but he saw the tears in her eyes.

"No, Marra," he said, with finality. "I must stay here. If I went with you to Moraine, I would draw this man after me. And he must not find you. Or—" He reached out and touched the tiny sheep-leather sack that hung between her breasts. "Or what you carry."

She looked down, then up at him again. "He wants Ma's old silver tube? The one all the fuss was about? Then why can't we just give it to him?"

"Giving him the tube would not be enough. He must have your silence, too. And your word will not be enough, for a man like that." He saw the flicker of fear in her eyes and gathered her hands in his own. "I won't let him harm you. I can hide you from him, block his access to the records he needs to find you. If he wants this thing so much, if it can hurt him, we should keep it. Linny will know how best to use it."

Marra looked down. "I'll—I'll start getting the children's things together."

He closed his eyes in relief and kissed her forehead.

Two hours later they still had not left for the transit station, and the flatloader he had hoped to catch was half an hour from departure. Asper had never realized how complicated it was to pack supplies for three children and a baby, for a road journey that might take four days with no chance to wash or buy food. Diapers alone . . . Marra was stuffing kitchen rags into the bag with the rest while

Asper hovered tensely. His older stepson Donie, thank God, was entertaining the baby for now—a boy of eleven with a clear head was worth his weight in trade credits. In the other bedroom Orry and Rosa were arguing over some game.

Marra had made it clear she was still angry. "And suppose we get there, and the old house has blown down in a storm?"

"Your mother's house," Asper said, "is perfectly fine. It's waiting for you. You know I've been paying to see it's maintained. You and the children should be comfortable—there's plenty of room."

"I know the house," Marra said. "I was born in it, married in it, I lived there for twenty-five years." She tugged closed the drawstring of the canvas bag. "Father Haveloe," she said, "is going to think I've left you, you know. He didn't want me to marry you in the first place."

"It was none of his business," Asper said. "He was your priest in Moraine, not here."

"And I've got to face Ma Stayart and the other bottom feeders," Marra said, "and their remarks about how my sister saved the village with her—"

"It's what must be, Marra."

"I won't be a widow again," she said stubbornly.

"Three months," he said. "In three months the man from Nexus will be gone. In three months you can come home. I must insist that you obey me in this, Marra. Will you?" He took her chin in his hands, tilted her face up to his. "Answer me!"

After a moment, hesitatingly, she nodded.

By the time Asper loaded Marra and the four children into the back of the flatloader, headed upcoast, its engine had been running on warm-up for ten minutes, and the big garage stank of fish-oil exhaust. With a layover in Outer Reach, it would be, he'd found, a five-day trip in the cold metal bed of the flatloader. That prospect alone was probably enough to explain Marra's tears as she hugged him good-bye in the gathering darkness. He did not let her see his own.

The 'loader ground into gear and lurched forward. Asper watched until its lights vanished in the swirling snow.

Then he turned, with little hope, to try to avert the disaster he had created for himself. To protect the wife and children he loved and had put in danger.

SIXTEEN

Linnea stepped back from the chart glowing on the wall of the front office, in the groundside pilot-training facility at Port Marie's skyport. *Progress.* More than a thousand new pilots were coming on duty, or close to it, or waiting for the refurbished ships Torin's "side yard" operation was turning out as fast as they could.

Not bad for five months' work. In three more months, or four more, anyway, orbital patrols would be in place above everyone of the Hidden Worlds.

She heard the main door rumble open out in the lobby, Torin coming through with the code she'd given him. She glanced at the wall chrono. Whatever his business was, she hoped he would make it quick. With luck she might be home and asleep by an hour after midnight, if the late tram was running on schedule.

Here was Torin—and the urgency in his eyes made her go still.

"Lin," he said. "Lin, out front—Line Security."

She stiffened. "Coming in?"

"Can't stop them. Thought I should warn you."

She set down the box of work she'd intended to take home tonight. Better to have empty hands when those men came in—they had neural fusers, and used them when it suited them.

But only one man appeared in the doorway. An officer she vaguely knew, one who'd served on Station Six. When he saw her, he looked visibly relieved. "Miss Kiaho. Please come with me."

She didn't move. "Where?"

"Station Six," he said. "I've just been called back on duty. An emergency. No, I've not been briefed. But I was told to bring you with me, in one of our fast shuttles."

"A Council order?" she asked.

"No. At the stationmaster's request." He looked at Torin. "This is not a Line matter."

"Well, that's reassuring," Torin said dryly. "I don't suppose you've got room for me on this fast shuttle?"

"Miss Kiaho's freedom is not at risk," the Security man said. "But her services, and not yours, are needed on Station Six. Please excuse us."

Linnea felt cold. Iain had been working, as ordered, on Station Six, but he'd obeyed the terms of his arrest: He'd never once sent word to her. She'd never once seen him. "Is Pilot sen Paolo involved in this?"

The officer gave her an opaque glance. "Are those your effects? Then let's go. The next launch window for Six is in less than thirty minutes."

"Torin," she said over her shoulder, "I'll be back as soon as I can. Tell Dorie the files she'll need are under the usual code."

"I don't like this," Torin said sourly.

She gave him an eloquent glance and followed the officer out through the lobby to the street. To the Security van in the street. She could not keep back a twinge of fear as she climbed in.

So Iain was involved. The officer's silence on that point as much as said so. Well, if she was going to see him, she would be calm; she would not let him see how angry she still was. Or how deeply and painfully she missed him. Sometimes, now, she woke in the night and ached for his warmth beside her, the warmth she had kept at a distance for so many wasted months.

The shuttle flight was rougher than any commercial flight she'd made. Good that Torin wasn't along—he always, always threw up, terrible in a small shuttle. When they arrived, the Security officer said a hasty farewell and disappeared, probably to his data center—leaving her unescorted. So she really was at liberty. She made her way to the stationmaster's office. Early morning, not much past dawn, it was, by station time, but the control section of the station buzzed with activity.

His assistant waved her through with a look of relief, and she entered the stationmaster's small, precisely arranged office. He rose from his work chair as she came in, but she was not looking at him. For Iain was there, standing up to greet her.

Iain, regarding her soberly. Iain in pilot black, his hair braided as she had learned to braid it so long ago, woven through with the crimson cord that marked him as his father's son. She saw the cord and understood it in the same moment, and her breath leaked away, as did her impulse to go to him.

The stationmaster looked from Iain to Linnea, and said, "Thank God you're here, Miss Kiaho."

She tore her eyes away from Iain, and asked, "What's happened?"

Segura looked terrified. "A ship just jumped in. High orbit. We've identified it as Cold Minds. And it beamed a message here, to this station. To this station *only*."

"Why hasn't it been destroyed?" Linnea demanded.

"It's small," Segura said. "One-man, two-man ship. Unarmed. And the message—" He swallowed hard. "Whatever is in that ship is asking for you by name. Both of you."

"They can't dock here," Iain said instantly.

"Of course not," Segura said. "Security procedures are being followed. We have warned the, the ship—if they pass within a thousand kilometers of any Terranovan installation, they're vapor." He licked his lips nervously. "But there's—a voice. Insisting on talking to you both."

It couldn't be Rafael. It couldn't be. She tried to catch her breath.

Iain looked at her. "Can you do this?"

She would not allow herself to think about it. "We have to," she said. "Where's a comm?"

"We've got a tight feed into the Line Security office," Segura said. "Let's go."

Dizzy with apprehension, Linnea found herself seated with Iain in front of a holoplate. He took her hand and gripped tight, below the pickup field, and, glad of the comfort, she did not draw back. "Put it through," Iain said.

A gritty image sparkled with static—it must be a small ship, crudely equipped. The image wavered in a moiré pattern as the algorithms worked through the signal, then flicked into something close to clarity. Linnea choked.

Rafael. Not the same, not the same, but it was Iain's cousin. He wore black rags, and his red-orange hair had been chopped to shoulder length. Untidy, greasy, it floated loose around his thin face, his oddly dark eyes.

Iain said nothing—she felt sure he was incapable of speaking. So it was the image of Rafael that spoke first. A strange voice, slow and dragging. "We are the Minds. We are before you."

"Relayed through that body," Iain said to her. "From a controlling Mind in the ship, I'd guess."

She swallowed against nausea. So Rafael was a corpse. The eyes did not seem to look at Iain or at her; but she knew something else looked out from inside them, something that was no longer Rafael.

"We see you," she said.

"Speak and get out of our space," Iain said.

"Free passage is offered," Rafael's body said.

"For whom?"

"All," the voice said, and the face grinned, baring black-slimed teeth. "Abandon these worlds, and all will be allowed to pass. All ships."

"No," Iain said. "These worlds are ours. We will defend them."

"We offer life for some," the face said, "or death for all. Choice is offered. It will not be offered again." Again it smiled, horribly.

"A threat," Iain said, "needs something to back it. If we do not accept your offer, what then?"

"Death," the face of Rafael said, "in many ships. You cannot fight. Too weak. Too few."

Linnea closed her eyes. It only made it worse, to hear the voice and not see.

"You have said enough," Iain said. "We refuse. Carry our answer back to your masters."

"You do not speak for all," Rafael's image said. "Carry our message to your superiors. This vessel will return."

"I know what the answer will be," Iain growled. "Save yourself the trouble. If you appear in our space again, you will be destroyed on sight."

"You and that corpse you're using," Linnea said. She

could not take her eyes from the face that had been Rafael's. Not the face she saw so often in nightmare. This face repelled and terrified her for a different reason. *He did not ask to become this.* The thought hung in her mind, and in a voice of terrified pity, she said, "It isn't yours, you know."

The thing's answer was an odd one. The head rolled on the shoulders, and it coughed. And when it came up again—

When it came up again the eyes looked straight into Linnea's, through the pickup, across the intervening space. For the first time his eyes looked blue.

The voice spoke. Different, weak and faltering. "Our sons still live," it said. "Tell them, Iain. Our sons still live."

The image vanished.

"That was Rafael," Linnea whispered. She turned to Iain. "Did you see? That wasn't those things, at the end. I saw his eyes. You were right, Iain. It's him. He's still in there."

Segura stepped into the little room. "We've got the record," he said. "What was that bit at the end? Whose sons still live?"

But Linnea was looking at Iain, whose face was sick with a dawning horror.

"That's what the other messages meant," Iain said. "*They are afraid.* The little boys—the sons of the Line. The Cold Minds are keeping them alive. Keeping them to pilot their new ships, to use them. Mutilate them—" His voice broke.

"They simply infested them, surely," Segura said.

"No," Linnea said. "Infested minds and machine minds can't pilot. They use—they use humans."

"If those children are alive," Iain said, his voice rough, "then they can be rescued."

Linnea moved to face Iain directly. "*If* they are alive.

If this is not a trap. Maybe that was Rafael, really Rafael—but maybe the Cold Minds *allowed* him to tell us this. For *their* purposes. Iain, listen to me!"

Iain raised his haggard face and looked at her. "You cannot expect my brothers to ignore this. To leave our children to die in despair, or be sealed into a Cold Minds jumpship. That is as inhuman as, as—"

"Unless you warn them," she said, her voice tight with urgency, "unless you make them understand, they will attack Nexus now. Before they're ready. Before we're ready. No matter the risk. No matter the cost. No matter what it does to every other one of the Hidden Worlds. Listen to me!" He was looking away, shaking his head, and she saw the grief in his face. "Listen to me!" she said again. "I know, if it's true, it's terrible to think of children left in the Cold Minds' hands, but—"

"It is the Line's decision," he said, and the anguish in his voice stopped her, broke her heart.

"Risking everything," she whispered. "Everything. For the chance of saving a few children—even a few hundred—"

"This is not a question of numbers," Iain said. "We must try to save them, Linnea."

Linnea bent her head in despair. She knew, deeply, though she could never speak the words to Iain, that this was the wrong decision. A bitter world it was, where sacrifices had to be made; but this was the wrong one. Living worlds—even for the sake of children, to abandon living worlds—

Disaster. She shivered. Disaster and death.

She would never see Iain again.

Hakon hit the switch that ended the recording and swung to face the Honormaster. "Well? Is there any doubt what we must do?"

The Honormaster's voice was dull, defeated. "If this is not a trap, not a lie, then when Nexus fell, we abandoned our sons to the Cold Minds. To fear and helplessness."

"Sen Paolo was right about that much," Hakon said. "We must attempt to rescue the sons of the Line."

Master sen Martin nodded slowly. "We cannot fail them again."

Hakon hoped the Master could not sense his trembling urgency. "We know from our own old records, from Earth, that intense radiation will disable and destroy the Cold Minds. I am certain they will have chosen to place their central Minds in the deep bunkers, far below the City. A strong radiation source, a fission explosion, down in the bunkers will do it. One man could carry the device down and place it. And then, with their central controlling Minds gone, we can wipe out the rest of them easily."

"It will take a large assault to get one man as far as the bunkers," Master sen Martin said, his voice sharp. "We cannot strip Terranova and the other worlds of their defenses."

"We can if we abandon sen Paolo's notions about patrols," Hakon said carefully. "We could return to the plan Council Lord Fridric sen David supported. Pull in the fringe patrols. Fall back to the five strategically important worlds. Protect those and those alone while we move against Nexus."

Master sen Martin looked impatient. "Too much risk."

Hakon took a frustrated breath. "Our spy patrols tell us that the Cold Minds are nowhere near prepared for any further attacks. The lack of metals and manufacturing on Nexus has hampered them. But all the same—Master, we have no time. Our sons are suffering. They are suffering *now*."

Master sen Martin's jaw tightened. "What do you need?"

"The men and ships that are already in transit here will be enough," Hakon said. "With them, we can answer the Cold Minds' challenge with a force they do not expect." Hakon lifted his chin. "We will prevail."

"I have faith in you, Pilot Master sen Efrem," the Honormaster said. But his voice was thin.

Hakon drew a breath, and said, "Then I may proceed? Is that the will of the Council?"

"It is," sen Martin said, "or you and I would not be discussing these matters."

"Very well," Hakon said, his heart swelling. "I will try to be worthy of the honor. But—sen Paolo. He may now support retaking Nexus, but I need a free hand. We have been rivals. I do not trust him. As there is a question of his—position in this, even if it does not rise to a matter of treason, I do not want him involved in this attack. In fact, I want him confined and watched."

"That seems excessive," Master sen Martin said. "He has requested permission to accompany the attack force, and I had thought to grant it."

"It is necessary," Hakon said. "We cannot risk that he will act against us. Or that there will be further contact between him and the Cold Minds." Hakon's eyes blazed. "This is no time for caution and half measures. If we are wrong, we can apologize later. After Nexus is ours again, and after our little brothers are free."

"Well," Master sen Martin said, "it is a small matter. Let it be as you say. And the woman Kiaho?"

"Have her kept groundside. She can work from there."

Master sen Martin considered, then nodded. "I will give the order. I will also summon the Council to authorize the attack, under your command. You do realize it will take some time to accumulate a sufficient force here."

"Yes," Hakon said, a twist of bitterness in his voice.

"Sen Paolo and the woman Kiaho have very efficiently scattered our forces, with their new patrols and additional linkers. But if we hold incoming ships for a time, we will have enough in a matter of weeks, I hope."

Master sen Martin rose, and Hakon rose as well. Sen Martin clapped a hand on his shoulder. "Good fortune to you, Pilot sen Efrem."

Hakon nodded, struggling to keep the triumph, the joy from his expression. *Little brothers, we are coming.*

At last, at last, his hands were free.

SEVENTEEN

Fridric stood looking down at the face of his future, and wondered why he was not moved.

The newborn slept, tightly swaddled in a thin yellow blanket, his hair (disappointing pale silk, not Rafael's red) a comical tuft atop his pink face. He was physically perfect, robust, exactly what Fridric had wished. Yet he felt no joy. Headaches, and the strain of keeping a constant careful watch over Yshana lest she come to some harm or try to escape him, had kept him from sleeping well for most of the month since their arrival on Santandru. And his heart troubles seemed to be worsening, not getting better. Worst of all was a feeling of distraction, of distance from the world, that had crept over him of late. Nothing seemed to ease it.

Rain pattered against the small plastic windows along one wall of the nursery. Fridric sensed the hovering disapproval of the nursery matron. Yshana had not wanted to relinquish the baby, as he had suspected would prove to be the case; and the people of this narrow-minded world would never be able to understand the complicated legal agreement she had signed before becoming pregnant, an agreement that terminated her rights at the moment the child was born.

The agreement was, he had to concede, recorded only in a destroyed city; still, as he had told the matron, a bargain was a bargain. And Yshana had been well paid, funds deposited to her account on her homeworld of Honua as soon as the pregnancy was confirmed.

Yesterday, when she was being discharged, Yshana had wept in a most unseemly way, and half the nursery staff with her. Yet she was going to a perfectly pleasant rooming house—he had given her (*given* her! entirely outside their contract) plenty of credit, enough to let her live as comfortably as this world allowed until she could buy passage toward home on the next jumpship that arrived.

Here was the matron, a short, blocky figure in a blue dress, with a sharply pleated blue cloth snugged over her white hair. "Do you wish to hold him yet?" she asked icily.

Fridric looked away. From the start he had felt an odd reluctance to touch the baby, and he saw no reason to begin now. "No. I'll hire an attendant for him."

"Why did you want him if—" She clamped her mouth shut and picked up the infant. "Time for his bath. Excuse me."

Outside in the dim hall, Fridric lowered himself onto a hard plastic bench. The noises of the ward—crying babies, happy chatter of women's voices, distantly a groan of complaint from a woman in labor—faded as he sank into thought.

The baby would do well enough here for a few days. So, at last, Fridric was free to take care of his remaining item of business on this world: finding the woman Marra

Saldanha, Linnea Kiaho's widowed sister and possessor of the proof of David sen Elkander's crime—his true genetic sample, stolen from the Line archives. The sample would not match Fridric's or that of his grandson. The samples for David sen Elkander's own paternal ancestors for several generations had been lost at the time, in a convenient storage mishap; the sample currently under sen Elkander's name was from Fridric and Paolo's actual father and so would match appropriately. So what the Saldanha woman possessed was a dangerous missing link that could be used to prove the illegitimacy of the infant's claim to the Line.

If, of course, anything was left of the Line archives after the invasion by the Cold Minds. But Fridric could not risk it. The stakes were too high. If Nexus was retaken, and sixty years from now this boy rose to the power Fridric hoped for him, there must be nothing that could threaten that power—Fridric's great and carefully built legacy.

He must be methodical. He dressed in shabby local clothes, a shirt and trousers and a frayed sweater purchased used at a tiny shop near the hospital. He tied his long, gray hair back unbraided, in the style the men of this miserable town seemed to favor. Then he walked out into the cool, watery sunlight of an early spring afternoon to begin his search. Surely there was no way for a living woman to hide from him long on this little world.

But apparently there was. He had known from the start that Asper Cogorth would be of no help in his search; and Fridric could not threaten him in any serious way, not when he himself had the extreme vulnerability of a baby heir, easily accessible. No, he would have to carry out his own search.

The comm directory, he already knew, had no listing for Marra Saldanha. When he went to the Vital Records office and paid for a search, he was presented after several hours with a thin sheaf of paper records, copies: the registration of Saldanha's birth as Marra Kiaho, the record of her marriage at sixteen to a Rowdy Saldanha, notes of five children born, three surviving; but there it ended. There was nothing for the past several years.

He sat in the parlor of his small house near the hospital, pondering. Perhaps it was true: Perhaps Saldanha was dead. But there would have been some record of that, surely, unless the death was quite recent.

The children. They would have been enrolled in school. He copied their names out of the records and trudged through rising wind and spattering rain to the city department of schools, a tin-roofed concrete shed.

The man behind the counter was quite unable to help him and seemed bewildered by the fact. "I know those names," he said, raising his voice over the clatter of rain on the roof. "The records should be here. But there's nothing in the files."

Fridric tried to smile casually. "No matter," he said. "Marra asked me to pick them up for her, but perhaps they've already been sent to the children's new school."

"Schools outside this city are mostly priest-schools," the man said. "Not much for records, those, and very small. But, wait, you said, Marra? You mean Marra Cogorth?"

Cogorth. A chain of cause and effect clicked neatly along in Fridric's mind. He smiled calmly. "Yes, Marra Cogorth." He could hardly ask where she was, not after claiming to know her; but he knew now how to find out. "It's no matter. Thank you for your time."

As he left, he had to restrain his steps to keep from hurrying visibly, arousing suspicion in the clerk's mind. Marra Cogorth. So she was married to Asper now, Asper who was a high official in the city government here.

Fridric knew he would find no records under "Marra

Cogorth." Asper would have covered his wife's trail most carefully.

But not quite carefully enough.

He would have a word with Asper.

M arra Cogorth stood tensely on her front porch in the gray light of evening, huddled in her shawl, looking out over the barren dirt yard of the house where she had been born. Evening had begun to creep over the village straggling down the hillside below her: a couple of streets lined with small stone houses, a little church, a few greenhouses and fish-processing sheds. And in the small harbor, snugged up tight against the coming storm, the village fishing boat, the *New Hope of Moraine*. Linnea's gift, or so people said. Linnea herself had never returned. Perhaps she had changed too much. Sold too much of herself. Or—or died. . . . *Better to forget her. Try.*

Try again.

After more than three standard years of living in Middlehaven, Marra thought Moraine seemed far too small. Not safe. The wind whistled around the corners of the little house, an echo to the shrilling of her nerves.

Asper was supposed to have commed her this afternoon, as he had every day for the past month. She had waited for more than an hour in Father Haveloe's study—with him hovering ungraciously, impatient for his dinner—but the call didn't come. She had to hide how afraid she was, to keep Father Haveloe from assuming something was wrong, spreading talk in the village.

At last she had paid the priest one of her last few coins for the charges and placed a call to Asper at home in Middlehaven. There had been no answer.

Asper would not fail to comm her if he was free and well. Not for anything. He'd promised.

The wind picked up, and she pulled the shawl tighter. Greenish gray clouds raced inland, low overhead. She could almost feel thunder under her feet, could guess at the size of the slow, greasy rollers that were striking the beach right now, on the other side of the ridge that sheltered the village and harbor. A big storm was coming. Soon all flyers would be down, maybe comms as well. And she did not know what was happening in Middlehaven, what was happening to Asper.

She went inside and barred the door behind her. At the scratched kitchen table, the boys sat working through some arithmetic on their school slates. The baby slept in a basket near the stove. Rosa sat on a stool beside the basket, tracing her way with a grubby finger through her assigned page of Marra's old reader. As Marra watched, Rosa got up and stirred the soup, seaweed broth with box clams. The new fishing boat was a good one, and Moraine prospered. Everything looked comfortable. Safe.

But Asper—

Marra hung her shawl on the peg by the door. "Donie, Orry. Go around and close the shutters, there's a storm coming. And check the shed door, be sure it's locked up tight."

They both got up and went out, and soon she heard the comforting thump of metal shutters closing over the windows. The boys came in windblown, Donie so tall now, looking more and more like his father Rowdy when he used to come in from the sea. Lost now.

She was alone. But this was only the edge of aloneness. Only the beginning, if Asper was dead.

He'd sent her away so quickly. He hadn't told her good-bye, the way Rowdy always had before he went to sea. He might be dead now, somewhere back there in Middlehaven. In their house, maybe. Or in the street.

Marra served soup for the children, took her own bowl, and sat. Rain pattered on the metal shutters as the wind gusted. The metal frame of the house creaked and popped. She was nearly finished, hardly tasting it, when Orry lifted his head, frowned, said, "Ma. Listen."

She cocked her head. A sound outside. A whistling roar like the storm wind, but more clear, more powerful, rising rapidly.

"A flyer," Orry said.

"Can't be a flyer," Donie said. "Not in this kind of wind."

Marra rushed through the dark mudroom to the back door. She opened it against a frigid press of wind, leaned out, and stared up toward the ridgetop, blinking in the cold.

It came over low, and the sound multiplied instantly as it appeared, huge and heavy and slow. A flyer on final approach, its body jet stepped down to a low rumble, its landing jets already hissing. Its running lights, red and green, cast swift shadows that leaped away from her as she watched. It passed over, heading for the little landing field at the lower end of the village by the bay shore.

Marra shut the door and leaned against it, thinking rapidly. No Middlehaven pilot would risk one of the flyers in this weather. It had to be the man from Nexus. They were all pilots, weren't they—a little wind wouldn't stop one of *them*.

Asper was missing. And now the man from Nexus had come here. "Asper," she whispered, in despair.

Then she caught her breath. "Bar the back door, Donie," she said to Donie, before she could think, before she could let herself be frightened.

"Why, Ma?"

"Just do it," she said sharply, wedging the front door's bar into its track. Meant to keep wind out, that was all it was, but it was better than nothing. Just then, in the distance, the sound of the flyer's jets cut off. It had landed.

"Oh, God," she said thinly. "Donie, take the little ones

into my bedroom." He hesitated, and she shouted, "You do it now! Orry can help you drag that old blanket chest in front of the door. No lights. Keep quiet, keep Rosa quiet."

Marra looked in despair toward the cradle where the baby was sleeping. She could not leave the baby to Donie to tend; if she woke, she'd wake hungry, and yell like a burned ghost, and nothing Donie could do about it. Quickly, Marra pulled an old quilt from her mending basket, draped it over the cradle. The baby didn't wake, thank God.

The knife, now. Rowdy's old fishing knife, kept in this house since he died. She reached up and took it from its old place on top of a tall cabinet, up out of reach of the children's curiosity.

She bent feverishly over the sharpening stone in the kitchen, putting a fresh edge on the knife. *Shifff, shifff, shifff.* How long now since the flyer came in? The children, at least, were quiet. Maybe it would work. Maybe it would work for long enough.

Or maybe not. She turned the knife over and made herself draw it more slowly over the stone. *Shifff.* Her hands shook, and the worn bone handle carved like fish ribs kept slipping in her sweaty grip. Any moment he might come. This knife was the only real weapon she had—a strong one, a workman's blade, not some worn, brittle kitchen knife. With this she could fight. . . . She swallowed hard and made her hand slow down some more. Finish this right. Then blow out the oil lamp and wait. If he found her here, even if he killed her, he might not look further for the children. Might not hurt anyone else.

With sudden panic she tore the little bag containing the metal cylinder loose from her neck. Asper had warned her not to try to buy her life with it. She, and he, were as good as dead once the Pilot Master knew where it was.

She pulled open her drawer of flour with a squeak, dropped the bag into it, smoothed over the surface. Best she could do.

The wind rose again, making the metal joints of the old house pop. She wiped the blade with a rag and touched the edge lightly with a fingertip. Almost sharp enough—

Outside, gravel crunched, and she snatched her finger away. A thump on the porch. She leaned to blow out the lamp through the top of the glass chimney, but her breath was thready with terror, and the flame only flickered.

The front door crashed open, the old metal bar bursting from its fittings. Marra gripped Rowdy's knife among the folds of her skirt. Her heart stuttered as wind and rain billowed in across the floor. Flickering light from the lamp caught the man in the doorway, shining wet in his dark rainsuit.

"Marra Cogorth," he said in a cold voice.

"Get out!" she screamed, and the black bile of rage choked her.

He didn't reply. He pushed the door to, but the broken latch didn't hold. The door gusted open again, letting in another spatter of rain. He stood looking at her as the door swung loose in the unsteady wind, the doorway a gulf of darkness framing him. "Where is it?"

Marra straightened, glad of the hidden knife. But kept her eyes away from the leather sheath and whetstone that lay plain to see on the table. "Where is what?"

The Pilot Master gave her a cold glance. "My patience is over," he said. "Where is the thing your sister went to Nexus to sell? It is my property. I require it from you."

Behind her skirt, Marra shifted her grip on the knife. Blade up, Rowdy had advised her once, to slip in between the ribs. "If you want it," she said steadily, "you have to promise to leave us alone."

"I need make no promises to the likes of you." He took a step toward her. "You will tell me where it is—now, or later. Now is less painful." He sounded out of breath.

"You'd better stop," she said, her voice shaking in spite of herself.

The Pilot Master's eyes narrowed. He had thrown back his hood, and the lamplight caught his heavy brows, the hard bones of his flushed face. "Give me the knife you're hiding. Now."

She kept her eyes on his face, slowly held out the knife in her right hand. He reached out to take it.

Snarling, in a single motion Marra snatched up the lamp in her left hand, her strong hand, and flung it at the Pilot Master. The oilpot shattered and gouts of oil splattered him, bursting into flame. With a roar he dropped to the rain-wet floor, rolled over and over.

And Asper—Asper, thank God!—appeared around the door frame, soaking wet, and threw himself down on the Pilot Master's legs. The man kicked and struggled, his scorched face terrifyingly red. Then he went limp.

"Get help," Asper gasped, one knee on the Pilot Master's back.

Marra dropped the knife and ran.

Zhen Kumar set her jumpship carefully down on Moraine's tiny field, glad that the storm had finally blown itself out. Amazing, it was, that this village—Linnea's home—was still standing. It looked so tiny, spread out below in the watery sunlight. Not big enough to be the only settlement in a hundred kilometers of coast. Little stone huts with metal roofs, a labyrinth of stone walls, a church at the foot of the village street near the bay. And rising above and behind, barren gravel slopes sweeping up and up toward the half-hidden glacier that gave the place its name, whose meltwater fed the bay a kilometer away, with pipes leading it down here to the village. She grimaced. Pretty primitive.

She'd lost two days to the storm, and another day talking the idiots at Middlehaven into partly fueling her ship. Not even the news of the Cold Minds had rocked their stubborn certainty that she could not possibly be the ship's pilot, even though they had seen her land. And they'd pointed out the other jumpship with evident pride—two jumpships in port at once was, she gathered, pretty much unprecedented.

Then they'd told her the pilot's name.

So here she was in Moraine, where she had finally managed to find out that Marra was, and where Fridric sen David had landed the flyer he'd stolen three days ago; and there was the flyer, of course—a little scorched from her ship landing so close, but that was his problem, not hers.

She had to find Linny's sister Marra. That was what she'd come for. But first she'd better find out what this sen David, what the leader of the Line itself, was doing in a fishing village on a world at the far end of the Rimini Fading, the farthest back of beyond.

She rather suspected it had something to do with Linnea. Gossip with Marra could wait.

Zhen locked down her control board. The landing jets pinged and popped under the ship as they cooled. She dressed hastily, although she was still dirty from the long jump that had ended three days ago; no place to wash in the skyport, short of a bucket of meltwater. . . . No time for nonsense, no time for anything except to comb her greasy hair and knot it back out of her face. Then she walked between the empty passenger shells to the hatch.

As she'd expected, a small crowd had gathered by now. At the front stood a tall, heavy, pink-faced man with grizzled hair, dressed all in black. She saw with surprise that he held a club. And that man there, a big knife of some kind, and over there—

They were all men, and all armed. She climbed down carefully. "This is Moraine?"

The man in front looked down at her in obvious puzzlement. "Where is the Pilot Master?"

"I'm the pilot," she said. "Zhenevra Kumar. From Terranova. Is there a man here named Fridric sen David?"

"How can you be a pilot when—"

She planted her feet. "Is he here?"

The man stepped back. "We have him," he said.

"What do you mean, you have him?"

"He threatened a village woman," the man said. "He's in custody, waiting for the magistrate to come through on rounds."

Zhen swore under her breath. "Can I talk to him? It's important."

The man did not move. "I don't think there's any need for that."

She set her fists on her hips. "That man is the Honored Voice of the Inner Council. The head of the Line, do you understand? And the Line is at war. Don't you think they'd like to know he's here? And why he's here?"

He pursed his lips. "At war?"

"The Cold Minds," she said. "They invaded Nexus. They captured it." Over the rising buzz of astonishment from the other men, Zhen asked, "Didn't he tell you any of this?"

"He said nothing."

The tall man glanced aside as a thin man with gray hair stepped forward to stand next to him. "The Council Lord jumped here from Nexus," the gray-haired man said. "Is there any chance that he—that the Cold Minds—that they infested him?" His eyes were dark with fear, and the men behind him looked just as afraid.

Zhen took a steadying breath. The same thought she'd had, the same that had brought her here in such a hurry. "Why don't we ask him?" she said.

Fridric sen David paced his prison, ignoring the pulsing ache in his head, the sting of his blistering burns. It had taken four men to get him in here, a storage shed behind the woman's house. It was lit only by a high strip of plastic window. They'd pulled out the fishing nets and other trash and left him in here with two blankets, a jug of water, and a warped plastic bucket to piss in. Days now, and no word of when he would be freed. It was an outrage.

An outrage. He kept waiting for the towering anger he knew he should feel. That the Honored Voice should be treated like this, when he had simply been trying to reclaim a piece of his own rightful property.

The magistrate here would not be able to prove that he had intended any harm to the woman, whatever her husband might suspect. So they would, in the end, have to free him.

They would pay, when proper law returned to this world. He would see to it, when he was back in power and the Cold Minds defeated.

He must be free. He *must* be free. His headache pulsed, pulsed, until finally his heart fluttered, leaving him gasping for breath, dizzy. He lowered himself carefully to the folded blankets, leaned back against the wall, tried to steady his breathing.

He closed his watering eyes against the gray light leaking in through the scratched plastic of the window above him. Flashes of blue burst against the insides of his eyelids, he had been seeing them for weeks. They were getting worse. And the strange, stretching ache in his belly.

And the whispers in his mind. Little, thin, whistling sounds, chattering sounds. They'd begun even before the invasion—

Voices outside, again. He knew that a man always guarded the door of the shed, and sometimes he heard their dull chatter when the guard changed; but—a woman's voice? And not an accent from this world, either. She sounded Terranovan.

He struggled to his feet. The door opened, and he shrank back from the light. A woman came in, small and black-haired, wearing a black coverall like some parody of a pilot. She wrinkled her nose in disgust.

And Cogorth. Cogorth was here, too. Fridric's headache got worse.

Cogorth spoke first. "Why didn't you tell us about the Cold Minds?"

Pain, pain—"Because," he said with a gasp, "it was irrelevant. I wanted to protect my heir." The pain eased a little.

"Are you ill?" the woman asked. She was frowning at him.

"A little," he said. "I'm an old man. And it's cold in here."

"Tell us," Cogorth said. "On Nexus, did the Cold Minds—did they come near you?"

"We left before they landed," Fridric said. "I never saw them."

"Did you see your son Rafael on Nexus?" the woman asked. "Were you ever near him, in the same room with him?"

Fridric remembered, then, Rafael smiling at him across a dinner table, smiling a little stiffly, his eyes oddly dark—

"What do you mean?" he asked thinly. The pain mounted again.

"We know that your son betrayed Nexus," the woman

said. "He did it because he was one of them. He was infested."

Terror took Fridric then, shaking him like some animal. He knew at last what in the deep places of his mind he had feared, known. Known for a long time. The Cold Minds had taken his son.

And Fridric had worked with Rafael, dined with him, again and again, helped and protected him, placed him in power, put him where he needed, where *they* wanted him to be—

Where Rafael would be able to prepare the way.

A scream crowded up Fridric's throat, burst out. Rage, terror, grief. *He* was the guilty one. *His* blindness the fatal flaw. The pain in his head built, cold, white, shrill, and through the fog of his thoughts he knew himself for what he was.

For what he had become.

No, his mouth said, but his voice was a raw hiss of air, tasting of blood from his torn throat. His legs gave way, and he slumped to the stone floor of the shed.

With his dimming sight he saw the man and woman watching, other faces crowding in behind. All stern, all stone. No one moved to touch him, to help.

He was polluted. Poisoned.

He collapsed onto his side. *No. No, no*—he did not know whether he spoke, or whether it was the voice of his mind—

Or the voice of another mind in his.

He cried out again in final horror, and his heart stuttered.

Stuttered.

Stopped.

His last thought was a flicker of gratitude, of relief—

EIGHTEEN

That afternoon, Asper Cogorth joined the men of the village, all those who were not at sea in the *New Hope*, in the yard of Marra's house to settle what would be done with the corpse of Fridric sen David. Covered with an old plastic sheet, it still lay in the small shed at the back of the yard, the shed where sen David had been imprisoned and where he had died. The door of the shed was locked tight, and the priest had wrapped the lock in a bit of plastic and scrawled his signature across it—an official seal, he being the nearest thing the village had to a magistrate until a real one could make the journey from Middlehaven.

A little rare sunlight failed to warm Asper, shivering in a borrowed coat. He'd brought nothing with him in the flyer. He hoped he'd forget that flight someday, or at least that it would fade from his nightmares: Fridric wrestling the battered old ship through the rising storm, and all the while Asper had never suspected that the real terror was not the storm—that the real terror was sitting in the cabin with him. A meter away. . . .

Father Haveloe stood in front of the sealed shed, facing Asper and the other dozen or so men—including Eddo, the medtech, who still steadfastly refused to hold an inquest on the body, or indeed to touch it. The priest's face had gone from pink to red during this discussion. "No," he was saying. "We cannot simply burn the corpse; then when the Pilot Masters come here and inquire, as they must, we will not be able to prove that the death of their Honored Voice was natural."

"There was nothing natural about that death," Eddo said in his dry voice. "If he'd gone and died of some contagion, something you'd call natural, Father, surely you'd let us burn him. And this is worse, by my lights."

"Examine him, then," Father Haveloe said coldly. "Produce a report. Be ready to testify when I must account for the death of so important a man while he was in my custody."

"That thing's no man. Burn it," the man beside Asper said in a slurred voice.

The man's companion relieved him of a flask of what looked like potato whiskey. "Listen, Father," he said. "We're all scared. I can't follow all this you say about being held to account, but it seems to me we're all to account for our wives and our families, and what has to be done to protect them is to burn that body in there, and do it now." A grumble of assent followed his words.

Father Haveloe stood looking from man to man, evidently gauging the depth of their anger and fear; then he straightened. "Burn it, then," he said shortly. "But I've nothing to do with it." He strode away.

Asper watched him go, then turned back to the other men. "I need oil," he said. "All you can spare. This has to burn hot."

A few minutes later Asper studied the locked door of

the shed. Three big jugs, two half jugs of lamp oil stood ranked in the mud; it would have to be enough. A few villagers had gathered outside the fence. No point in delaying any further.

Asper broke the seal on the shed's padlock, opened it, and removed it. With a tremor of nervousness he pulled the door open. The hinges screeched. Then Asper sighed, relieved. The old gray-plastic sheet lay undisturbed on the floor of the shed.

Beside him, Eddo the medtech bent to pick up a jug of oil. Asper stopped him with a hand on his arm. "Wait," he said carefully. "Something is wrong." The sheet looked—*flattened*.

Asper picked up a narrow-bladed shovel from the heap of goods that had been cleared from the shed. He reached out with the handle and flipped back the edge of the plastic. He should have seen the dead man's booted feet.

Instead he saw bones.

Yellowish bones shaved thin, worn translucent, greasily smooth. Nothing else. Even the gristle that had held the joints together was gone; the bones of the feet, ankles, shins lay in loose heaps.

"God save us," Eddo gasped. Behind them, Asper heard a man cough rackingly and begin to vomit.

Gingerly, Asper pulled off the rest of the sheet, revealing only more bones. By then he knew it was too late. Whatever had happened, whatever had . . . *eaten*, Asper supposed, was the only word—whatever had eaten the body was gone. In the back of the shed, at ground level, Asper found a small round hole, no more than five centimeters across, cut straight through the corrugated metal wall of the shed. The edges of the hole shone like mirrors, they were so smooth. Behind the shed the bare rocky slope rose away toward the mountains. There was no track, no sign that anything had passed. But, Asper supposed, there wouldn't be.

Asper piled what would burn of the furnishings of the house on top of the fire inside the shed, to keep it going hot and long, and to dilute the smell. When the flames had begun to die down, he turned to the priest. "I am getting my family out of here."

"Go with my blessing," the priest said heavily. He had said very little all morning, his gray face clear testament to the horror he must feel.

The other men began to leave, muttering together. Eddo walked past Asper with a significant glance. As the medtech left the yard, Asper realized that Marra was standing outside the gate, her old blue shawl clutched nervously around her. His heart sank. Eddo politely held the gate open for her, but Asper called out, "No! No, Marra. Don't come near. Stay outside the gate."

He saw her give Eddo a frightened look as he passed her, and Eddo paused and touched her hand. But he said nothing, and Marra turned back to her husband. "Asper! What's this?"

"That man who brought me here is dead," he began.

"I heard," she said. "And something about the Cold Minds, but what's that got to do with keeping me away from our own house?" Her voice was trembling.

"He might have been infectious," Asper said. When her eyes showed incomprehension, he said, "I mean, he might have been able to spread the, the little machines that infested him to people he touched."

He saw her grip the shawl tighter, saw her chin tremble, but then she took a breath and said steadily, "That's you, then. He touched you. You rode in that flyer with him. So you're, what they call, infested now?"

"I hope not," Asper said, struggling to speak in a steady voice. "But until we know that, know I am clear, I mustn't come near you or the children again."

"But you touched me already," she said. "You're my

husband. You slept in my bed last night. If you have those things, then I do, too."

He'd hoped she wouldn't see that, but she was as canny as her sister, in her way. "All we can do is hope that you don't," Asper said. "And we can keep it from happening now." He made his expression stern. "I want you to go back to the children now. You're still at the Stayarts'? Pack. Be ready to leave tonight."

She nodded and turned away. As he watched her walk away, he wished he'd had the courage to tell her how far away he was sending her. But first it had to be arranged.

G lumly, Zhen watched the burning from the bottom of the street. The smoke didn't rise very high before the strong wind from the ocean took it. What a dank, nasty, bitter cold place this was, this place Linny had come from. And the people treated Zhen so strangely. Maybe it was the way she was dressed. Maybe she just didn't fit into their idea of the world.

Well, Linny didn't either, then. Zhen wondered, again, what made Linny miss this place so much. Could just being born in a place, and never seeing anywhere better, make you love it?

Before Zhen left, which would be as soon as she could possibly manage it, she would record some images of Linny's sister and the children on her palmscreen, show that they were all right. For now. But the future didn't look promising.

Zhen was turning away to go back to the cold little guest house, where at least she could get out of the wind, when a man coming down the slope waved at her, and called out. "Pilot Kumar!"

Well. Politeness at last. She stood and waited while he approached: Asper Cogorth, Marra's new husband. Not new, old—so old he had gray hair. But he was what passed for a city man on this world, she supposed. Something they had in common.

As he approached, she said, "Just call me Zhen. I'm not a passed pilot yet."

He looked surprised, then concerned. "But you piloted all this distance, all the way from Terranova, on your own, didn't you?"

"I wasn't supposed to." She jammed her cold hands into the pockets of her tunic. "Can I help you with something?"

"I hope so." He was standing a good five meters away, and when she stepped toward him he backed up. "I want to send my wife and children back to Terranova with you."

"Why?" she asked bluntly.

"To protect them," Asper said. "I can't, here. I can't even go near them. I don't know if I ever will again."

"There are tests now," Zhen said. "They can look at your blood and see if you're infested. They've sent ships out from Terranova with stocks of them. Only a few months, and you'll be able to get an answer."

"Not soon enough," Asper said. "I want my family on their way to safety, *now.*"

"Terranova is a lot closer to Nexus than this place is," Zhen said. "And Nexus is where the Cold Minds are."

"But we're undefended, and Nexus is not," Asper said. "And Linnea Kiaho is on Terranova. Marra will want to go where she has family."

"All right," Zhen said abruptly. It would make Linny happier, that much was sure; and it cost Zhen nothing. Except—"I need fuel."

"Middlehaven Skyport will refuel you completely," Asper said. "I'll see to it. Pay for it if I must. As for my family's passage—"

"That fuel will cover it," Zhen said. "Marra and four children."

"Fair enough," Asper said. "When will you leave?"

Zhen squinted at the lowering sun. "Morning," she said. "I don't like landing in the dark."

"Then we have an agreement," Asper said, then, with more feeling than she'd thought so gray a man could express, he said, "Thank you." And turned away.

She watched him go. Odd man. Odd place. It would be so good to get home.

A nd now Asper had only to tell Marra. Daylight was fading. He walked to the gate outside the Stayarts' house, which was the largest in the village and nearest the church, and called for Marra to come out. He saw Ma Stayart's watchful, suspicious face in the shadows of the porch, and he knew she would listen, but there was nothing to be done about that.

Marra appeared, wrapped in a shawl against the evening cold, her brown eyes smiling. "Asper! We're packed. I'll be glad to get back to Middlehaven."

Asper wasted no time. "Not Middlehaven, Marra. I'm sending you and the children to a place where you'll be safe."

He saw her eyes widen.

"A place where you can be tested," he said, "you and the children, and know that you're not contaminated. Where you will be protected. Those things will never come near you again."

"If you aren't there, too, I'm not going. Why can't you come and be tested, too?"

"I won't get near you," he said. "Not until I know it's safe. And I want you on the ship, out of danger.

She planted her feet. "A ship! I am not getting on one of those ships. I am not going all that way away from you. To live with strangers! Asper, I don't want to leave my home."

"You won't be with strangers," he said. "I'm sending you with Pilot Kumar to Linny, on Terranova. It's all arranged."

"You never asked me! You never asked me one word. You want me to get in a box, to put my children in a box, trust myself to that woman who thinks she's a pilot—" Her voice had dropped; she probably sensed Ma Stayart's lurking presence. "They're my children, Asper. I won't do this, I won't."

"They're your children," Asper said mildly, "but you are my wife, and as I remember, you promised to obey me."

She stood very straight. "I didn't promise to do every mad thing you ask of me."

"For the children," he said, "you must risk it." He knew how afraid she was for the children.

Unshed tears shone in her eyes. "No," she whispered.

If he could have taken her in his arms, it would be over; he would have won. But he could not touch her.

She was crying openly now. "I don't know how to do this," she said. "When Rowdy died on the *Hope*, he just didn't come back. I didn't ever have to look at him and know I'd never see him again."

"I promise," he said urgently, "that as soon as I know it's safe, I will send for you. Or come to you. I didn't marry you to be apart from you. It won't be for long. And then, not ever again."

She shook her head, her face twisted with weeping. It hurt, standing here well back from her, it hurt not to go to her. But he kept his face set, his voice steady. "I won't die," he said, knowing it was a promise he should not make. "I will send for you, or come to you, as soon as I can. Marra—Marra, love, don't, it doesn't help."

She squared her shoulders and took a long, shaking breath. "I'll—" She took another steadying breath. "I'll go."

He closed his eyes for a moment. "I'm glad."

"How soon?"

"Tomorrow morning," he said reluctantly, and saw his words take her breath away, saw her lips tremble.

But she did not break down this time. "The children's things," she said. "And m-mine, in our house—"

"They'll still be here when you come back," he said.

"The—necklace I wear," she said. It's "—she glanced back at Ma Stayart, leaned closer to Asper and hissed—"in the flour drawer. I need it. I want to give it to Linny."

And get it, finally, away from her family—Asper understood. "I'll fetch it, Marra. As for the rest, we'll repay the Stayarts for what you need for the journey. You won't need much. And when you get to Terranova, Linny will be there."

"Terranova's a big world, I hear." Marra rubbed at her eyes with the edge of the shawl. "Lots of cities bigger than Middlehaven, even."

"Pilot Kumar knows Linny well," Asper said firmly, confidently. "She'll tell her you've come, and Linny will see to you."

"Linny mostly needs seeing to, herself," Marra said, and Asper knew with deep relief that she was going to be all right.

S hivering in the morning cold in the basement of the stone church, Zhen Kumar dipped her spoon into the gray fish stew, held her breath, and took a bite.

The broth was strong, the strips of eel chewy. Bits of potato thickened it a bit. She'd had worse.

She set her spoon down and smiled across the table in the church's basement refectory at Linnea's sister—soon to be Zhen's passenger. "Very nice," she said.

Marra set her strong brown hands on the table and looked both ways. A couple of old women chatted together in the kitchen, preparing breakfast for the old, unmarried people of the village, but the dim, chilly refectory itself was empty except for Zhen and Marra. Marra lowered her voice, leaned forward, and said, "Please. I have to know. How is Linny?"

"She's very well. Busy. She's a pilot now, you know."

Marra's eyes widened. "She is what?"

"A pilot," Zhen said. "Training other pilots, in fact. She trained me."

"But—the Pilot Masters surely wouldn't allow that."

"They'd rather not," Zhen said, and grinned. "Linnea's hard to intimidate, after—well." How to put it. "She spent some time on an infested world, right before it was destroyed. Iain rescued her. Not much scares her now."

Zhen almost saw Marra's ears prick up. "Who's this Iain?"

"Iain sen Paolo," Zhen said. "A former Pilot Master. Linnea's lover, at least he was for a while."

Marra tapped her fingers lightly on the table. "Lover. Not husband."

"Pilot Masters don't marry," Zhen said.

"Pilot Masters only love men," Marra said.

"Some do, some don't, some don't care." Zhen shrugged. "Iain's pretty set with Linnea, has been for a long time now."

"If Linny's a pilot," Marra said, "why hasn't she ever flown her ship back here?"

"To go and come back," Zhen said, "takes a big part of a year. The jump feels like a few weeks but lasts more than three months, each way. . . . She *wants* to be here. She talks about you and the children."

"But she sent you instead," Marra said.

"*She* didn't send me," Zhen said. "I asked to come, to see you. She's been worrying about you and the children—it hurts to see it."

Marra bit her lip and looked away. Then coughed, and said, "A long way, then. And not much like here."

Zhen smothered a burst of gratitude at that thought. "You'll be all right there," she said. "Linnea will be over-joyed to see you." She suddenly felt an overwhelming urge to be out of here, in otherspace, on her way home. To Torin. "Can you be ready to leave in an hour?"

"To Terranova?" Marra asked cautiously.

"Not yet. Back to Middlehaven this morning, for fuel."

"Middlehaven," Marra said. "I wonder what's going to happen to that baby."

"Baby?"

"The baby Asper told me about. The Council Lord's baby, or his son's I mean."

"Wait," Zhen said. "You mean sen David's got an heir? *Here?* In Middlehaven?"

"Whole reason he came," she said, then shot Zhen a glance. "Mostly."

"Maybe—maybe the Council would be grateful, then, if we brought the baby back with us."

"His mother, too," Marra said. "You've room?"

"Just," Zhen said. She sighed gustily. "I'll take her. If she'll come."

"She'll come," Marra said. "Asper says she's from Ho-nua. It's warm there. She probably doesn't like Santandru much."

Zhen nodded. One stop. Then they would jump for home. For warm places. She shivered. Then smiled, reas-suringly, at Linnea's sister.

It would be all right.

It had to be.

NINETEEN

TERRANOVA
THREE MONTHS LATER

Linnea slept, in the room on Sunrose Street. *Thunder*.
Thunder, and Linnea was back in the truck on
Freija, in the warm, endless rain, riding toward infesta-
tion and death—

Thunder—

She woke with a gasp and sat up. The light came on,
dizzying in the depth of the night. Someone was pounding on the door. Her thought went instantly to Line Security.

"A moment!" she called out angrily, and the pounding
stopped. She threw on a sleep robe and went to the door.
Lifting the hanging away from the window, she peered
out. A dark figure, alone. Not Security. Then a muffled
voice said, "Lin! Let me in!" She turned to the door, unlocked it, threw it open.

Torin, rumpled and rain-soaked, stood outside. Grinning wildly. "Did you hear the news?"

She grabbed his arm and pulled him into the room,

closing the door behind him. "Do you know what time it is? Are you drunk? Are you *crazy*?"

"Not one bit." He grinned. "Zhen is back from Santandru. Back safe."

The words knocked the breath out of her. She gaped at him. "Back. She's alive!" And then, ridiculously, she started to cry.

Torin pushed her down into the work chair, then sat down across from her on the foot of the bed. She dragged her sleeve across her eyes, and said, "Torin. Tell it straight."

"She's at Station Six," Torin said, leaning forward, elbows on his knees, hands dangling. He was still grinning. "I talked to her just now. She made the whole trip both ways perfectly, no problems. And—" He broke off. "Linny, you're all right?"

She nodded, struggling to smile.

"Because she's got some people with her. Your sister, she said. And some little ones."

Shock slapped Linnea's breath away again, left her speechless. *Marra.* Linnea tried to catch her breath, find words. *Marra, here*—"Why is Marra here?"

"Don't know much, you know the charges for orbit-to-ground. But Zhen says she's well, they're all well. She's coming groundside in the morning. The others, they haven't got papers, they need immigration processing, refugees, something like that. And testing for bots, they're not priority like Zhen. Like a pilot." He smiled, and Linnea saw the flash of pride in his eyes. "Anyway. Be a couple of days before they can come down."

"I'll go up," Linnea said at once.

"But you can't," Torin said. "Council order."

"They're welcome," Linnea said icily, "to arrest me, once I've seen my sister."

In the end, she waited until Zhen arrived, late the next day. Eager as Linnea was to get to Marra's side, she couldn't stand the thought of crossing shuttles with Zhen—not seeing her for days, maybe, if there was some delay in bringing Marra's family down.

That morning Torin had leased the old flat downstairs again, and he'd moved in by simply dumping his few possessions on the bed. Then he went out to the skyport to wait for Zhen's shuttle.

On an impulse, once Torin was gone, Linnea went out to the market and filled his flat with spring flowers, stocked the kitchen with food and two bottles of wine as Torin had not thought to do, and made the bed up with clean linens. Then she went upstairs and waited, filled with a jittery mixture of relief over Zhen, nervousness over Marra. Wondering what Zhen had told her, what she would think of Port Marie. She'd find them a flat down by the park, Marra would like that. . . .

Zhen and Torin knocked on the door in the late afternoon. They both radiated joy. Linnea blinked back tears as she welcomed them. She set her hand on Zhen's arm. "Is it true you brought me my sister? How is she?"

Zhen covered Linnea's hand with her own and grinned. "She's well. A little jumpsick yesterday, but better this morning."

"And the children?"

"Fine and healthy. Two boys, tall, and two girls—"

"*Two* girls!"

"There's a new baby, you know," Zhen said.

Linnea blinked. "How?"

"The usual way, I suppose," Zhen said. She stared at Linnea. "Oh. You wouldn't know. Marra's married to a man named Asper."

Linnea sat down suddenly. Fortunately, the end of the bed was there to catch her. Marra. Married again. Married to *Asper*. She felt dizzy.

After a moment, Torin said, "Zhen, pour Linnea a glass of water. Maybe she'll close her mouth."

"I'm sorry," Linnea said, blinking hard. "Married. To Asper Cogorth. Yes. But why is she *here*?"

Torin handed Linnea a glass of water. "That brings us to other news," he said gently. "Not all of it so good." He straightened. "Fridric sen David was there, on Santandru. Took his son's woman so his grandson could be born someplace out of the way, out of the fight. But he died there. And it turned out he was infested by the Cold Minds. Just like Rafael."

Linnea shuddered, feeling pity for the woman and baby who had been caught up in this. "Did they burn his body?"

"Yes," Zhen said. "But it was too late. When they went to do it, nothing was left of him but bones."

Linnea shivered. "So the Cold Minds are there. Somewhere."

"If they are, they've got no ships. I spent a whole day scanning from orbit. Nothing." Zhen rolled her eyes. "The bones—that's *why* Asper wanted Marra out of there, off that world. Safe. Marra and the children, and Yshana and the baby. That instant. No reasoning with him."

"The baby," Linnea said cautiously. "You mean, Rafael's son?"

"Yes. He's up at the station with his mother. Didn't you know? I told Torin all the details last night—"

Linnea managed a grin. "I think Torin heard only your voice. Not your words." She set down her glass. "I want to catch the shuttle at four. And you two probably need to continue your reunion in private." Her heart caught at the pure happiness in Torin's answering smile.

As Torin and Zhen disappeared down the steps outside, Torin called back, "Too damn many flowers, Linnea!"

Linnea stood looking after them, then closed the door slowly. What would Iain think about this news? With

Fridric dead and Rafael gone—that meant *Iain* was the head of the family. So this baby was his responsibility, by Line custom.

But this was Terranova, and the laws here probably gave Yshana some rights. Best to leave it at that, maybe.

Though Iain would have to be told.

Since the day they spoke to Rafael, she had not tried to see him again. But she had to go up there now; she would find a way to get around the rules.

She could not decide whether she dreaded seeing him—or whether this odd, unsteady feeling was happiness.

Marra waited nervously in the confusion of the shuttle passenger bay, Lily asleep in her carry-basket at Donie's feet, the other three lined up beside her. Yshana'd been asleep when Marra left their room, and what with the baby and how tired Yshana was, it didn't seem fair to leave the children behind with her.

But Marra hadn't thought it would be this *long*.

Linny'd said this shuttle for sure, but the passengers were streaming out and there was no one who could be—

There.

Marra caught her breath at the woman striding confidently toward her, smiling. "Linny, my God," Marra said thinly. Then they were embracing, hard, and Marra was crying and kissing Linny's cheek. "You're so pretty!" Marra said. And she was, all in elegant deep blue, her hair past her shoulders now, silky black. She did something to her eyes now, too.

Linny turned and stuck out her hand to Donie. "It's been a long time, Donie Saldanha," she said. He shook it and nodded, looking abashed; Orry did the same. Rosa accepted a kiss on the forehead with solemn wonder.

"That's Lily," Marra said, as Linnea crouched by the basket.

"Asper's daughter, I hear," Linny said, offering a finger for the baby to grip.

"We've been married since a little after you left," Marra said. "He was—you know he was coming by and seeing we were all right, and more and more he'd stay to dinner, and, and finally when he offered for me, it just felt right." She shrugged. "He's a good man. I know he tangled you up in—in a lot of things, but he wants to do right by you now."

Linny got up and smiled at Marra. "I can do right by myself, these days. Which way to your room?"

Marra led them off, Linny carrying the sleeping baby in her basket, not much of a burden in the light gravity, in this place. When the two sisters were settled at last in Marra's little sitting room, with the children playing next door, Marra finally was able to ask the question that had been burning in her mind. "This Iain sen Paolo. That's the man who sent for you from Nexus, at the beginning of it all?"

Linny flushed a little. "Not exactly. We, we got together on Nexus, when I first arrived there." She looked down, the way she always used to when she didn't really want to answer; then looked up again, straight into Marra's eyes. "We both—lost a lot, then and later. But we found each other. We were good together. We did good work."

"*Were* together." Marra didn't like the sadness in Linny's eyes.

Linny's eyes went hard, the same way they always had when anyone showed sympathy. "He has his work, and I have mine."

There was a brief, dangerous silence. Then Linny's face changed again, a smile, still hard, but a smile. "I understand Iain's got a little cousin here, next door."

Marra smiled back, relieved to be getting on to a comfortable subject. "A very little one. He's, what, six weeks old? He's with his mother, she's a quiet thing, pretty though. He's pale and blond like her—didn't you say Iain has black hair?"

"I don't recall saying." Linny's voice was flat.

"Zhen must have said, then," Marra said. "We talked a lot on the jump. Through that shipmind thing." She looked at her sister, curious. "What's Iain going to do about this baby? Orphaned and all, and a relative of his."

Linny's face was shadowed for a minute. "I don't know. I haven't told him yet."

"Best you do. He might want to provide for the boy," Marra said practically.

"I'm sure he would," Linny said, "if he had anything to do it with. But he doesn't." She shrugged.

"I thought they were all rich," Marra said. "The Pilot Masters."

"No more. And Iain's not one of them." She looked at Marra, the same unreadable Linny she had always been; but there was a depth of sadness there that took Marra's breath away. "Things have changed, Marra. Changed a lot. You'll see."

In the morning, Linnea helped Marra get the children's bags packed for the shuttle trip groundside. It felt strange, like pretending, to try to fit into her old place as Marra's sister, the children's auntie. They'd all gotten their blood tests, and they'd all passed, thank God, though Linnea didn't let them see her relief; better Marra didn't know how dangerous it had been, to be so close to a man who was infested.

Marra had decided, apparently on her own, that the woman named Yshana would travel down with Marra and stay with them until she could decide what to do next. With passenger travel shut down, Yshana couldn't go home to Honua yet, probably not for a long time. Quiet and timid, Yshana clung to her baby and did not seem to object to having matters decided for her. But she did not seem . . . damaged, as Linnea had been. Maybe Yshana's experience, a simple matter of business as far as the Pilot Masters were concerned, had been different.

Yshana was, of course, beautiful, though she wore a plain, serviceable blue-gray dress that she must have bought in Middlehaven, judging by the awkward fit, and her pale hair was cut quite short. She sat quietly in a corner of the sitting room, her bag and the baby's set at her feet. The clinic here had been trying to make her milk come in again, and she had been nursing the baby, but judging from his frustrated whimpers, it hadn't worked completely yet.

When he had settled a little, Linnea squared her shoulders and went to look at him. He seemed like all babies his age: a soft pink face with a tuft of blond hair and tiny ears that looked squashed. Linnea glanced at Yshana for permission, then touched his cheek shyly. Like warm silk.

Then he stirred, fuffed, blinked his eyes open. And she jerked back her hand, because he had Rafael's eyes—that same deep, icy blue, colder than the slaty blue of a newborn. Linnea passionately hoped he would inherit nothing else from his father. She forced a smile for Yshana. "He's beautiful. What's his name?"

Her eyes, not quite the same blue, widened. "I don't know. That's for my mother to find, when I get home. Maybe in a year or two she'll have the right dream."

"What do you call him?" Gingerly, Linnea touched his blanket.

Yshana turned as pink as the baby. "His milk-name is Moth," she said very softly.

Linnea drew back her hand again. "Will it be a problem for you, when you come home with a child?"

Her mouth tightened. "Not's long as I've got the money, too. I've got brothers need schooling."

"You should get some schooling, too," Linnea said.

Yshana turned pinker. "Maybe someday. . . . Marra said you're a pilot's lady."

"Oh ho?" Linnea shot Marra a look; Marra, who was focused on packing, merely looked puzzled. "I'm no one's lady. I'm a pilot myself."

"So it was a mistake," Yshana said. "I thought so. A pilot taking a lady. Everyone knows they don't, they just hire . . . us."

"That's ending," Linnea said. "They'll have to find a new way to make their families."

Yshana flushed pink. "He talked about you."

"Who?" Linnea stared at the girl.

"Rafael," Yshana said very softly. "I don't think he could—*not* talk about you. What you looked like. What you—said to him, one time or another." She licked her lips. "I think he loved you. In his way."

Linnea jerked to her feet and walked away. When the nausea had faded, she turned and looked at Yshana. "There was no love about it," she said flatly. "Not one shred. He hurt me. He—" She broke off, looking at the baby in Yshana's lap—Rafael's son.

An innocent.

If he was not to be poisoned by his father's legacy, it must begin now. With her silence.

She sighed. "There's no need to remember it, now."

"No need to remember what's true?" Yshana asked.

Linnea was trying to find a reply to this when the station's evacuation alarm went off.

She got Marra and Yshana and the children safely up to the passenger loading area and made sure they were assigned to the first shuttle out, before she stopped a white-lipped passenger-bay attendant, and asked quietly, "What's up?"

She knew the attendant, an older man, from her work on the station and her many trips groundside and back. He looked at her with fear plain in his eyes, and said, "Word is, there's a linker ship come in from Kattayar, says the Cold Minds tried for the yards there. Seems like they're off Nexus, out in the Worlds. Standing orders, we get everyone nonessential groundside, first thing."

"Right," she said. "Thanks." She hurried back to where Marra and the others were encamped, near the boarding ramp. Marra was clutching Rosa in her lap; the girl was crying with gulping sobs. Donie sat in the next chair with Marra's baby sucking on his finger, but his eyes were wide and frightened.

Linnea dropped to her knees beside Marra's chair. "Listen," she said over Rosa's noise—and others, Rosa was not the only crying child in the room. "Marra, I'm not coming on the shuttle."

Marra stared at her, outraged. "You most certainly are!"

Linnea reached out and stroked Rosa's dark hair. The little girl's sobbing quieted, and she opened her eyes. Linnea smiled into them. "I need to stay here. There's no immediate danger, but we may need every pilot we can get."

"Stop playing games, Linny," Marra said, so vehemently that Rosa started crying again. "This is real. We need you."

Linnea lifted Rosa out of Marra's lap and held her, patting her back as she gulped for air. "Look," Linnea said, "you get in touch with Torin Dimarco, first thing, he's got the address where you'll be staying. His comm code's in the palmscreen I gave you. You have it? Good.

I'll come down as soon as the emergency is over, and I'll find you right away. I promise, Marra."

"You send me down to a city full of strangers with all these children?" Marra demanded. "And Yshana, she's not much use, just another child really."

"There's nothing I can do, Marra." Linnea glanced over at Yshana, who sat huddled in a corner, her baby across her lap. Moth was not crying; he stared solemnly at nothing, his blue gaze unfocused.

Marra seemed near tears. "Don't I have any say in this?"

"No. Sorry." Linnea set Rosa down in Marra's lap, leaned over, and kissed Marra's cheek. "Take care."

She ran for the stationmaster's office. The small outer office was jammed with Line pilots demanding news. As she arrived, the stationmaster came out, red-faced, waving for quiet. She joined the group as silence fell.

Stationmaster Segura spotted her, and a hint of relief showed in his eyes. "Pilot Kiaho," he said. "Please tell these gentlemen that they can rely on our orbital control facility. We will have adequate warning of any—"

"We need to get out in our ships," one of the younger pilots said firmly. "That's where we can see the situation clearly."

"That's where you can deplete your maneuvering fuel," Linnea said, "and maybe be out of position to respond if they do show up." She looked around at their closed, resentful faces, and hurried on. "Look, I know you don't like being limited to indirect data. I don't, either. But that's how it has to be. We stand by our ships, and we launch on the word the Cold Minds've appeared in Terranova space. Not until."

The stationmaster nodded vigorously. "Analysts groundside are saying this may be a feint. It may be meant to draw us out, even draw us into a trap."

"A trap where? Kattayar?" an older pilot asked. "They say they beat them back at Kattayar already. We need to keep our focus on the Nexus attack. Rescuing our sons."

"Yes," Linnea said, "but first we have to be sure they've not timed an attack on Terranova to hit while we're panicking over Kattayar." She looked around at the pilots. "You've all read the bulletins, I'm sure?"

"That's all speculation," the young pilot said. "Pilot sen Efrem says what we need is action. He says we need to take it to *them*. Strike Nexus while they're busy elsewhere, while their defenses are weak!"

"It's a feint," Linnea said. "If they had what they needed to take Kattayar, they'd have tried for Terranova instead."

"Thank you for your expert insight," a dry voice said from the doorway, and Linnea turned. It was, of course, Hakon sen Efrem. He strode to the center of the group and addressed his fellow Line pilots, not even glancing at Linnea. "I've consulted with the Inner Council. I've sent the signal. We have the forces we need. The attack on Nexus begins now. Complements from all stations will form up for jump at the established coordinates out-orbit. Gentlemen, to your ships."

Linnea grabbed his tunic. "You can't do this!"

Sen Efrem struck her hands away. "You've lost," he said coldly. "And Iain sen Paolo has lost. Or—perhaps he didn't tell you? He's staying behind with you and the other women."

No, he had not told her. Relief hollowed her out, anger made her flush.

And sen Efrem saw it, of course. "Go to sen Paolo and try to comfort him. I know you know how." He strode out of the room.

She stared after him, then turned to Stationmaster Segura. "I need to get to Orbital Control."

"Of course," he said with obvious gratitude for her company. "I was going there myself."

"There might as well be witnesses," she said grimly.

W hen she arrived at Orbital Control, to her surprise Iain was already there, standing tensely in the back of the room, his arms folded over his chest. He turned and saw her, and her breath caught. He had gone back to his old gray tunic and trousers, his hair tied plainly back, but his face looked haggard with grief and worry. Without another thought she hurried to him and embraced him, feeling the firm warmth of his back under her hands.

And he pushed her gently away. "It's good to see you, Linnea."

She let go, took a step back, and tried to catch his tone: remote, neutral. "And you." She took a breath. "Hakon sen Efrem tells me—"

"That I will not, after all, be traveling to Nexus with the attack force," Iain said. "I'm sure that's some comfort to you."

"Iain, there's family news," she said. "We need to go somewhere private." She glanced at the control display. "Nothing will happen for a while. They've got to fuel up, form up."

He led her to an office that must be his own—smaller than the one the two of them had once shared, and outside Orbital Control itself. When the door had closed, she faced him, and said, "Fridric is dead. He died on Santandru, infested. And Rafael has a son. A baby son, here on Terranova, with his mother."

She saw in Iain's eyes the world changing.

"My uncle—dead," he said slowly. "It's—strange. I'm the only one left. The only one of my family."

"You and that baby," she said.

He shook his head. "No. If I have any choice in this, our line ends with me. Let that baby grow up on some other world, as far from Line influence as possible. As far from his father's memory as possible."

"That may not be your decision, Iain," she said. "Yshana has rights over her son."

"Then I will explain it to her," Iain said.

She looked at him sadly, at the pain in his eyes. *It goes on,* she wanted to say. *Family goes on. Whether we want it to or not.*

But Iain had already moved on. He touched his commscreen to life. "How many armed ships do we have left?" he asked. "Counting what's close to coming off the yards."

"Sen Efrem took everything he could get, pulled ships in from every close-in world," she said. "We don't have enough, yet, to defend Terranova. The other worlds are better off—I sent ships off as fast as I could, to keep them out of sen Efrem's reach."

"So you don't have enough to go on with, if you have to," Iain said.

You. She sighed. "We're building more."

"Too much lag," he said. "This is too perfect a time for an attack."

"Would the Cold Minds really leave Nexus vulnerable?"

He was silent for a few moments. Then he said, "No. I think you're right. I think they're on Nexus to stay. Their message through Rafael, telling us to leave—they want these worlds, just as they wanted Earth. Because they are ours."

"So it's ambush," she said slowly.

Iain stood with his back to her, toying with the controls of the commscreen. "What could be better? Manipulate us into attacking them. Wait to disable our ships as fast as we emerge from jump." She heard the raw fear in his voice. "Take our pilots captive—more human pilots for Cold Minds ships. Once they've been—modified." He turned away from the commscreen, stood with his closed fist resting on the wall.

"You've told them this?"

"Everyone has told them."

She went to him and set her hand on his shoulder, and he looked down at her with a flicker of surprise. "There's nothing we can do from here," she said. "And maybe sen Efrem's frontal assault idea *will* work—maybe he'll be able to get the bomb down into the deep shelters."

She could feel Iain struggling to calm his breathing. Then he said, "It was an insane plan from the beginning. The weapon will never reach the bunkers."

"We have to hope it will. That's all we can do." She moved around to face him, looked up into his anguished eyes. "We *have* to hope, Iain."

"I can't," he said in a broken voice, and began to weep. She pulled him against her, tightened her embrace, helpless here as anywhere. Helpless to avert the disaster Iain feared; helpless even to comfort him.

TWENTY

TERRANOVA ORBIT

The moment had come. As Linnea and the stationmaster entered the high, domed room that housed Orbital Control, the huge display over the central holoplate showed a slowly expanding cloud of ships around the station, all flagged blue for traffic that was departing and tracked. A few incoming ships showed yellow, trainees and new pilots who would assume the orbital patrol duties the Line pilots were abandoning. Linnea touched her palmscreen to search the main display and found Zhen's call sign attached to the registration number of an incoming ship, listed as a newly repaired linker. Linnea hoped she'd had time to be properly installed in it; linkers were more maneuverable. Safer, if they had to fight.

There had been no more departures from the docking bays for several minutes now. More and more of the outgoing ships flicked from blue to green as they reached the radius beyond which a jump was allowed. Linnea listened silently to the minimal, businesslike orders and responses on the Line channels. Finally, all the flags were green, and Hakon's voice cut in. "All ships, all stations, report readiness to jump for rendezvous point."

Stationmaster Segura touched the comm control in front of him, and said, "Good fortune, pilots." He glanced at Linnea, but she shook her head. She could say nothing to Hakon now.

"We thank you, Stationmaster," Hakon said. "We will return with our sons and brothers in just over three months."

"May it be so," the stationmaster replied, his voice husky.

There was a pause, then Hakon's voice said, "All ships, all stations, jump for rendezvous on my mark, standard arrival scatter. *Jump.*"

Almost too quickly to follow, the green lights winked out. Linnea turned and looked at the flat display showing all seven orbital stations. All had lost their clouds of green. "He did it," she said emptily.

"Maybe they'll succeed," Segura said, then sighed.

"We have to make plans," Linnea said. "We have to assume that none of them will ever return."

"I know," Segura said, still gazing at the nearly empty orbital display.

Linnea touched his arm. "I need to talk by comm, to-day, with the shipyard owners and the unions. We need more ships, built faster, even if we have to draft people off the streets to do the work. We need more pilots found and trained."

"I will see what I can arrange," the stationmaster said. He still seemed lost.

Linnea put out a general call to the ships coming up from Terranova—the new, makeshift orbital patrol—for a meeting by comm, as soon as they'd all docked. Then she stood for a while, silently, watching the main display. The scale had been changed and it now showed Terranova, a nearly transparent blue sphere marked with the faint traceries of coastlines, the lights of skyports and cities. Around it and through it she saw near-orbital space, the seven orbital stations, the flock of manufacturing satellites. All seemed quiet, the few moving ships—not visibly moving at this scale, of course—flagged green or yellow.

She turned away from it, her throat aching. After all this time, after all she had learned about the Line, how strange it was that their final abandonment of their ancient duties could hurt *her*. That *she* would feel as if the universe had become larger, colder, more frightening.

She wondered, briefly, how Iain must feel. Then hurried away to his empty office to rough out a patrol schedule for the ships she still had.

There was no way, she finally concluded, to squeeze out even one more ship. A better guard would have to wait for more ships to be placed in service.

She checked in with Torin, groundside. With the rest of the union leadership, he was scrambling to fill emergency shifts with at least partly trained workers, scrambling to spread out the skilled personnel as far as possible. Depressing, all of it, but also the best she could have expected. She told him so.

His image, over her holoplate, shrugged. "How's Iain?"

"Tired," she said. "Worried. We all are."

"It's up to you and Zhen, then," Torin said. "And the rest of the new pilots." He pursed his lips. "Tough test."

"I know," she said. "But they're up to it. . . . Look, I need to check in on Iain. I'll comm if anything changes."

"See that it doesn't, will you? I could use a full night's sleep." And he signed off.

Linnea stopped to buy two packaged dinners at the nearest employee refectory, then hurried to Iain's quarters.

The ones they'd shared for a while. She found the right door, let herself in—her palm still admitted her. Maybe he was asleep—

The lights came on as she entered. No Iain.

She set the bag of food on the small table. "Iain?" The refresher closet stood open and dark; she looked in. No sign of him. Then her glance sharpened. No sign at all. His travel bag was gone from its peg on the wall.

Fear bit into her, hard. She left at a dead run. No sense waiting for the lift; she half slid down the gangways in the light pseudograv, sped up in the corridors, ending at last in the docking bay where her ship and Iain's were kept. Then stopped, frozen. "Ah, no. . . ."

Over the hatch where his personal ship had been docked the status light burned severely red, and an orange alarm light flashed—signaling damage, an unusable docking station.

Iain was gone. He had blown the docking clamps and escaped.

She pressed her hands to her mouth, took a shaking breath that was half a sob. She knew where he'd gone. Where he had to go. To face—what? His own demons of damaged pride? His father's failure?

To face Rafael?

She caught her breath. Did he imagine he could still reach Rafael?

But in that strange comm conversation with the infested Rafael, the real one had not spoken to Iain.

He had spoken to her.

She straightened and ran to her own ship's dockside panel, laid her palm on it to unlock it, started the emergency warm-up sequence. Then she touched the wall comm and called Zhen.

Zhen appeared at Iain's quarters half an hour after that, her expression fearful and questioning. "You're sure he's gone with them?"

"They traced his call sign, in Orbital Control," Linnea said, stuffing a clean jumpsuit into her travel bag. "He jumped with the rest. He must have timed his breakaway for the minute the jumps began. No one spotted the alarm."

"Torin said—" Zhen cleared her throat and went on. "When they commed last, Torin said, Iain didn't seem at all like himself—he seemed like one of *them*. A Line pilot. Hard and cold."

Linnea laughed. "He *is* one of them," she said bitterly. "Or so he has decided."

"And yet you're going after him," Zhen said. "To Nexus. To the Cold Minds. Lin, have you thought about this for one single moment?"

"I have been thinking of nothing else." She heard the tremor in her voice. Nothing to be done about that. "I have to go. Zhen, I think I am the best weapon we have."

"*You* are?" Zhen leaned on her clenched fists, her eyes blazing at Linnea across the table. "Don't you see that's the same stupid thinking that made Iain go? We can't lose you both!"

"I can talk to Rafael," she said.

"Are you out of your mind? Rafael is dead! Infested."

"He's still there," Linnea said. "It's not much hope. But it's the only hope we have if the attack fails. And you and I both know it will." She picked up her bag. "I've left instructions for—for handing out the new ships as they come off the lines," she said. "Who's readiest, who's best. Work with Torin on it, will you?"

"You're walking away from what matters most," Zhen said, her voice bitter. "Following Iain off to die. I know you love him, but do you have to hurt us to prove it?"

"It's not that," Linnea said. "It's nothing to do with that. I'm trying to keep a disaster from getting worse."

"I'll never see you again," Zhen said, fighting for

control. As Linnea watched, she won. She lifted her chin and extended her hand. "Make it be worth it, Pilot."

Linnea took Zhen's hand in both of her own and looked down into the other woman's angry eyes. "Hope for that," she said bleakly, "with everything you have."

TWENTY-ONE

NEXUS NEARSPACE

Tension sang in Hakon sen Efrem's mind as he waited for the calculated moment to drop back into normal space, into Nexus close orbit. A risky maneuver with so many ships, even jumping from a rendezvous point within the system.

Everything, everything depended on the events of the next few minutes: neutralizing orbital defenses, then a headlong descent into atmosphere, landing in force around the City. And, at the same time, a second secret landing in the deep desert near the tunnel opening Honormaster sen Martin had told him of: the long-hidden back door to the deep bunkers under the City. A few picked men led by Hakon himself would take to the tunnel, deliver one of the small nuclear devices patrol ships carried, and, perhaps, escape before the blast. . . .

The moment to jump ticked in Hakon's mind, and he *flexed* and folded in on himself, bracing for the burst of normal space, real light, real stars, Nexus filling his vision—

Jumped into chaos, shock, confusion: ships scattered, their formation widening, swirling as they drifted—dead ships. Their electronics must have been killed by the electromagnetic pulse of a nuclear blast, crippling them, trapping the pilots inside. His ship's radiation warning pulsed yellow.

The Cold Minds had been waiting for them.

Hakon knew with shattering pain, knew now that it was too late, that he had been manipulated. Played.

At the same instant a missile burst, kilometers away but near enough. Black blindness took him as his ship's systems blinked out. Hakon felt the sinking, sick emptiness in his belly that meant his jump engine had de-spun. He could not jump away. He could not even see. He fought to maneuver manually, but the jets did not answer—melted, or disabled by the EMP. He was helpless.

A long time later his ship jerked, jerked again, waking him from a dreary fog of despair and postjump exhaustion. He winced as metal scraped, hard, along the skin of his ship.

Hakon swayed in his shell, feeling a growing tug of acceleration. And then he understood: A larger ship had taken his own aboard. Into custody.

Hakon was hanging head down, and as the acceleration grew, he felt the restraining straps digging into his bare skin. The entry to atmosphere and the landing left him sick and dizzy. The heat in his shell built up without relief, until he felt confused, smothered. Drops of sweat pattered against the inside of his shell. His ship held enough oxygen to last him for hours, he knew that, and in any case death was not his enemy, not now—yet fear still chilled him, the pilot's fear of darkness, suffocation, a slow, drifting end.

But the worst came when he knew they had landed on the surface of Nexus, and he heard only silence as he hung there. He tried to release himself from the shell, resigning himself to a two-meter drop in complete darkness. But his head-down position disoriented him, as it should not, *should* not, if he had been in proper condition. Politics had pulled him in, too long since he'd flown regularly, and now he was paying for it. . . . Alone in the dark, despairing, he tried again and again to free himself until, overheated and short of oxygen, he passed out.

Hakon's mind floated slowly up from warm dreams: brief flashes of home when it was still undefiled. The trickle of water in the cool perfumed shade of cedar trees—sun on a stone wall. . . . The dreams faded, then the memory of the dreams, and he found himself half-lying on a cold floor, leaning against a metal wall. He blinked hard to clear his vision. Shapes—men were kneeling around him. He remembered then—gasped in horror and struggled to get to his feet. Hands gripped him, held him down, and a sharp voice said, "Quiet, sen Efrem. You are as safe as any of us. And they don't like it when we shout."

Hakon's head ached, terribly, and he touched his temple, feeling crusted blood where the links to his ship had been roughly pulled free. "So they have us," he said, struggling to keep his voice steady.

"They have us," a haggard older pilot said.

Hakon sniffed the air. Oil, fuel, dry concrete. "Is this the port?"

"It is," a voice said. "It's handy for their ships. They can measure and cut, measure and cut, until we fit—"

"Be quiet, brother," the older pilot said.

"You're the last to wake, sen Efrem," the sharp-voiced man said. Hakon stared at him and finally saw, through the man's bruises, that it was sen Akkila, the leader of the second flight.

"We're home," sen Akkila said. "You've put us in a hard place, Hakon sen Efrem. It's too bad it isn't just you who has to pay the accounting."

Hakon stared up at sen Akkila, discovering a new truth: His power to persuade such men to follow him, of which he had been so proud, had not meant he was *right*.

NEXUS NEARSPACE

Iain's jumpship dropped into normal space over Nexus, and into the disaster he had feared: a slowly expanding drift of ships that his shipmind struggled to sort out, flagging one after another as unpowered and uncontrolled. Without the jump coordinates the other pilots had, he'd had to jump in blind. Blind, and hours too late it seemed.

At once he shut down all systems to minimal, cut off his lights and transponder, let himself drift while he studied the situation.

Several moving ships shone orange, unknowns, and tagged with high mass. They moved among the drifting Line ships with obvious purpose. Cold Minds ships—they had to be.

Not all his brothers could have been destroyed. Not with so many jumping in at once. Some must have made it to ground. He would follow.

He would live.

His ship jerked itself out of the path of a tumbling piece of debris, slamming Iain against his restraints, then in the confused scatter of labeled dots one abruptly showed red—collision course. Missile. He gathered his mind and jumped. Too far, Nexus a pale disk. He collected his thoughts, made himself see it this time, made sure he knew, in his hands and feet and the center of his mind, where he had to come out.

Then, carefully, he touched the maneuvering engines to full hissing life an instant before he jumped.

He burst back into normal space, so close to Nexus that the planet filled half his vision, *overhead*—so close that the thin upper atmosphere screamed along his hull.

He rolled into the correct orientation for entry and let the velocity he'd bought with the maneuvering engines punch him through the upper atmosphere. The shipmind told him where he was: coming in from east of the City, and already below the orbital defenses. He smiled grimly as he battled the first high winds of the atmosphere. He would bet his life—he already had—that their mutilated semihuman pilots could not, would not try the same trick.

Cold Minds on the ground would track his ship all the way in, no way to avoid that. But by the time anything, any infested human, reached his ship, he'd be nowhere near it. He'd lose himself in a city he'd known all his life, where he'd played running and chasing games with a mob of other boys, weaving in and out of parks and buildings and city transport tunnels, on and on for kilometers.

Let them *try* to track him.

It took Iain two days to reach the center of the City. By then he had developed an inner sense for when to go to ground—to lie still in the shade of a stand of dead shrubs while a monitor drone purred by overhead; to press himself into the shadows behind a low stone wall as booted footsteps echoed down the street on the other side.

By then he had seen enough horror to last him a lifetime. Enough death. From the clothing that remained on the dry bones, the papery mummies, he knew them mostly for servants, men and women, and many older men of the Line. He was glad the faces were gone.

He saw few small bodies, and almost no pilot black. They must have been taken up for another purpose. . . .

The City itself was bones, dried bones: Without the climate shield, the sun burned close overhead, intimate, fierce, dimmed only by veils of dust on the wind from the desert. The City's gardens and broad lawns and gracious parks stood brown as the dust, brown as the bones, dead.

He'd found water in the lower levels of a few houses, reserve cisterns, still sealed and cool. One other had been tapped. It seemed to be visited regularly, but the muddy footprints leading away from it were small. His heart lifted when he saw them. Some of the young boys must be alive and free. He saw no other sign of them, nor did he expect to. To live in this desolation of horror for almost a standard year, they must have gone feral.

Once, at night, he froze at the sight of two eyes glowing blue from the shadows. The hair on his neck prickled as he waited for it to move, show itself—

Then it hissed at him, fiercely, and flashed past his feet into the night. A cat, an ordinary cat. He wondered how it had survived. A few kinds of small reptilian animals lived in the open desert. Maybe they were coming into the City now. There was nothing to stop them.

In the center of the City's central park, near the Council Tower, he found the first sign that other men had made it to ground and were still free: symbols scratched in the parched soil at the base of what had been a monument to the First Fathers to land here. The noble grouping of ancestral pilots had been sliced off at the ankles, the metal taken for other uses.

Iain squatted in the deepening shadows of evening, trying to grasp the meaning of the marks while he could still see them.

His breath caught. That was a sunball formation. A

classic, the slip play—every Line schoolboy knew it.
Sunball and—he stared at the last symbol. A tall rectangle topped by an arc, a slash through the arc aiming up at
an angle—

And up there to the right, a star.

Iain straightened. Sunball meant a school. And only
one of the City's four schools had its own observatory.

He knew now where to find some of his brothers. Free
to move, in the city . . . so there was still hope. At full
dark he would go there and see for himself.

While he crouched in the corner of a walled garden,
well out of sight from all around, he heard the scream of
a jumpship high overhead, decelerating hard. The Cold
Minds ships were using the skyport south of the
City—they didn't cross overhead any more than Line
ships used to. This one would not make the field. Coming
in too fast, something wrong, some raw pilot—

The bright spark vanished from sight, blocked by a
building across the park, and a moment later the sound of
the engine stopped abruptly, slapping echoes from the
buildings around him.

Two days after the attack—it had to be some inexperienced pilot, a bad hyperdesic, jumped in too late. Iain
hoped he'd survived. There was nothing anyone could do
for him.

Linnea crawled from the hatch of her jumpship high in
the hills above the City. She straightened carefully—
nothing broken—and examined the ship. What was left
of it. Not wrecked, exactly, but she wouldn't be leaving in
it, that was for sure; her long, scraping landing across a
field of rock had done the old ship no good. It would take
a good shipyard to repair it. No going back.

There never had been. She swallowed, her throat dry
already in the heat. She'd filled the water pouch in her

emergency pack, but it might have to last her a long time.

She swung the pack onto her back and looked down at the dusty expanse of the City. An oddly familiar view—at least, she knew the outlines of the buildings.

With a shock she realized that she must not be far from Iain's old house in the Cloudshadow district. But the view had changed in one way: All the City's polish and color were gone, scoured away by almost a year of sandstorms. Some of the places she remembered as parks and fields had been filled with domes and pipes and coils of greasy-dark metal—factories, storage, she couldn't guess.

She wondered, numbly, whether Iain was alive down there somewhere. Well, even if he was, now, there was not much chance they would both survive this. No point in thinking about it.

She had to get to the center, to the Council Tower that still loomed over all the rest. That was where the deep bunkers were, where the controlling Minds would be hiding—and where she had the best chance of finding Rafael.

The invasion had failed, and Iain most likely was dead, or captured with the rest. But there was still a chance if she could find Rafael. If she found the strength to face him and wake him to a new, twisted hope.

If she could give him a reason to die.

In the last of the light, she began climbing down toward the cluster of mountainside houses just below.

I ain stumbled as his captors shoved him through a wide door, into a vast, dark space dimly lit by dawn filtering through slitted metal shutters high above. He should have expected a rough welcome from his brothers when they'd caught him creeping up toward the school. He looked around, careful of his bruised head, smelling dust and sweat.

From the sound of it there were only half a dozen men in this huge space. He blinked again and at last could make them out, even see their faces. Faces he knew, most of them. He struggled to remember the name of the man standing nearest. "Pilot sen Larans." A senior pilot, well past thirty. He'd been near to retirement.

"Sen Paolo," sen Larans said. "Why are you here, and free? Did you warn the Cold Minds of this attack?"

Iain winced and rubbed the bridge of his nose. "Pilot sen Larans, if I had done that, would I be here in the middle of it? Or would I have stayed safe on Terranova, where the Chairman himself ordered me to remain? As for why I'm free—" He tugged aside the neck of his black tunic, showing the stark bruises left by the restraints in his piloting shell. "I landed. Not too well."

"Not too well at all," sen Larans agreed. "But what made you track us down?"

Iain looked around at the other men. "My place is with the Line," he said quietly.

Sen Larans raised an eyebrow. "You are a stubborn man, sen Paolo."

Iain chose not to answer this. "Where are the other pilots?"

"Most of us, they took in orbit," a younger pilot said. Iain knew him, too: Arek sen Pol. "They took our brothers down to the skyport. Jumpships and all, in carriers. We think they must still be there, if they're alive; there have only been a couple of small ground transports in and out of there. We've got men watching it."

"I came in from the eastern edge," Iain said. "I didn't pass the port."

"Most of us here are from the landing by the bunker entrance," sen Pol said. "We came in from the south on foot, at night, so we saw them working at the unloading, under big blue lights. Piling up the ships like so much scrap."

Iain looked at sen Larans. "And Hakon sen Efrem's plan—"

"When we landed, the tunnel was blocked." Sen Larans shook his head. "No chance." He glanced toward a dark shape in a distant corner of the room. "We got one bomb this far. We had to abandon the rest, or die."

One bomb. Enough, maybe. "Is Hakon here?"

"He never made it down," sen Larans said. He sounded utterly indifferent. "If he's alive, he's at the port with the rest of the pilots. The boys who are still alive are somewhere in the Council Tower."

Iain blinked. "It's true, then?"

"Sen Pol, here—he heard them last night. He got into the Tower grounds, barely got out—but now we know. The bait in the trap was real."

"Then they need our help," Iain said.

Sen Larans snorted. "A dozen of us against the Council Tower! They've got infested men on guard. We've got our fusers, but there are mobile machines to worry about, too, more and more as you get closer to the Tower. Remote eyes."

"Then what is your plan?" Iain asked quietly.

"Now we know we can get right to the base of the Tower," sen Larans said. He met Iain's look, his eyes hard. "We can't kill the Cold Minds down in the bunkers. We can't end this war. But we can save our little brothers from those monsters' ships." He glanced aside at the bomb. "We can give them a clean death."

Iain looked down at his hands. What had he hoped to accomplish if he ever saw Rafael? If Rafael was even alive?

What hope did he have of living to see Linnea again, here in an infested city, without ships, without real weapons?

One real weapon.

It had become a matter of choosing the best way to die.

He looked up at sen Larans. "Maybe that's best," he said. "When?"

"Tonight," sen Larans said. "And we can't time-detonate. If they find it before it goes, we've lost our last chance." He looked at Iain. "Sen Pol says we'll need two men to get the bomb safely over some of the rough ground."

"I'm one," Iain said. "I'm not of the Line. Expendable."

"Well." Sen Larans looked uncomfortable. "That's true enough. You're with me, then."

"Good." So he would have a hand in one small victory.

But it felt like defeat. He could almost hear Linnea say that, in her dry voice.

He wondered if she would ever know how he had died.

Night, and Linnea crouched tensely in the central hallway of a dead man's house. She'd found the corpse on the way in, bones and a braid slumped in a chair, a shattered crystal goblet at his still-booted feet. Honorable death, he'd chosen: pilot suicide by poison, no doubt from the proper glass.

She'd gone straight past him into the tomb smell of the house, sealed tight against dust, heavy with the heat of unfiltered desert summer. No time to find a better place to hide: Something circled in the sky above the house this minute, the drone of its engine growing and fading, growing and fading. They'd caught some sign of her, clearly. If she didn't move, if she didn't move, surely they would give up, go on, go after some other trace. . . .

They're machines. They don't give up.

She closed her eyes, tried to breathe shallowly, tried to remember a prayer.

This hall was the only part of the house that could not be seen from a window. *So if they know I'm in here, they know where I am.* But she did not dare move.

Something scuttled along the floor against the wall. An automatic, one of the little cleaners—she'd seen them in Iain's house. Nothing to be afraid of—

It skittered away from the wall, weaving a sinuous path toward her over the stone tiles.

An automatic, in a house that hadn't had power for almost a year?

She froze, hopelessly. It stopped near her feet. Reared up, and she saw the glint of a tiny lens on the front of its body.

Harsh blue light washed over her.

Shadows in the hall—

They took her.

TWENTY-TWO

NEXUS: THE CITY
TWO DAYS LATER

Cold. Standing with bare feet in a puddle of icy water. Darkness pressing against his open eyes. Iain could not rub his eyes to clear them of whatever was blinding him. He was bound, his arms pulled back around something rough and twisted, wood that scraped against his back as he tried to free himself. But his wrists were firmly held by a metal strap that cut into his skin if he twisted too hard. He stopped struggling. If he lost his footing and slid down, he might not be able to straighten himself again.

The back of his head hurt, and he could feel a crust of dried blood on his neck, a cold, sticky patch on the right shoulder of his coveralls. He heard his own ragged breathing, the rush of blood in his veins. He heard water dripping, dripping, all around him, echoing in vastness. And far off, faint clattering sounds, little ticks and whispers.

His eyes began to focus. He saw one source of weak light, an oval directly overhead, shimmering faint gray-blue. He could not judge how large it was, or how far above him. But the light seemed to be slowly increasing. Now he could make out some of his surroundings.

He stood on a wet, buckled wood floor. A few meters away, a little higher, a round surface glistened. A bowl two meters across, brimful of water. And between himself and the bowl, almost at his feet, a meter-high pile of sapphire splinters, half-buried in a mound of blackened metal chain.

Iain's slow thoughts worried, worried at the things he was seeing. He should know them. He should know them, though he had no memory of this dark, ghastly chamber—

Then he understood, and his breath caught in a whimper.

That pile of shards was Earth. The crystal image of lost Earth that had hung for centuries in the shaft above him—now fallen and shattered.

This was the Inmost Place. This the central dais.

He was tied to the Tree.

And there, off to the side—he saw with a wave of horror a dull gray metal cylinder a meter long, with a handle at each end: the small nuclear bomb, stripped from a Line pulse-missile, that was to have put an end to this place, given the sons of the Line the gift, the freedom, of death. Sen Larans's plan had failed.

The Line had failed.

He was the last.

He wept for a while, in despair, in loneliness. He wondered when they would come for him.

If he were free, that bomb would open to his touch, to the family code embedded in his palm that still marked him as Line. He would carry it down and down, far under this chamber, to the dark places. He would set it off, and die, cleaning all this filth away forever.

But he was not free.

The light grew and grew as morning came to the world
he had thought never to see again, to the sky of Nexus far
above him. In time he could see most of the great chamber, the huge murals of the swirling dust and bright stars
of the Hidden Worlds now faded, smeared with vertical
runnels of glistening darkness. The empty ranks of ledges
where the gathered Line had stood. In the rustles and
whispers around him, the patter of water on wood and
stone, he heard the faint shivering dream echo of the
great summoning bell at the top of the shaft above him.
Music rose in his mind: the Line Chant, the Line's long
history, always sung by a hundred men, always heard in
reverent silence.

It would be forgotten now. Deservedly so. But he had
loved it once. He wept again, for a long time.

Thirsty, shaking with chills, he must have slept. He
jerked awake when something cold touched his face, and
he twisted away from it in panic. The pain in his wrenched
shoulders cleared his head. The light was strong now, full
daylight beating down from the shaft. Someone stood in
front of him—

He straightened against the Tree. Silently facing him
was Rafael. Hair a little longer than when Iain had seen
his image at Terranova, but still filthy. His neck glistened,
raw with a weeping rash. He was thinner than Iain had
ever seen him, the bones of his face almost pressing
through his pale skin. He held a neural fuser, Iain's neural fuser, in one skeletal hand.

"Is it you, cousin?" Iain choked.

The thing that spoke was not Rafael. "We are the
Minds. We are before you." The inside of its mouth was
black. Bots.

Terror made Iain strain against his bonds, and he felt
the metal cut into his wrists again. Not deeply enough to
kill him. "That body is dying," he said raggedly.

"We are the Minds. We do not die. Another will be

used in this one's place." It smiled, lips stretching back over black-slimed teeth. "Your attack has failed. Your pilots, your weapons, your ships will be put to our use."

"More will come," Iain said.

"They will also be put to our use. Now," Rafael's voice said, "we will learn of the orbital defenses of Terranova, and what reinforcement they are to be given."

Iain felt a faint echo of gratitude for the months he had spent on Station Six, out of contact. "I know nothing of that." Few of the pilots would know the overall design; that had been under the control of the stationmasters, working with Linnea.

"You are not here to tell us," Rafael's voice said. He opened his mouth and a thin chittering sound, painfully loud, filled the huge chamber. Iain winced. When it stopped he heard footsteps, coming up the steps that led to the platform, up from below.

Two infested humans appeared, gripping a black-clad prisoner between them. Iain saw who it was and cried out in wordless anguish.

Linnea. Not safe, not on Terranova—here in the pit with him. Doomed with him. She was dirty and bruised, bleeding from one temple, and the eyes she turned to him were deep pits of fear.

"Don't—" Iain's voice broke. "Don't be afraid."

"I'm sorry," she said in a dull voice. "I had to come." Her eyes were hollow with grief. "I had to try—" She stopped and looked away.

Iain looked at her. So did she, too, have some mad idea that she could waken Rafael? That some part of Rafael still lingered inside that infested brain?

"This one is here to tell us what we require," Rafael's voice continued, relentlessly. "If this one does not speak, you will suffer. You have no weapons that can defeat the Minds. Aid us. Accept peace. Your deaths will bring purity to these worlds."

Iain saw Linnea's eyes go cold. She turned to Rafael's body. "Rafael," she said. "These things can only kill us. They cannot make us unhuman. They cannot make you unhuman. Listen to me!"

But Rafael's head turned away from her. "You will provide the information," Rafael's voice said. Dulled, hoarse. Not his living voice, the sharp, flexible weapon he had used so well.

Linnea gave Iain a frightened glance. Then tried again. "Rafael. Your father is dead. These things killed him. But you have a son. He is alive on Terranova. If these things attack there, he will die."

The thing's head tilted again, oddly. The mouth worked, and a rope of black drool stretched down from its chin. Then a weak voice said, "No son."

Iain saw Linnea fight for breath, her legs trembling as she faced the man who had scarred her body and her life—trying to call him back, to speak to him. Iain had never seen such revulsion in anyone's eyes.

"Be strong," Iain said in a frayed thread of a voice. "You can be so strong."

She closed her eyes. And when she opened them, he did not know her. Pity. A terrifying pity. Iain held his breath again.

"Rafael," she said. "I saw your son. I touched him. Tiny and new. A clean beginning, Rafael. Nothing that hurt you will ever touch him. I swear it to you."

The stronger voice spoke again. "The information."

Her voice sharpened. "Rafael! Listen to me. Listen to my voice. Remember me. You remember *me*."

It stirred, turned its head. Iain saw its black, aimless gaze rest on Linnea—and stay there. He held his breath. *Keep its attention, love. Keep trying.* Though he, too, was remembering—the image Rafael had showed him once, in prison, of Linnea under his power, Linnea's spirit crushed to ash. The scar between her breasts, the shape of the Tree he was tied to—sometimes Iain used to cover it with his hand when they made love, as if he could make it not true, make it never have happened—

The head rolled on Rafael's shoulders, the eyes wandered loosely, then sharpened, focusing: Something inside was using the eyes again, in a human way.

Rafael.

Rafael looked around at the Inmost Place, though his body trembled with some internal struggle for mastery. The gaunt face frowned. "Dirty."

"It will be cleansed," Linnea said, that same terrifying intensity burning in her eyes. "You can cleanse it. Clean fire."

The red-rimmed eyes turned toward Iain. "Little . . . c-cousin."

"Rafael," Iain said through tears—tears for Linnea.

"So far away," Rafael said dreamily. "Pure—pure—purity of—" His face contorted.

Iain caught his breath. "Linnea!" She had to keep trying, no matter what it did to her. Their last hope hung by the fraying thread of her compassion—for the man who had broken her life.

He saw her straighten, an act of pure courage that caught at his heart. "Rafael," she said. "Listen! Listen to me! You're in pain. End it. Take the fire to the roots of the Tree. Cleanse the roots." The things holding her were tightening their grip, and she winced and struggled. "The dark, Rafael. Take it down to the dark. Rest in the dark. Find death." She swallowed hard. "And we will keep your son in the light."

Rafael turned his face to her again. Paused. Then walked, slowly, toward the two bodies holding her. Touched the fuser to their heads, one then the other. *Flash. Flash.* The sharp odor of singed hair and flesh.

Both bodies released their grip on Linnea and fell limp. One slid silently off the platform into the dark depths below.

Rafael looked straight into Linnea's eyes. Iain saw her trembling, her throat working with revulsion, but she held Rafael's steady gaze. "It can't be forgiven, you know," she said, her voice shaking. "I can't forgive it. But it can be erased."

"Erased," Rafael breathed. The fuser slid from his hold, landed with a thump on the platform. He turned to Iain, held up his scorched hands. "Cleansed." The sunlight reflected down the shaft from far above lit his hair with the old fire, and Rafael smiled at Iain, a sweet, open smile like a child's, like the child Rafael whom Iain had never known. The child Rafael who had never been. "Little cousin," he said calmly. "Run and find them, little cousin." He lifted his face to the sunlight. "Up."

Rafael turned and, with a strength Iain would not have believed he still had, lifted the bomb with his burned hands, lifted the dark weapon the weight of a child. Cradling it, almost tenderly, he descended into the darkness under the platform.

TWENTY-THREE

Her hands trembling with fear and urgency, Linnea unfastened Iain's bleeding wrists from around the twisted white stub of the Tree, and he straightened with a groan. He swayed, off balance, and she caught him to steady him. He pulled her against him and held her tightly, muttering, "Never risk this again—never again."

She pushed away from him, glared up into his face. "Never leave me behind again, you bastard!"

"Never again," he said, and pulled her into his arms once more. For a moment she let herself hold him, burrowing her face into his chest. Let her face twist, for one instant, into raw fear, while he could not see it. He held on so hard she felt they were melting into one. She pulled back to breathe, to say, "No time. Let's go."

"He said *up*." And Iain was off, staggering first, then running. She ran close behind him down the narrow wooden steps from the platform, then up the broad stone stairs to the rim of the Inmost Place. At the top he looked back at her. "The children are here in the Tower. The bomb—"

"We'll find them," she said. "Stairs."

He nodded and led her off to an alcove, palmed a door. It opened for him. Stairs led up. "Half a kilometer high," he said.

"No power," she said. "No lifts. No water. They won't be far up."

As they ran up the stairs, Iain opened the door at each landing, shouted. "Little brothers! Little brothers, we're here! Answer!"

On the third level up he swung the door open—and Linnea seized his arm. An old man was walking away up the long dark hall inside. An old man carrying a bucket, heavy white plastic. He seemed not to have heard Iain's shouts.

"Infested," Linnea said.

Iain raised the fuser, and together they followed, quietly, twenty meters behind. Halfway up the hall the man turned aside, unbarred a door. It swung open; the old man shuffled inside.

Linnea followed Iain closer to the doorway, and as she did the stench caught her throat. Ammonia. Human excrement. They looked at each other—stepped around the corner.

Froze in shock.

They are quiet, they are good. Quiet and good. Quiet and good. Raymi hugs his littlebrothers close and whispers to them, *Quiet and good. Quiet and good.* He has kept these two alive for a hundred feedings now, more, it's hard to count.

The water is coming. Unless they are not quiet and good. Then the water is spilled, and the little ones go thirsty, those without brothers to help them scoop it up, lap it up, from the dirty floor.

Always when the sunrays slide to *that* wall, and they have been quiet and good, always then the water comes. The slow steps, the white-haired water-man whose eyes flicker blue, whose face twitches.

Quiet and good. If Raymi tells himself the words, he's not so scared.

They are all so quiet, and so good, that Raymi hears the water coming before it does, before the bucket goes *thump* beside the door. He walks his littlebrothers closer to the center, where the water will be. They whimper and squinch, and one of them soils the floor in fear. But they know he's right. He's kept them alive.

The door opens, and the other littlebrothers scrabble back, but not Raymi's. Sometimes it's a feeding for the ones that come in, sometimes little ones go and stay gone. But not this time.

Raymi stays. This is the water. His littlebrothers need it. Hot hot hot their skin is, their eyes sunk back. Like his. Pissing orange like him. His mouth aches, lips cracked, tongue dry. Something was wrong with the water-man. It had to be that because they have all been

quiet and good

Now maybe they've fixed him. The water is here.

In the center of the room, the water-man sets down the bucket with a *thump*, and water goes *sloosh* on the floor. Raymi thinks, good, more for the little ones without big-brothers; they get the last, and there will be more last. Raymi's eyes are on the water, jiggling jiggling, shiny wet. His hands grip his littlebrothers' necks. Quiet and good. No one moves until the door closes. Raymi used to have to say it. Now everyone knows.

The door doesn't close.

Raymi looks over and sees two people. An oldbrother, one of the ones who went away. Black cloth, tied hair. His mouth is shut. A mama, the other, her mouth going oh oh oh, water coming out of her eyes. *Tears,* Raymi remembers. He remembers *crying*.

Their eyes are alive. They're alive.

And one of them touches the water-man with a thing in his hand

and the water-man dies.

He *dies*.

Raymi screams.

His littlebrothers jump forward for the last water ever.

As soon as it's gone, spilled, soaked in, when the last boy has licked up the last drop from the dirt on the floor, Raymi hears the oldbrother. He talks. *Go run hurry.* Stands by the door waving hands. *Go run through.*

But if they go run through, they are not quiet and good.

But if they stay, there will be no more water.

Raymi pulls his littlebrothers close. Pushes them forward. They squeak and stumble. *Go run hurry,* says the oldbrother. *Go run hurry,* says the mama.

They go. The rest follow. Out to the bright. To the blue. The first sky Raymi has seen in a year.

Run, he says, rusty. *Run!* he coughs. Then he waves them past, all the littlebrothers, all the bigbrothers, even the lost.

"Run!"

*H*e is Rafael again.

He walks with his burden through the deep, narrow halls. His eyes do not require light. He walks as if through deep water, through a resistance he knows is of them, of his enemies, striving to control his limbs. But this body is his again, for the moment, for the last time.

That which has spoken through him, at times, is far away now, in the Inmost Place; its words are weak in his mind. And that which lives in him is simple and does not understand what he carries.

The gift. Fire from the world above.

A winding and a winding and his steps suddenly echo in a high, wide chamber. Dark shapes sprawl up the walls, lights shooting along the tendrils that twist along walls and floor and ceiling, that join Mind to Mind. In a blue flicker, they confer. He feels words crowding into his mind, words this body would speak if he allowed it.

He stumbles. His bones are crumbling away; he is dust. Far enough. He lays his burden down. Lies close beside it, the cold stone holding him embraced, the dark he has loved echoing all around. He presses his singed palm against the smooth metal flank of the gift he has brought. It knows him for what he once was. It opens for him. Sharp white light in this dark place. He sets his palm against an inner screen, taps out a code he learned when he was twelve years old. One that means: *All is lost. Death must come.*

But he feels triumphant. He brings clean light. He will be cleanly erased.

He thinks for the last time of *her*, seeing into his darkness with her eyes he could not change, her compassion he could not twist or break.

Because he was weak? Or because she was strong?

One finger moves, the last. Now there will be
Light

Almost a kilometer from the Council Tower, well out of sight in the narrow canyons of the streets, the ground leaped and bucked under Linnea's running feet, throwing her and Iain to the ground. Some of the boys running with them screamed. Dust choked her. She heard the rippling tinkle of glass falling from high in the towers around and lay with her face buried in her hands.

She raised her head, saw Iain close beside her. "The Council Tower—" A distant grating roar, a bass shuddering, a sliding sound that shook the ground again. "Breathe shallowly." And in a moment even through closed eyes she could sense that most of the light was gone. A rush of hot air played along her body. More screams, and boys weeping in strange, raw voices. Only a few of them had yet spoken in words.

"Radiation," she said in a strangled voice.

"No," Iain said. "Too far below. We're safe from it. But the tower's foundations must be broken." His arms were strong and solid around her, and she tried to breathe steadily.

"He did it," she said.

"He did it," Iain said, and with a shock she realized that his cheek pressed against hers was wet. Could he, did he, even now, weep for Rafael? Who had once, long ago, used Iain, hurt him as badly as she had been hurt?

She got to her knees, then stood with Iain and looked around at the dust-hazed street littered with glass. The boys, still huddled together in terror, could not walk over this with bare feet. "The school," Iain said. "We'll take them to the school. There's water there, and mats to sleep on—"

"Clothes?" Linnea asked. "Shoes?" Iain's feet were bare, too. She licked her lips. "Food?"

"Maybe."

She set her hand on his chest, got his attention. "Iain. The Cold Minds. How safe are we?"

"The controlling Minds, the masters, must be vapor," Iain said. "The rest will be confused, disorganized, for the moment. But we don't dare expect it to last."

She looked around. The boys were beginning to stand

up, but weak as they were, and naked, and filthy, they could not go far.

"Only forty still alive," she said, despairing.

"Forty more than we had," Iain said. "The other pilots, if they're alive, are at the skyport. If we get to them before the Cold Minds reorganize—"

"We can move," Linnea said fiercely, "exactly as fast as these children. Your brothers are on their own."

He took a breath as if to argue, then looked beyond her to the children. And was silent.

They spent the night at the school, found food in deep storage that was still safe to eat; found water to drink, and a swimming pool indoors that was half-full of warm, cloudy water. Not clean, but cleaner than the boys. Some jumped in without hesitation; some had to be led in and washed. She heard their voices in the night, trying out words again.

The boys started out in the morning in puffy sunball shoes, and shining singlets and shorts in indigo and yellow. "A team at last," Iain said, and Linnea laughed helplessly.

Their way after that was treacherous. They could not travel by stealth with so many, Linnea knew; they were certainly being watched and tracked. But Iain had been right that there seemed, for now, to be no organized Cold Minds resistance to their progress. The few infested they saw moved like confused animals, huddling in shade where they could find it, waiting to die. Automatics saw the odd procession, clicked, moved on.

Without the central Minds, the infested humans could not coordinate, could not resist a determined attack, but neither could the Line pilots ever feel safe. The skyport, Iain said, could be cleaned of infestations. It had power they might be able to restart, an independent water supply, and a stock of food. Enough to last them until they could be evacuated. If they could take the port—

At the south edge of the City, Iain led Linnea and the boys to a place with water, under a house half-wrecked by the strong southern-desert storms. That night a dozen older boys came up to the edge of the camp—boys who had escaped from custody or had never been caught and had led a nightmare feral existence for almost a year, scavenging food from abandoned houses and dodging Cold Minds monitor flyers and salvage patrols. Offered food, they came in and sat across the dark room from the boys from the Tower. Some of the little ones growled at each other, until Iain explained, calmly, simply, that there was going to be food, water, fine new clothes for everyone. Soon.

Seeing the coldness of their eyes, all these boys, Linnea felt dread. These children had seen their younger, weaker brothers die of starvation and neglect. They had seen horror upon horror in the ways of the City, and in the houses where mummified bodies of old men and children lay where the Cold Minds patrols had left them. These would be grim enemies for the Cold Minds, when they grew up; grim warriors, and a grim weapon for the wrong hand. She hoped they would heal, in time.

The long trek to the skyport on foot took most of a hot desert night. Linnea walked beside Iain, along the service road beneath the high tube that had brought her into the city so long ago. Now it stood dark, unpowered, far above, a stark line against the cloudy nebulae of the Hidden Worlds, and the long procession shuffled along the hard, smooth pavement in its shadow. The boys from the Tower were good at being quiet. . . .

In the morning they came down from the ridge that separated the skyport and the City, and found the Line's disabled jumpships stockpiled on the ground. To Iain's joy, Line sentries met them: The prisoners had broken out and taken the port when the moment came, when the controlling Minds fell.

Trailing the long string of boys, she and Iain approached the low building, mostly underground, where passengers in transit had once found food and rest. As they came nearer, Linnea heard voices. Men's voices, human voices, a confusion of them. They came to the main doors, unpowered and heavy, and she looked at Iain.

He hauled on one side, she on the other, and the way was opened. The boys spilled into the broad white room where most of the Line survivors waited.

For most of the children there was no homecoming; she hadn't expected it. But here two brothers embraced; there a father wept over a son. "This is good," she said, numb with tiredness.

Iain looked down at her. "It is."

And here was Hakon. She almost did not recognize him, tired and untidy; and his arrogance seemed quite gone. He met them both with an uncertain expression, at the center of a ring of pilots. "You," he said. Then, "Iain. Iain sen Paolo." He looked dazed.

"Hakon sen Efrem," Iain said, with a courteous bow of his head that looked insanely incongruous to Linnea, among these marooned and powerless men. "I bring good news. The central Minds are destroyed. The bomb was placed according to your plan."

The room fell silent. "Placed by whom?" Hakon demanded.

"By my cousin Rafael sen Fridric," Iain said, "who died in the act."

"That is impossible," Hakon said. "Sen Fridric was infested."

"Incompletely," Iain said. "You remember the old rumors. Spiderweave." Linnea saw the flash of disgust on more faces than Hakon's. Iain went on, unperturbed. "His mind was imperfect, and imperfectly controlled. Linnea could speak to him. She woke him back to humanity, for just long enough."

Hakon glanced at Linnea, but spoke to Iain. "How?"

"By reminding him," Iain said, "of the worst thing he ever did. And telling him of the best."

Hakon looked puzzled, then shook his head dismissively. "So we've won," he said. "Nexus is ours." The men around them kept silent. Somewhere, a child whimpered.

"It is not," Iain said. "We are still a long way from home. And still not safe."

"No place is safe," Linnea said. "Or will be ever again. The Cold Minds are still here. They can take root again. We can never eliminate them."

"We *will* find a way," Hakon said. But no one spoke up to support him. "We *will* rebuild this City."

"If it is rebuilt, it will not be here," Iain said. He smiled at a small boy in the arms of the man next to Hakon. The boy burrowed his face into the man's shoulder.

Hakon watched, too, and smiled almost reluctantly. "We've gained something."

"I am happy for you all," Linnea said quietly, and saw, startled, that he looked at her with clear acknowledgment. Iain put his arm around her, and she leaned against him, exhausted at the thought of all the work that still must be done to get these men, and these wounded children, back to safety on Terranova.

TWENTY-FOUR

Linnea was not surprised when the Line pilots had to fight off three assaults by infested men the first week. There was food at the port, and their simple inbuilt guidance drove them to seek it. After each attack, men walked among the dead who had been infested, noting and mourning those they had known. And then the corpses were burned. Pyre after pyre for days.

The Line found and sorted out their ships—abused wrecks, most of them. Linnea shared the other pilots' distress over that. In the months she'd used her ship it had become almost a companion, the intimate interface a link she had never before felt to a machine. And some of these pilots had flown in the same ship for twenty years.

No one went near the strange bulks of the Cold Minds ships. Everyone knew what might be inside. And what surely lay in the piloting compartments.

While armed Line patrols cleared out the dark corridors underground, others made a careful search through

the sand-blown hulks. They uncovered two intact training ships, overlooked by the Cold Minds.

That same day, in those two ships, two of the younger
pilots were dispatched home to Terranova, carrying two
of the sickest boys with them, to report the news and
bring back ships, tools, medtechs—aid that would take
more than three months to arrive. Linnea hoped that the
sickest boys would have recovered enough by then to
travel in otherspace, home to Terranova and safety.

Iain and Linnea found a room in the transient hotel
and settled in. Even after a year of desert exposure, the
room was the best they'd shared since Iain's house on
Nexus: spacious, windowed, with a soft bed, running
water, even power for three hours every evening. They
both slept hard, exhausted.

On a morning three days after the ships departed,
Linnea knelt at a low table off the main concourse, bent
over a scrap of paper, totaling food supply numbers and
longing for her palmscreen. Arithmetic was still a struggle for her, and it shamed her. Someday, she'd promised
herself, someday when there was peace, she would learn
everything she had ever wanted to know.

She felt a hand stroke her hair and looked up to see Iain
smiling at her, looking cleaner than he had for a long time,
in his own clothes of plain gray. They had been able to recover clothing and supplies from their ships, though the
ships themselves were useless, unrepairable with the tools
still available here. The Cold Minds had stripped the repair yard nearly bare.

"Can't you see I'm busy?" she demanded, but an answering grin escaped her control.

He poked at the paper. "You forgot to carry a one
here." She stabbed at his finger with her stylus, and he
snatched it back.

Then he knelt down beside her. Sunlight streamed in

through the dusty glass wall behind them, and in its harsh light she saw the lines of worry his smile had temporarily concealed. He seemed to be searching for words.

"Iain, what is it?" She set down her stylus, pushed the paper away.

"They're going to burn the Cold Minds ships," Iain said.

She studied him. "Well. You expected that, didn't you? Even with the drives disabled, they're a threat. Probably full of bots."

"They have human pilots," Iain said. "Humans from Earth."

"Dead by now, surely," she said cautiously.

"I don't think so," Iain said. "Those ships maintain their pilots. They must—the pilots never leave them."

"Still—" She searched for words. "How human are they, really? Grown in tanks, maybe. Surgically modified, if that Inner Council report is right. Didn't it say their brains aren't normal?"

Iain grimaced. "The brain of the one intact subject the Line managed to recover at Freija was not normal, no. But, Linnea—" He shook his head. "These are humans who were born on lost Earth, or near to it. How can we just let them die? If they *can* recover, if they can speak, think what they might be able to tell us!"

She looked at him sharply. "You've been to the pilots about this already, haven't you." It was not a question.

He looked away. "They're holding off for twenty-two hours. They said I could ask for volunteers."

"Oh, no." She got to her feet and looked down at him. "You want to go into one of those ships. You want me to go in with you. And pull out one of those half-human things—"

He stood up. "You're the last one I'm going to ask. Then I'll try it alone."

She closed her eyes. *Unfair.* Then looked up into his. "One attempt. In daylight."

"Good enough," Iain said.

They wore quarantine suits to board the ship Iain chose, one of the smaller ones. Inside was mostly a solid mass of machinery—weaponry and jump engines, Linnea guessed—pierced by tubes and crevices too small for anything human to move through. She did not touch anything, followed close behind Iain, tried not to think of the distance this ship had traveled. Thousands of dark light-years out from Old Earth. . . .

The one human-sized passageway led, of course, to the piloting compartment. The beams of their handlights slid harshly along equipment, tubing, walls. Shadows jumped and swayed.

"Down," Linnea said in a strained voice, aiming her handlight.

The pilot lay in a long pit set into the deck. After one long look, Linnea turned her eyes away, counted and breathed as Iain had taught her to do to fight nausea. But she remembered the silver leads that snaked into the empty eye sockets, the atrophied arms and legs, the bald head and slack, finely wrinkled face.

Iain crouched and touched it with a gloved hand. "He's still alive." The body did not move at the muffled sound of his voice.

"How do we—" She had to stop and breathe again. She must not vomit inside a sealed suit. "How do we disconnect him, if he has no eyes to see with? I don't think he can hear or see, or move."

Iain slid a finger past the tubes leading into the mouth. "He's got no teeth."

"What else doesn't he have?" She wrapped her arms around herself. "Iain, this is a bad idea."

Iain shined the handlight along the edge of the pilot's shell. "Do you see a disconnect control?"

"I don't think he's meant to come out of there," she said, dread half-choking her. "Not until he dies."

Iain slid his hand down the bare chest of the pilot. The face didn't change, it couldn't change, pierced by tubes. Then the skin of the belly shivered.

She barely made it out of the ship, barely tore off her helmet in time. Iain came out to her as she stood shaking, spitting, wishing she had some way to wipe her mouth. "I'm sorry," he said quietly. "I think you are right—these people cannot survive when removed from their ships. But we should at least look at as many as we can. Record their images. These are our distant cousins. They should be remembered."

"J-just don't touch them again," she said tensely. "I can't stand it."

By sunset they had visited seventeen of the thirty-two ships that remained on the skyport field. By sunset even Iain was sure that nothing could be done for the Cold Minds pilots. All of them had been modified, radically, to fit their various ships; even those least changed did not seem capable of, or interested in, human communication or even touch. And no Line pilot, of course, would dare risk linking his brain to a Cold Minds ship in an attempt to communicate.

Some of the pilots had visible tumors, products of their years in space. All of them were older than pilots should be. "They hoped to replace them in the Hidden Worlds," Iain said. "With us."

They stood outside the eighteenth ship, as the sun of Nexus sank out of sight behind them. "One more," Iain said.

"The last," Linnea said. "Please."

They made their way to the piloting compartment as before. "A woman again," Iain said, and moved the beam of his handlight away from the reclining body, along the banks of support machinery that lined the bulkheads.

Linnea frowned and focused her own handlight on the pilot. Knelt beside—her. She was small, with dark brown skin, hairless as they all were. But there was something—

It was hard to see against the dark skin. But Linnea lifted the woman's left arm from its limp position on her belly, and said, "Iain."

He must have heard the terror in her voice, because he knelt at once beside her. Looked at the woman's wrist in the trembling beam of Linnea's handlight. "That's—"

A tattoo circling the wrist. A tattoo of a garland of flowers. *Daisies,* Linnea thought. The dark outline had spread, fuzzing the white and yellow and green of the flowers and leaves.

"She used to be free," Linnea whispered.

As Linnea knew they would, the Line burned the ships anyway. The senior pilots seemed to shrug off the news that the Cold Minds pilots had come from a stock of free, normal humans—that there were humans alive, if not on Old Earth, then in its system. "Our problem is more immediate," one of them, Bran sen Oliver, said testily. "You say the pilots can't be saved. Then ending them is an act of mercy. And destroying those ships is the only way to clean them."

It took most of a day systematically to burn out the insides of the ships. Linnea had begged that the human pilots first be killed by the same injection a Line pilot would use to end his life in a hopeless situation. "Don't let them burn alive," she said. Hakon sen Efrem, to her surprise, backed her in this; and in the end they prevailed. So when the ships burned, and she stood with Iain watching the fuel-fed flames mounting high into the night sky, she knew that at least whatever had lived inside them felt nothing now.

What happened to the soul, when the body was made into a tool, when the mind was closed into itself forever? What would happen to her, or to Iain, if they found themselves in such a place? Madness almost at once, she thought. Or a withdrawal into an inner place, away from the body, away from thought and memory. She had learned that place in prison on this world. She had learned it from Rafael. Who, also, was burned. Gone.

In the evening she went again, alone, to see the smoking pyres of the ships, the stirring of dust among them. Dead. The Hidden Worlds were safer than they had been. For now. Black smoke mounted to the dusty sky.

Rafael was dead.

Rafael was dead, certainly dead, and the fear that had circumscribed her had begun to go clear, like glass. She could see out. She could see Iain. All his mistakes with her, all hers with him, flicked through her mind. But this time she did not gather them, count them, store them where she could find them again; this time she let them lie.

They had both almost died. That meant it was time for forgiveness, before another piece of their lives was wasted.

She went in, late, and found him asleep in their room. Power was out again, the commscreen dead, but the light from the stars and dust of the Hidden Worlds cast a pale glow across the bed.

She slid in beside Iain, slid her arms around him and kissed his cheek. He stirred, woke—turned toward her and kissed her back, hungrily.

This was the time. This was right. His hand slid down the curves of her body, caressing. She opened to him, urged herself up against him. Now she could see. Now she could understand.

Urgency, need took her. There was only this, only this moment, breathing Iain's breath, holding him closer, closer, closer. . . .

She went to sleep with Iain curled warm against her back. She wanted to go home. So desperately, she longed for home.

But for the first time, it was not Santandru that filled her mind. It was Terranova.

TWENTY-FIVE

Linnea reached Terranova with Iain more than seven months, objective, after the invasion had been launched. As she brought her ship into its docking space, the repair bays of Station Six swarmed with activity. She could only hope she wouldn't be caught up in it. She wanted to go groundside as soon as she'd rested—see Marra and the children and how they had settled in.

Linnea rushed through the docking procedures, dressed hastily, and emerged into the wide space of the docking bay. Up and down the bay she saw crews at work on the ships, fine-tuning the crude repairs that had been made on Nexus. Iain's ship had been in for an hour already, and a crew was already at work on it.

She passed a pressurized repair bay where more seriously damaged ships, carried as cargo from Nexus, had been brought inboard for better access. More crews hard at work. Torin's people must be swamped. She had missed him, and Zhen. Maybe she'd see them tomorrow, too.

Tonight, though, she was limp with postjump exhaustion—and with the long strain of what had happened on Nexus. Too tired to code a call, to try to talk to anyone, to try to explain to Marra why she had gone, what had happened. . . . *Home. Bed.*

Iain was sound asleep when she reached their quarters. She took a shower, then slid into bed beside him, and into peace. This was right. . . .

I ain was gone when she woke, probably off to check on the progress of his ship's repairs. Linnea made the mistake of going to the station office first, before she commed anyone groundside. There was no sign of her staff or Iain's, just a harassed assistant to the stationmaster, who practically fell at her feet with relief when she walked in. "It's all the new ships we've been building, while the Line was at Nexus," he said. "Now that the Line pilots are back, some of them want to step ahead of *our* pilots, take the new ships right out of their hands. And the yard owners are letting it happen."

Linnea sighed and dug into the stack of current messages. Zhen had done her best, but the fact that the owners thought of Zhen as a shipyard worker's woman first and a pilot second, if at all, had clearly kept her from prevailing with them, or with the Line. Linnea spent half an hour composing a series of sharply worded messages protesting recent events, then, with a pang of guilt, put up a notice that she would be groundside, out of reach, for several days. She had to track Marra down. She'd dispatched a message, but she'd found no code for a live call.

To her delight, Iain decided to go with her. "I could use a rest, too," he said. "Before we start in again."

Zhen met them at the Port Marie skyport and hugged them both enthusiastically. "Thank all the gods you're back," she said. "We've been waiting and waiting."

"So have we," Iain said. "What's the rush?"

"Torin and I want five days off," Zhen said dramatically, as they headed for the exit. "Just five. That's all we ask."

"I'm sure we can work that out," Linnea said, puzzled. "What's it for?"

Zhen grinned. "Remember I told you once that we wanted to make a wedding? We don't have half the money we need for the party we thought we wanted. But there's a war on, so it's time to buy flowers and food. The ceremony will start next week."

Linnea laughed for pure happiness and flung her arms around Zhen. "To think Iain and I almost didn't get back in time!"

"We were waiting for you," Zhen said smugly. "Or I was. Torin was all gloom, but I knew you would manage."

"I wish I'd known that," Linnea said, and met Iain's serious look with a half smile. "Now. Take me to my sister!"

After Iain and Linnea dropped their bags at their room in Sunrose Street, Zhen led them off down the hill to the flat Torin had found for Marra, Yshana, and the children, on a pleasant, shady street near a waterfront park. Zhen tapped on the door, and called out, "Company here!"

The door opened, and there was Marra, looking strange to Linnea's eyes in a bright sleeveless shift, with her black hair loose and streaming down her back. Her eyes lit. "Linny! Oh, thank God, Linny, come in, come in!"

Linnea stood her ground. "Marra. This is Iain."

Marra's face went still, and she turned to Iain. "You are welcome to my house," she said stiffly, and stood back so they could all enter.

"You're lucky, it's a school holiday, the children are all here," Marra said to Linnea. "And Yshana and the baby. . . ."

Yshana got to her feet to meet Iain, with Moth in her arms. In the seven months of their absence, Rafael's son had grown long-limbed and wiry, with thick silky blond hair. But he was still fish-pale, still had those troubling blue eyes. He stared, silently, at Iain and Linnea.

"We've finished lunch," Marra said. "Are you hungry? Thirsty?" She spoke to Linnea, but her glance kept sliding aside at Iain.

"Some water, perhaps," she said.

"You should stay to supper," Marra said abruptly. "You can help cook, Linny. You probably know all these odd vegetables and fish better than I do."

"I don't cook much," Linnea said. "No kitchen." But in obedience to Marra's glare, she rose and followed her into the flat's little kitchen. Back in the sitting room, Zhen began a bright-voiced conversation with Iain.

"Why did you bring him here?" Marra hissed.

"Marra?" Linnea blinked at her. "We're together. We live together."

"You aren't married! You bring him around where Rosa and Lily can see, and the boys—who do you think you are, Linny? Who do you think *we* are? We're decent people!"

All the warmth Linnea had felt at seeing her sister safe and comfortable had fled. "I'm sorry you're upset," she said. "But I won't pretend anything for you. Or even for the children. This is my life now."

Marra turned away and angrily began pulling root vegetables down from a hanging basket. "Everything's wrong here," she said. "I miss decent fish. Good, strong-tasting fish that holds up in a stew." Her shoulders slumped. "I miss Asper."

"Word will come soon," Linnea said.

"So they tell me." Marra turned and faced her, her expression tight. "I don't understand all this otherspace talk, the weeks here and the months there. I just know that I don't know whether my husband is alive or dead. And that I can't go home yet."

"Not until we know it's safe," Linnea said. She felt the weakness of her words, because, of course, nowhere was safe.

"And when I go," Marra said, dropping her voice again, "you won't come with me. Will you?"

"I can't," Linnea said. "This is home."

"Father Haveloe still hasn't married," Marra said. "I think he still thinks of waiting for you."

Linnea laughed, painfully. "Then he will be waiting a long time." She folded her arms, looked down at the wooden floor. "I think we won't stay for supper. Not if you're afraid of what seeing Iain will do to the children."

"Linny, don't," Marra said firmly. "I—we'll manage. It's just a lot to understand. In a strange world. And you're strange now, too." She sighed. "Even the children. Donie's always at the shipyards whenever he can go, tagging around after that Torin. He's obsessed with those ships, he tells everyone his auntie is a pilot. It's ridiculous, Linny!"

"It's true," Linnea said. "Maybe Donie will be a pilot, too. They can start training at about his age."

"Donie will come home with me to Santandru." Marra's voice preempted argument, but her eyes were on Iain, who was huddled in the sitting room with Donie, discussing technical aspects of a model jumpship the boy had evidently built in school.

"The world is bigger than you think, Marra," Linnea said. "And it's changing."

"I don't see any reason for it to change," Marra said. "Why can't we all just go our own ways in peace?"

There was no answer to that. Linnea took some of the root vegetables to the sink and began to wash them. "You want these diced?"

"The sweet yellow ones? I'll bake them whole," Marra

said. After a moment, she looked at Linnea, then set her face firmly and pulled out the little sheepskin sack she always wore around her neck, under her blouse. "Linny. Listen. I've got something I need to give you." She opened the drawstring, shook the sack's contents onto her palm: two thin gold rings, and a small silver cylinder. She picked up the larger of the two rings. "My wedding ring from Rowdy," she said, and poked it back into the sack. "That's for Rosa someday; he was her da. But these—" She held out her palm to Linnea. "Ma's wedding ring. And that thing the Pilot Masters wanted so much, that caused you so much trouble. Take them both. Use them as you like. I don't care."

Linnea looked at them, then up at Marra. "Ma's ring? Are you sure?"

"Someday, maybe, you'll have a use for it," Marra said. "But that silver thing—everything bad in our whole lives came from that. If I had my choice, I'd smash it to dust and pretend it never existed. But it isn't mine. It isn't mine to choose."

"It belongs to Iain," Linnea said. "He'll choose." She took them from Marra and tucked them away in a pocket.

Marra straightened her shoulders, as if a burden had been taken from her. Then turned away to the little powered cooler on the counter. "Have you ever cooked any of this red fish? It turns to mush when I try. . . ."

Linnea gave the cylinder to Iain in private that night in their room. He looked at it with the same distaste Marra had shown. "So this is it. What Fridric killed for. Why my father lied to me."

"It's also truth," Linnea said. "I think you should keep it. Without it, you can't prove your ancestry isn't from the Line."

"No one can prove that it is, either," Iain said. "The genetic archives were in the Council Tower. Gone. This means nothing now." He closed his fist over it. "Less than nothing."

"Then you're free of it," she said softly.

He was silent for a long time. "I think—I think I always was. I only wish I'd known it sooner."

She put her arms around him, laid her head on his shoulder. The room seemed crowded with memory, her mind crowded with words she could not say. Questions she could not ask. She lifted her face to his and kissed him gently. That was an answer.

Four days later, a liveried Line messenger brought a handwritten notice to Linnea and Iain's door. They were summoned, officially, to the ingathering of the Line. Iain stood looking down at the elaborately scrolled writing. "Not a trial, I suppose."

"Not in the literal sense," Linnea said grimly. "They'd just have arrested you, not handed you a gold-edged invitation."

"I wish they would leave us alone," Iain said bleakly.

Linnea looked again at the date written on the notice. "Maybe that's the day they're going to vote about abandoning Nexus," she said. "About officially moving the Line to Terranova. I suppose they'd want to let us see it happen. We were there."

On the day, they both dressed with care—Iain, his hair tied back in a smooth silken tail with a black cord, wore his formal dark blue tunic and trousers; Linnea chose her wine-colored dress, the best of the three she owned.

The ingathering, such as it was with only a few hundred Line men of any age groundside, was held in the Line's headquarters, in the largest of its meeting rooms.

Linnea had heard Line men talk of building a new Council Tower on the bluffs above the southern end of the city, but she knew there was no money for anything so elaborate, perhaps never would be again.

No one, even Hakon, was proposing a return to the ruins of Nexus. The Inner Council had agreed in principle: The Line could no longer keep itself remote from the rest of the human race. That had nearly ended in disaster.

Iain and Linnea waited outside the closed doors while the Line convened and formally opened its proceedings. When the Line Chant began, Linnea looked at Iain. The line of his jaw tightened as the massed male voices rose, but his expression stayed serene. She clasped her hands behind her back. *Whatever comes, let Iain be safe.* No one, probably, was listening, whatever Father Haveloe might have said; but, then, they had come this far. Which must be some kind of miracle.

Silence. The doors opened before them, and a strong-voiced man called out their names: *Iain sen Paolo, pilot, late of the Line,* and then, to Linnea's astonishment, *Linnea Katerina Kiaho, pilot.* A Line escort led them down to the front of the room. Master sen Martin waited there, in Council robes of pale amethyst; his formal election as Honored Voice had come immediately after the news of the victory on Nexus. Beside him, in flawless black, stood Hakon—still, somehow, the head of the Line pilots. The victory he hadn't earned had gone to his credit, as Linnea had known it would. Both men watched their approach unsmiling. There was no Tree, no fire, no chain, none of the symbols Iain had described to her long ago, which had been ruined by the Cold Minds and consumed by fire.

They stopped, flanked by their escort, facing the Honored Voice. Sen Martin spoke first. "Iain sen Paolo," he said. "Linnea Kiaho. We welcome you among us." She felt Iain's faint start of surprise, but his expression stayed calm. He bowed deeply in acknowledgment of the greeting, and Linnea gave a slow, formal nod.

The Honored Voice stretched a hand toward the assembled men of the Line, a sea of black, and in the foreground a sprinkling of older men in deep-toned robes of office. "This assembly," he said, "has seen the record of your actions on Nexus. We have heard the testimony of our brothers, old and young, whom you saved from death or worse than death. We have come to regret the actions of the former Council—I personally, no less than any. And therefore we propose an unprecedented action."

He turned toward Linnea. "You are called here as a witness to justice, and as one who has suffered in the past from the actions of the Line. In restitution, we give you an honor no woman has ever had: We ask you to present this to Iain sen Paolo." He turned to a man who stepped forward holding a silver tray. Across it lay a thick cord of crimson silk. She knew it at once: a lineage-mark, worn in the braid of every Line pilot. Its color marked his family. She had woven it into Iain's braid long ago, in their first days together, when she had been his servant.

Sen Martin raised his voice. "Iain sen Paolo, son of Paolo sen David, is restored to our brotherhood." Behind her Linnea heard the rumble of the gathered men's voices: *He is restored.*

Her heart was pounding. Odd: that she should feel grief and worry, at this moment she knew Iain had dreamed of, hoped for, for long months and years.

She looked at Iain, expecting joy, acceptance; but his eyes were dark, and when she raised her hand toward the cord, he caught it in his. "Council Lord sen Martin," he said clearly, so all could hear. "Your offer honors me. I will hold it in trust for the son of my cousin Rafael, if he should ever wish to claim it. But I cannot accept it for myself."

Sen Martin looked grave. Beside him, Hakon blinked.

"Perhaps in time all of my former brothers will accept merit, rather than blood, as the qualification for this honor," Iain said. "But that time is not yet. And proof exists, in my possession, that I am not of the Line."

"This is known to us," sen Martin said. "Yet it is still the will of your brothers that you rejoin them as an equal."

"They honor me," Iain said. He looked up and met sen Martin's eyes. "But although I remain a pilot, I will not serve the Line. I am a son of Santandru."

Linnea heard the stir and mutter of voices behind her. The figure of the Honored Voice in his amethyst robes shimmered through tears, and for a moment she thought she saw Fridric standing there, Fridric who was dead; but that was ended. The dishonor had been undone—whatever that meant, now. Iain had refused the gift. Refused to return to the brotherhood that had once been his life. He was whole, in himself. She could believe that at last. He was not a broken piece of anything.

He was healed.

She stood by his side, her head high, and felt the beginning of hope.

TWENTY-SIX

That night they had supper at Marra's flat again. Linnea could tell that her sister was trying to be warm to Iain, to let go of her years-long dream that Linnea would marry the village priest and settle on Santandru forever.

After supper, while Donie and Orry did the washing up, Iain brought out a small silk-wrapped package and laid it in Yshana's lap. Moth was sleeping in another room, and as usual Yshana seemed a little at a loss in her son's absence. Now she stared down at the package. "For me?"

"Unwrap it," Iain said.

Yshana untied it carefully and unfolded the black silk. Linnea caught her breath. The crimson cord of Moth's lineage, of Iain's lineage, lay neatly coiled at its center. Yshana looked up. "It's pretty," she said shyly, "but—"

"It's the sign of your son's family," Iain said. "Of my family. Men of the Line weave these into their braids, when they are formally dressed. I want you to keep it for Moth."

Yshana's blue eyes went wide. "Don't you want this for yourself? Won't you have sons someday?"

Linnea, watching, saw him hesitate. Then he said, "I will have no sons, or daughters, for the Line." He kept his eyes on Yshana. "This cord is the symbol of your son's birthright, should he care to claim it. If, when he is older, he ever asks about his father—send him to me. I will tell him the truth." And here he looked at Linnea. "All of it."

"I hope he won't want it," Yshana said quietly.

"Yshana, it must be Moth's decision to accept this lineage or reject it," Iain said. "As it was mine."

She nodded, and folded the silk over the bright cord again. Linnea watched, troubled. But Iain's expression was peaceful. It had been, as he said, his decision.

And he had chosen Linnea.

One week later, Zhen and Torin's wedding began. To Linnea the three-day party was a confusion of color and scent: Everyone wore bright-colored new clothes, according to custom, and flowers around their necks, in their hair, floating in the beer, mixed into salads and soups and curries and underfoot everywhere. Linnea had to keep shaking flower petals down from inside her dress, and they flew everywhere when she danced.

At night they set fireworks off in the street, highly illegal but highly gratifying to Marra's children—and secretly to Linnea; she had never seen anything like them in her life. Bands of musicians had been hired for dancing at the waterfront park, and Linnea learned new dances and taught old ones until she had to drop down, exhausted, at a table with Iain and order another beer.

On the third day it all culminated in a street procession, with Zhen and Torin half-buried in flowers in the back of a pedicab, followed by another with Linnea and Iain as principal witnesses and trailed by a noisy parade of all the guests, singing—not all of them the same song. At the front steps of the neighborhood records office, the procession was met by a cheerful official in a gaudy shirt special for the occasion, who accepted his own load of flower garlands from Zhen and Torin. Then he listened solemnly to the couple's formal promises to care for each other's children if any, to share the products of their work, to care for each other in all times good and bad. When they were finished, the official read out, in a fine round voice, their full names of Torin Gavriel Dimarco and Zhenevra Anamaria Kumar, and pronounced them married.

Finally he signed, with a flourish, the colorful certificate of marriage Zhen had had made to be a family keepsake, and collected a kiss from Zhen and a tip from Torin while Iain and Linnea added their signatures as witnesses. Then the whole clamorous procession rolled off for the final party. By now Linnea was pleasantly numb, and her memories of Nexus and other places had dwindled, faded. Danger seemed far away, for now.

For now, Linnea sat in the curve of Iain's arm, leaning against his shoulder watching half the neighborhood children whirling with sparklers, making streaks of light that danced in front of her eyes even when she closed them. Zhen and Torin had vanished half an hour ago, according to plan, and the party was coming to a close. She looked over at Iain and indulgently brushed away a streak of yellow-orange pollen that had somehow smeared itself onto his cheek from one of his garlands of yellow flowers.

He smiled down at her. "Did you enjoy the party?"

"There weren't enough really big firecrackers," she said, assuming a plaintive expression. "And they ran out of those grilled melon bits on sticks you liked so much, which was a pity. Otherwise, it was adequate, I suppose."

He kissed her, and she tasted sweet herbed wine. "Ready for a rest?"

She looked at her hands. "Maybe—maybe we could

spend a few days at a quiet place down by the water. Just the two of us."

He lifted an eyebrow. "No more firecrackers?"

"I promise."

"Agreed, then." He kissed her.

"No regrets?" she asked softly, thinking, not for the first time, of the crimson cord—of the door that had been opened for Iain. That he had closed, for her.

In answer, laughing, he kissed her again. It was enough. For now.

Linnea woke smiling, in their room at a quiet waterfront inn. She had fallen asleep after a long swim over the reefs with Iain, and a long, shared bath, and warm, sleepy lovemaking. Now it was sunset. She got up and went out onto the balcony, which was built on pillars over the gentle sea. Iain stood there looking out at the dancing dazzle of level orange sunlight on the sea. She went to him and leaned on the rail at his side. He looked down at her and smiled.

Gently, she twined her fingers in the loose black hair that hung down his back. She had liked this time of rest and peace, when each day contained its own purpose, when they could share each moment without fear or worry. But—"It's time to get back to work, Iain."

He looked out at the sea, then down at her. "So soon."

She leaned against him. "You know I'm right. Work to do, years of it. Teaching, and training." She looked down at the dark water below. "Watching, and fighting."

She heard him sigh. "And after that?"

She pulled back and looked at him. "There is no after. This is life."

He looked serious. "No peace, ever?"

"Ask the Cold Minds when they will give up," Linnea said. "Then we'll know when we can have peace."

"I am at peace now," he said, and caressed her.

"I know." She touched his cheek. "I've been happy here, too. But we aren't finished, Iain."

He slid his arm around her, drew her close against his side. "Sometimes I like to dream."

She only smiled at him, then laid her head against his shoulder. They stood there together while the sun melted into the sea, into the trail of fire.

But they did not watch the sun, or the sea. Her eyes, and his, were raised higher: to the warm blue depths of evening. To the glimmer of the earliest stars.

ABOUT THE AUTHOR

Kristin Landon lives in Oregon with her husband and any of their children who happen to be home from college at the moment. In addition to writing, she works as a freelance copy editor of medical, scientific, and technical books. Visit her website at http://kristinlandon.com.